NEWPORT

A Fairy Tale of Sorts

A novel by   Timothy N. Thomas

T H E O D O R E   P U B L I S H I N G

Theodore PUBLISHING, INC. 12582 Ranchwood, Santa Ana, California   92705

Printed in the United States of America
First printing: July 2007

ISBN: 978-0-6151-4998-1

For Cindy,
who never ceases to inspire and mystify

Newport

A dim chandelier awakens me as I kindly slip out from beneath my slumber. I see my son walk with the effort of infancy, towards me, broadly smiled.

My wife speaks to me in dreamy tones, behind her a gradual burst of first light grants her angelic. And silkin curtains breeze about voluminous.

Nightmares of past loss and losing dissolve in the dawn as my daughter covers my face with satin sheets, her laughter soothes me, my ache.

I rush out open window as bird—quick lunging sweeps of my wings to a good height. The skies swirl and churn slow, ominous, with dark purple and gray clouds. The sun breaks through landing bold to my chest as I perceive Newport with dove nested towers of prince and princess. Newport rising from deep sleep serene, yet dying, crumbling in its majesty..............

Author unknown

4

Newport

Excerpt from one of Karen Vambert's many journals

That summer haunts me still, to this day. It was not that long ago yet it feels like a whole different time entirely. My friends and I talk about it occasionally but we seem to lack a depth of understanding which is a little tough for us to admit.

Some of what happened I just heard about but I have known these people all my life, the ones it happened to and the ones who told me. A lot of it I saw first hand. But the ones who told me, well, this isn't something they would lie about.

Sometimes I forget all about it, even the horrible parts. But then I will hear a wind chime, a simple wind chime brings it all in on me again. A sunset will do it too but a particular sort I cannot put my finger on. A writer friend of mine, who also lives here, wanted to hear my thoughts about what happened as he was considering a novel about that summer in Newport. His exact words were "I think the world would get a kick out of what happened." He even asked me how he should write it, a style. I wondered why on earth he would ask me that. He even asked me how I think it should be framed. I almost got mad at him. What do I know? But then I realized, I may never have an opportunity like this again. So I gave it some thought while he made coffee.

When he came back in I had a nasty little smirk for him. I told him "Do you think you could write it as though you were looking through a kaleidoscope? And maybe like a fairy tale, a kind of macabre one?" Because that is the way it comes to me. Because like I said, it haunts me—to this day. He gave me a pained grin and said he'd try.

> Karen Vambert
> Office Manager
> Union Bank

"I'll have something for you in a couple weeks, prologue maybe." John says on his way out. "I'll leave it under your concrete duck if you're not here."

"Great." Karen replies as she cleared off the coffee table.

PROLOGUE

Two weeks ago three young men from the state of Ohio rumbled into town, the town of Newport. Just about every summer they get themselves in enough trouble to necessitate a vacation. Unfortunately they got into a lot more trouble on their cross-country trip and they plan on hiding in Newport for a while. That is not a good plan.

Local police took immediate notice. The driver slid low in the seat, only his greasy long brown hair, sunglasses and conquering grin are visible. Another can barely be made out in the back seat playing the drums in the air as the music blares 'Whaoo black Betty…ram..a..lam!….Whaoo black Betty..ram..a..lam!' The other next to the driver sits up fairly straight with his right arm resting on the window ledge. An unfinished tattoo sculpts up his muscular arm. Wicked ensnarled little creatures and a busty naked girl evolve into a skull on the meaty cap of his shoulder, which transforms into an abstract series of thorny vines that envelop his neck. His expression is numb and resentful, his demeanor unapologetic. His knuckles are scared and thick as they tap on the doorframe to the music. The car is dirty but a classic 1965 Pontiac G.T.O and very powerful. There are two bumper stickers at the rear. One is very old, faded and says 'Disco sucks.' The other was applied last summer and says with empathy 'Support your local police.'

Two of the three young men left the bar earlier with the girls they met. An hour or so later the third young man by the name of Jim made his way back to the bungalow alone but decided to stop off at a market open all night. There wasn't anything he really needed just a faint impulse to look around. He grabbed some bread, ham, mustard and one plastic knife. He unraveled his crinkled bills and laid them on the counter. Jim sat down on the curb outside the store by himself and made a couple of sandwiches. The serenity that has crept up on him while being in Newport was with him once again. A drowsy saltin mist carries overhead leisurely moving eastward.

Jim stood up with little effort for his body was light and easy. He began to slowly make his way back home enjoying the gentle sparkle of the evening. Jim barely lifted his feet as he shuffled past ten feet or so of tall rose plants. There were five or six different colors and of course Jim was familiar with only about two of them. He stopped, made a quick glance around to spot if anyone may be watching, stuck his nose deep within the middle of a peach colored rose and breathed in robustly. His reaction was near that of inhaling a drug. The effect raced through his mortal body as his senses respond riotous. Jim had rarely felt better, as alive, as he did that very moment. He took another deep breath as deep as the first and the sensation intensified. As he walked on the feeling stayed with him, his senses now heightened some as though an arcane hand reached into his soul and lifted him up a notch from apathy to an honest possibility of sweet sensation by example.

Instead of making the usual left turn Jim made a right towards the beach. The telephone lines above crackle and run

just like back home but the whole of him stayed in the
moment. He arrived at the boardwalk as the moist air wrapped
itself around him. Jim stopped.

"If I take my boots off and walk to the oceans edge I
may never go home." Jim utters wistfully to himself. He
stepped off the concrete and sank in the sand and struggled to
move through it, he laughed quietly to himself. He listened to
and felt the 'kursh kursh' sound of the sand under his boots.
Attention that Jim had attached way too far inward was
brought out suddenly to the enthralling coastal environment. It
seemed as though there was simply more of him available and
present. There is an occasional sharp chill in the air and even
that is welcome.

Pier lights dotting out into the immense ambient abyss
and the whispered roar of waves crashing in measured intervals
assault him gently. The air in its saline sweetness and the
pungent odor of seaweed scattered on the beach blend in
rapturous entanglement with wood burning in the fireplaces
from the homes butted up to the sand. He spots a seagull
perched on top of a lifeguard stand. The white bird with black
tipped wings paying no attention to Jim as he appears
transfixed on the upcoming swells. "Hey there Mr. seagull, no
date tonight?" The bird does not flinch or look down. "Wha
cha lookin at buddy?" The young man squints out to the
oceans churning and rumbling. "Well—see ya later, hope she
shows up."

There is an occasional blinking light out at sea which
Jim figured to be maybe a buoy or a mermaids wink as he
approached the shore. It felt like the end of the line as well as a

new start as he took quick inventory of his last five years since graduating from high school. The endless girl chasing, the voracious drinking and fussing over his several cars up to his current Pontiac. That was it, that was honestly it, he realized. That alone is forgivable but he knew there was nothing to make him think he wouldn't be somewhere five years from now sitting alone in some crummy hotel room on a dreadful rainy night realizing the same thing.

Two girls walked by arm in arm giggling like girls do as Jim sat down in the sand.

Just as Jim looked to his right a wave hit the jetty, sending white foamed water jutting straight up thirty feet. Jim marvels at the sight. He pulls his knees up close to his chest. A moment earlier when Jim bent down to sit a piece of paper and pen used for keeping track of his conquests fell out of his breast pocket. He looked over at the paper and pen in the sand and felt that those two just lying there could mean something if one were inclined to attached a significance to it. As he pulled his knees tight to his chest he felt something dig into his ribs. They were two prescription bottles.

"I almost forgot to take these." When Jim was fourteen he was disruptive in class and the attention he had trouble putting on his studies was very easily placed upon what truly interested him: girls, sports, cars and girls. The school nurse caught wind of his supposed 'attention deficit' and persuaded his parents on an intense regimen of psychiatric drugs. Jim has been taking pills of the psychiatric variety for seven years now. All the pills do for him is make him either dull and lifeless or erratic and semi-delusional and then eventually dull and lifeless again. And unfortunately has caused some permanent brain damage along with a chronic twitch around his left eye and predisposed him to addictions of all sorts. Jim focuses hard to read the label. "No, no I'm not going to screw up how I feel right now with this shit. In fact........." He unscrews the lid and pours the tablets in the sand then unscrews the second and does the same. "Fuck those pasty white bastard doctors." He says harshly as he grinds them deep into the sand with his boot. Jim throws the bottles in the general direction of a trash can some ninety feet away. "Fuck them—pills don't solve problems every body knows that, fuck them."

A large gray dense cloud moved itself slowly and confidently in front of the moon leaving the young man in the subdued dirty silver glow of darkness, which he chuckled to himself could mean something too. Jim considered taking off his boots again but again decides against it. He recalled a time when he was twelve which seemed like centuries ago. A time when he and his parents took a Christmas vacation to a beach house in Virginia. One night Jim sat on the beach alone with a note book and pen. He had an assignment to dream up, a poem for his English class for the following week and what better place his young mind figured than on the beach late at night.

The memory of that evening embarrassed the tough and hardened twenty-three year old but he still tried to remember what he had written. Jim closed his eyes to concentrate. "Oh yes, yes, yes, yes," He softly said to himself. "Ghost ship, wow, the only 'A' I ever got, son of a bitch. Let me see how does that go again........ah 'Wet glazened rocks, seagulls perched' Right!

Jim reached down and picked up the paper and pen and started to write his poem again, he wanted to see the words, he wanted to see the words at night like they were a decade ago. The thick low slung cloud stood sentry in front of the moon and made a murky mess of the very faint Pacific horizon. Jim could barely see now or remember the rest of the poem so he closed his eyes and slipped back to that winter in Virginia. He recalled the handsome summer homes that scattered along the coastline. He tried hard to recall the activities and adventures but was only presented with a doleful, dismal and heavy darkness. Only the beach and the first line from his little poem about a ghost ship surfaced. A segment of another memory began to tease Jim as he straightened his back some from concentration. "Something about a mouse." He kept his eyes closed and tried to relax and let the memories come of their own volition. "Something about a mouse and a man." Jim tightened his brow as the odd little memory refused to coalesce. Jim rested his head on his drawn up knees and gave up.

"Oh, it was a book, yes right a book I read that summer and probably the last book I ever read." Jim smiles to himself. Off to his left Jim could hear a young couple throwing wood on a pit fire and laughing down the beach. The red-hot embers explode delicately from the impact as he fell into a deeper reverie. The faint illumination from the fire flickers up his face exposing an aging, a weariness that he is not aware of. "'Of

Mice and Men', that's it! I loved that, I mean I really loved that book. I wonder if that guy wrote any thing else. I recall it well now, I found it in a drawer in my room, the small tattered little book. The first page, the very first page, I can see it and feel it just like I did that summer. It blew me away how he described that gully or valley. There is no way on earth I would have ever thought of that if it hadn't of been for the softening that's been going on with on me lately in this little town here."

Without opening his eyes Jim slipped his boots off then sank and pushed his feet deep in the sand. He felt the most peace and pleasure of any kind since that night in Virginia alone on the beach.

Jim opened his eyes and just as he did the thick gray cloud parted some and exposed the direct light of the moon illuminating through the back of a seven foot wave. Jim could see into the wave with astonishing clarity. His eyes bug open wide as two seals turned and tumble inside the wave and rode it for thrill. Jim fell back in the sand and laughed and even cried a little while looking up at the suddenly alive sky of sparkling stars that he swore just winked at him. His mind was not necessarily opened through the vastness of the galaxies or beyond but he did feel a small kinship with it if only by fascination. He gripped the sand with both hands and felt nothing but his new found serenity.

Jim awoke three hours later in a dense fog to a sea lions soft-echoed bark in calling for his mate. Jim sits uneasy massaging his temples. As extroverted as he was when he arrived at midnight he was equally introverted, veiled with a weighted shroud of discontent pulled down tight around his ears and locked on him, his usual state. The young man from Ohio stands up.

Jim began to head back with boots in hand. The thick damp air of early morning feels as an unwelcome pressure upon his senses. His attention darts down the beach where the fog has lifted some. He tries to make out the motion of a man, which seems to have odd movements to his exhausted perceptions. He looks to his left quick and thinks he sees another human form moving about through squinting eyes and sudden alertness. Jim jerks his head right as the radiance of a flashlight throws a hard beam slicing through the heavy fog. The dark figure sweeps the light slowly over the sand and shore, stops at a large lump of seaweed then continues to sweep.

The young man steps on the boardwalk and takes his sox off to shake out the sand. Again he takes quick concerned glances in all directions while slipping on his sox and boots in this now strange city where he feels very alone. For the first time in a long time Jim feels a little fear as he mistakenly takes an unfamiliar route, he is worried he may get lost. The telephone lines above are silent. He stops at what he recognizes as the main street and looks for something familiar. A pay phone about fifty feet to his left rings four times then falls silent. Jim moves across the street within a thick mist, figures at least he is headed in the right direction. The traffic light above switches eerily in the mist, red, yellow, green, by its own lonely mechanism, no cars in sight.

Jim stops, exhales, closes his eyes and flutters his lips in relief. He sees the big white fender of his Pontiac less than a block down the street. Jim reaches into his breast pocket for a half cigarette he extinguished earlier and his right pant pocket for a match. As he lights it a quick flash illuminates his immediate surroundings for a fraction of a second. He is standing in front of the long row of tall roses that he inhaled deeply a few hours ago but has no interest. He doesn't even bother with a glance, keeps walking. The pay phone rings again but is soon silent. Jim stops abrupt, looks over his shoulder peering into the fog. "Come on ya wimp." He chastises himself and keeps going.

The young man passes in front of a home with the faint synthetic glow of a television giving the bedroom a ghostly feel as thin white satin curtains breeze about. He passes the rest of the houses with stiff quick steps, darts across the street and is home. He strolls up the worn brick entry way then changes his mind on instant. He back tracks and hops on his fender for another smoke. He reaches into his breast pocket pulls out a package of Winston's, peels the thin tab around then pulls the clear wrapper off. He crunches it up in his fist and drops it to the gutter. The wrapper does not stay crunched up, they never do. Jim smacks the pack to the meaty part of his open palm to drive the tobacco toward the filter. He pulls one out breaks off the filter and lights it with an old chrome lighter his father gave him years ago. The flame flickers with barely enough fluid to light his cigarette; he clicks the lid shut hard with his thumb and sits hunched over.

Jim can see the guys and their girls drinking and laughing inside through an old sash window. He lets out a little huffed laugh as he blows smoke out as a quick stream from the left corner of his mouth. His attention darts to rustling from a few bushes and a tree and then the rushed whine from the quick approach of a helicopter. The blades whirl and chop directly above him as two powerful lights bear down on him.

The three young men from Ohio were subdued brutally. Three policemen converged on Jim fast and threw him face first into the neighbor's garden. Rich moist soil crammed into his nostrils. Because of his impulse to struggle he was hit so hard in the head with a heavy baton that a crack to his skull exposed brain matter. Another was pinned and kneed so hard in the ribs eight of them were fractured and that was before they cuffed him. He was cuffed so roughly his collar bone was fractured and his left elbow dislocated. The last to be apprehended was the worst though. The toughest of the threesome by the name of Tony was apparently subdued and lying face to the concrete. In one final burst of strength he threw one officer off to the side and was about to jump up to go after another when a size fourteen boot came crashing down on his face shattering his nose and breaking sixteen teeth. Another boot kicked him so hard in the crotch the impact fractured his pelvic bone, not to mention crushing any future hopes of procreation. And of course all were Tasered—twice.

One may ask "Why so brutal an arrest?" The answer is quite understandable even reasonable by Newport standards. The three young men killed a state trooper on their merry way to Newport Beach, California.

"You three cock suckers are under arrest for the murder of Kansas State Tropper William T. Hansloget. And if you survive the evening I hope they fry you freak bastards." The senior officer says in a thick bitter tone.

If one is a criminal and considers hiding out in Newport, well, that is just not a good plan.

An old man ventures out of his house a while after the three are hauled off. He inspects the damage to his garden. He rubs his chin and shakes his head in disgust. The old man reaches down slowly and picks up a folded piece of paper. He unfolds it as his hands tremble and the cold, moist night air permeates his frail frame. He reads quietly and softly to himself with an old mans crackle in his voice.

Ghost Ship

Wet glazened rock, seagulls perched
As phantom winds blow over restless
     indigo tides
Ghost ship's sails snap and whip
Direction known only to stance of happen
Sea foam green, gray and blue
White sands silken grains stretch far and beyond
While palmed trees rustle by salted winds
     merriment
Streamed clouds above so pure and unburdened
     as blued skies echo grand oceans reverie
Through ghost ship's hull of creaks and dry
     rotten a faint sailors whisper can be heard

And wet glazened rock, seagulls perched while
    ship's sails snap and whip by winds of trade
    and tragedy

   The old man scratches his forehead slowly with a
puzzled glare to his eyes. He folds up the poem and slides it
into his bathrobe pocket. He walks out to the edge of the
sidewalk and looks keenly down the street both ways. He
shivers mightily from the chill of early morning as he pulls the
lapels of his bath rob under his chin tight. "What the hell is
going on around here?" He says with a twinge of irritation as
he looks back at his ravaged garden. He walks back into his
house and turns off the porch light.
   Back out on the beach atop lifeguard tower 32 a lone
seagull sits, peering intently into the upcoming swell. It is a
good one, he knows. He digs his small talons into the edge of
the gray weathered wood roof. The swell waves up quick as
the moon beams through and illuminates the wave's contents.
But only seaweed churns, swirls about then tumbles. The
seagull squawks disapprovingly then flies away. He'll have to
wait another month for the moon to be in just the right spot
for the show.

Karen's place

Karen calls John.

"Oh, I really like that."

"It's not really about them but I thought it would be a good place to start. Ya know, everyone comes to California— eventually?"

"I remember reading something about them, never heard much else though."

"Me either. I'll leave a few chapters on your porch under Mr. Duck next week."

"Great."

....ONE

_____NEWPORT_____

Union Bank in Newport Beach, California is
physically positioned well as in perfect in the heart of Fashion
Island. It stands at the apex of the horseshoe shaped life style
Mecca of Southern California. Its fifty-two floors tower above
all other structures. From the fifth floor on up all occupants
enjoy the shimmering cobalt blue and deep sapphire currents of
the Pacific Ocean. And if a long breeze from a distant sea falls
to Newport the surf is capped with a milky froth. Quite a view.
Any deal that is a big deal with regard to Newport is struck in
that tower. Of course there are other banks in the Island but
Union Bank has had the upper hand for about two decades.
Yet the brain trust at each, somewhat minor banking
institution, have a firm hold on some fraction of Newport
Beach. And the ratio of holdings and power can change
overnight which is basically the reason for this story.

Fashion Island, its splendid and grand self was constructed in 1964 in heart of Newport but over the years it has become *the* heart of Newport Beach. And it is truly an Island of fashion. The finest and most expensive garments south of Los Angeles call their home Fashion Island. This locale is where the affluent shop and the super affluent send someone to shop. At Fashion Island there are no 'sale' signs permitted. If one must be that human one may consider shopping at South Coast Plaza in Costa Mesa, a quaint little town directly behind, east and well in the shadow of Newport.

Only beautiful people live in Newport and shop at Fashion Island, man, woman and child. For this is the standard of expectancy from birth in Newport Beach. If you are not born beautiful it is ones obligation to make damn sure you get beautiful. In Newport alone two hundred and fifty million dollars a year is spent on cosmetic surgery. It is spent because the standard of existence must be met. Therapy is needed and vital but not flaunted like it is north of this resonant coastal community in county of Los Angeles. The money spent on psychiatrist, therapist of all denominations and psychiatric drugs would equal the GDP of many small countries.

The difference between a city like Newport and one in let's say, Arizona, is that when a woman in Newport has a large bandage over her nose it is most likely not because some guy named Gus smacked her one for burning the macaroni and cheese. The woman of Newport is merely holding up her end as the proper and expected human landscape of beauty, however derived, natural or otherwise. For the standard of existence must be met. As only beautiful people live in Newport.

Down on and around the beaches of Newport people
bristle with activity and warm generous sunrays play delicately
upon its creatures. At a stoplight a family on vacation from
Missouri is looking for a place to park—a challenge of epic
proportions. A young man of thirteen riding in the back seat
sees a girl in a bikini coming their way within the crosswalk.
This is a first for him. He slides down some in his seat so that
only his nose on up can be seen through the window. He sets
his 'Boy's Life' magazine and bag of chips to his left. He did
not simply watch her, he could not simply watch her as all the
senses he possessed and even others that awaken from the
numbing of their two thousand mile trip rev to life. All his
perceptions are engulfed by the girl walking now in front of the
Plymouth van. His mother spies out the corner of her eye to
see if his father is paying a little bit too much attention to the
girl in the bikini. He is.

Since the young boys mind was in overwhelm at first
blush, the first thing about her he could decipher singularly was
her hair, it was blonde but seem to take on the color of the
sand on the beach. It whisked on and off her face then swept
across her shoulders. When a warm thick breeze hits it just
right it waves around and over like it might under water. It
would then appear to dance on her shoulders and on instant
pretend to behave. The sun would have its fun too as it found
places to hide only to burst out a second later. Her face is
strikingly alive and tan with little freckles and her teeth are pure
white. Her skin looked so smooth and tan the young boy
almost couldn't stand it as he lets out a shrilled gasp as quietly
as he could manage. Her curves assault him, he felt and was
nearly paralyzed by powerful sensation sparkles racing through

his body. He squirms some in his seat. She was not overly curvy though, more the thin athletic type, surfer type.

'Surfer girl' breaks barely audible from the boy's lips. She wore this funny little smile and one can only wonder what she is happy about. He supposed if god is going to make a creature this gorgeous then he is going to make her pretty damn happy about it. The boy tries to mouth something, some word to frame the experience; he has no words for this moment. The breeze took a sample of her and kindly made its way through the car to back seat, at least he dreamed it did. It was a magnificent blend of suntan oil, young women and salty air. His father did possess a word and that word was 'Wow' as mom hits him hard on the arm and the light turns green and they pull away. But the young boy is still riveted to her as he whips his head around and gazes intensely at her through the back window. A common occurrence.

But if fortune has found one and they live in Newport, Fashion Island is the heart that pumps desire and expectation. The life style is laid out neatly, in a nice package; it must be bought regardless of price. The more spent—the better one should feel. Standards of existence must be met and Fashion Island must define them.

Outside but in step with fashion there are a number of classy restaurants and hotels that help make up the three-quarter circle of Fashion Island. And the two of worthy mention are the Ritz and the Four Seasons which happen to be in a perennial war for supremacy. A story could be written on the events surrounding the drama of just one calendar year with regard to conflict and excess if one were so inclined. Regardless, there are some extraordinary parties of dripping fortune and privileged circumstance. These parties began in a big way in the 1920's and have roared and occasionally whimpered their way to present day.

Indeed Fashion Island is a wonderful place for the wealth to play but there is a tight grip on Newport Beach, California and the wrist, hand and fingers is Union Bank. But oddly enough there is another business that resides in the Union Bank tower. You see Union Bank officers are not superstitious so they *do* have a thirteenth floor but it is not used by the bank.

4:13 am, one Saturday morning

The time is 4:13 am Saturday morning at Union Bank on the thirteenth floor. Neil Landitt's office faces the interior of Fashion Island. But that is merely what his eyes perceive, void of any viable emotion and interest. If you look into his eyes you can see the fog that has crept in leaving only the top portions of the buildings visible or nothing at all. Neil has seen this fog a hundred times but this morning he senses and evil flow of movement and presence.

It feels evil because Neil has had a body in his trunk for two days and he honestly has no clue as to how it got there or what to do with it. Neil peers into the fog, the evil fog, thick and churning. His feels it rolling over him, he feels its cold apathy passing through his rigid mortal body. His eyes are sullen and weary, very sullen very weary.

"Just go to the police and tell the truth." He mutters to himself, his face ghostly pale, expression gaunt, eyes squinting haunted.

Without time enough worth measuring, the mechanism of the mind that gives reasons why one should *not* do something kicks in and serves up five stellar ones to keep his mouth shut. And Neil agrees with all five. Neil lowers his head and says very softly and solemnly "Sweet Jesus, this is bad, really bad."

......TWO

THREE MONTHS EARLIER

The Newport Auto Show

There are two events that take place once a year in Newport which are the major underpinnings to social status and interaction on a grand scale. If you are seen there, you belong. If you skip either of them for nearly any reason (death in the family will not do) you not only won't be allowed to live it down for some time but chances are you missed something important regarding Newport's future. And it is usually a comment that was merely overheard but the message rifles through Newport Beach at speeds Bill Gates would blush over.

The Taste of Newport and the Newport Auto Show are those two events which must be attended if one may truly claim to be Newport. But to be fair to the readers in the furthest reaches of let's say, Oklahoma, The Taste of Newport is boring as a story. I will lay it out quick: A bunch of rich people sample food all day (ok, really good food) from local restaurants and drink as they boast and boast as they drink. And it is a sloppy boast due to the amount of wine ingested with no real advantage taken from what is overheard. And who wants to be drug through that if they are enjoying a summer night on ones porch in Enid, Oklahoma. Some how the rich folks are found to be a bit more tolerable at the auto show.

The Newport Auto Show, this is where the players of wealth all come together once a year intentionally or by the insistence of their equally well-to-do neighbors. Sure, there are plenty of martinis consumed but the mysticism of creation challenges their arrogance and holds it stifled. Amazingly enough they are kept in check to a degree by the sheer brilliance of fabrication, engineering and design. Somehow they feel a little less than the automobiles displayed but these are not just any automobiles. These are the finest machines ever created this side of the 1920's.

In fact the first of the year in Newport does not begin January first as in any other region of the United States. The first of the year begins the day *after* the Newport Auto Show. That is when the game begins once again, the game of fabulous prosperity and power. And that means property, the golden coast variety and the right business model built and operated on that property. For some of the most expensive land on earth resides in and is Newport Beach, California.

Today, it is all about automobiles though. As these are the finest in the nation or world for that matter and again the ownership of such excellence is a standard of existence for the wealthy local natives. But in reality -the cold and unapologetic type- for most, the show is no more than a blinding gloss of deception for the players to find out what the other players are up to in the chess game for the domination of Newport. And if something big happens during the year to follow the germ usually took its first breath at this event.

Then again, just as one is known as and by their beauty, ones automobile is also a metal skin form that is held to a high standard. For the term 'you are what you drive' is alive and thriving in the city of Newport as coveted scripture and the standard of expectancy must be met.

May Bach—Mercedes new entrance into ultra luxury. Rolls Royce—more fun and theater since BMW took over and many others like the brilliant Bentley, Continental G.T. But the Aston Martin Vanquish and the new startling Ferrari Enzo steal the show. One must understand though, a social and psychological framework exists and lurks in life's relation to these absurdly priced rolling Rembrandts. Take a fifty year old man working at, let's say, a home improvement store, standing over there earning maybe—thirty five thousand a year. Then take the fifty year old multi millionaire who has earned his money- however they pull it off. By some chance of fate, they are both admiring the new Enzo, side by side. The walk around it, inspect with intense wonder and focus. There may even be an exchange between the two men.

One is holding a beer, the other a martini. The Ferrari salesman spots the two, gives a quick tug on his lapels and grins devilishly to himself as he approaches. The salesman arrives on cue next to the men and the Ferrari displayed on the rolling plush of a small man made knoll and lush green grass.

"She's something isn't she." The salesman offers.

The not so wealthy fifty year old plumbing 'associate' smiles broadly and says, "You're right about that, you're sure right about that."

The fifty year old millionaire does not answer or acknowledge the salesman's presence. He is not available for conversation—he does not have to be. The salesman knows he has his man. He cuts off communication with the man with the beer in his hand. The salesman nods only out of reflex or social compulsion when ever the man makes a comment.

The man of modest means yet graciousness of spirit is completely alone standing five feet from the wealthy man and the Ferrari salesman. He feels the dull pulse of isolation gradually and he feels uneasy. Yet he continues to smile minus the sweet emotion and continues to comment on the Enzo as the enthusiasm slowly drains from him. Not all of it, but enough.

The sun is bright and generous and a sudden breeze whips through with just enough power to ruffle the collars of the men engrossed in the machine. And the dance begins.

"Do you have any idea how long I have waited for the Enzo? I heard about it three years ago and I have had two

Ferraris in between." The millionaire enlightens as the salesman feels the sensation of impending triumph and the other man shrinks into oblivion even further.

"Well, here it is!" The salesman knowing a minimum of wordage is appropriate and vital.

"It has got to be blue and I need a selection of blues."

"And so you shall have." The salesman states as he lowers his head in a partial bowing gesture.

The suction of mediocre means and apathy draws the other fifty-year old man into the parking lot and to his 1992 Dodge. He sits for a moment and looks at the back of his hands holding the steering wheel. He reaches into his left breast pocket and pulls out a cigarette, which he lights. Unfortunately payday is not till next Friday so it is the generic brand he will be smoking for the next few days. He takes a long look at himself in the rear view mirror. It is the kind of long look that includes a judgment of self—the worst kind. He is unsure whether he likes himself or not. Usually he does and is uneasy how it can be displaced so easily by spending a few minutes with guys like those.

He starts the car and heads out of the parking lot and drives in the direction of Costa Mesa, the small town east of Newport, where the store and his shift awaits. "5:00 to midnight, on a Saturday night? What a lousy stinkin shift." He grumbles to himself. But he will dream about that Ferrari tonight and several months down the road he will begin to look forward to, with much anticipation, the next Newport Auto Show.

There is a chasm, a spectacular chasm, between those who can only admire and those who know only the sensations of desire and subsequent purchase.

Make no mistake or gaffe, the Newport Auto Show in Newport Beach, California is meant, designed and brought into being for the wealthy and beautiful people who reside there.

_____

The glorious frolic of Beethoven's ninth, second movement, thrills the air with measured strides of elegance as a legion of trumpets and strings swirl up to the heavens in rising staccato, surging triumph. The propulsive rhythms captivate for a short while, then the beauty of the opus falls kindly back to earth in a sleepy wavering of horns but never lets one touch ground as the melody lulls the senses into tranquil submission before the orchestral movement lifts off again for the acquiescent brilliance of the Newport sky. The spirit of richness, gathered richness permeates all space and function as the accentuating drums thunder in. The spirit of gathered richness hovers above, interwoven so delicately within the equally opulent melody. The graceful dominance is now in place. And the people—the people are beautiful.

This is the realm, dominion and empire of beauty and wealth. And its high order may manifest anywhere. Any item of clothing or jewelry that may be worn or draped or fastened to one is done so to communicate fortune. The finest brands of watches and clothing too numerous to list and just about any style of diamond will do and the largest of any brand or style of diamond will do better. The idea is to display as much wealth as possible, aesthetically as possible, as all self absorbed royalty is compelled to do. If there is a baby then that baby is flaunted as well and will be done so from the cozy confines of a Silver Cross stroller no doubt. And of course there are those shy souls who flash down to only a conservative opulence displayed—old money.

A human existence is a funny thing to observe though. It is the source of all things creation. It designs and builds to perfection then in turn considers itself and others as defined by that thing created. One conceives and builds a Bentley today then the next day a man is considered to be an extension of or judged in proximity to that Bentley by mere ownership. Man creates a store the likes of Neiman Marcus one week and the woman buying the Prada purse is elevated to a new status or maintains her current status simply by virtue of one dangling from her wrist.

This is the day when the creation itself is more revered than the creator and the ability to create is over shadowed by the elevating powers of that fabrication.

The sweet and gentle grace of the family cat creates nothing yet is held in such high esteem and respect for its elegant nature—man should be so lucky.

......THREE

As the martinis flow and the rich peruse, Davis Rothman saw, felt, perceived none of this for his eyes and interest were intensely focused fifty yards north to the Fletcher Jones display of near fifteen silver Mercedes, all models, of course. Davis is jealous because he has a fledgling Mercedes dealership of his own —and was lucky to get some space today- while Fletcher Jones is the number two dealership in the entire United States with eyes on the number one spot no doubt within the year. Davis Rothman of 'Imports of Newport' has exactly four on display. To add injury to insult, Jones has the new two hundred thousand dollar SLR McClaren roadster right smack dab in the middle of all the German engineered glory, Davis has never even seen the SLR before today. But Davis may still sell a Mercedes today, maybe even two. He also knows he has about enough operating capital to last for one year, at best.

Davis knows full well he has to move more Mercedes more often or find himself in bankruptcy. But for a brief moment he stands with his hands in his pockets with a somber squint, head tilted some to the left with lips perched out, tight. All of that is directed and fixed on those fifteen silver

Mercedes. "How the hell did he get every single model in silver, I can't get near that many silver or otherwise and his salesman, look at them, they could sell Eskimos to ice cubes!" Davis Rothman mumbles and grumbles to himself. "And those flowers, all those flowers, why didn't I think of that?" He continues.

Davis Rothman is brought out of his self-abasement by a tap on the shoulder.

"Hello sir, I sure like that gold one right there, well I mean it's not gold, gold but wow that's a neat looking sedan," A man about thirty five blurts. First and foremost, Davis is a salesman, so it's an easy switch to tear his attention away from Jones' display and put it squarely on this attractive couple, attractive *interested* couple.

The man and woman standing in front of Davis are Neil and Kaisty Landitt and they are players but merely on the cusp for now. And Kaisty drives Neil hard because standards must be met. Right now though, Kaisty is embarrassed because her husband is talking way too much and a bit sloppily for her tastes.

"Gee, this is great, when I was fifteen my father pulled up the driveway in a gold Mercedes, ah, man that was the best." Neil rambles on.

"And you know Neil, Jones only has silver ones over there."

"I know, that's why I dragged Kaisty over here."

Kaisty's face flushes with embarrassment around her permanent set pout. But well dressed with her Prada purse, purple/ginger paisley skirt and blouse and of course Dior eye wear. Unfortunately it is all eloquence on a budget and she hates that. Sure, they can afford to be well dressed, even every day, they can probably even lease that Mercedes Benz over there. But little else can they afford and Kaisty's patience is running thin.

Neil gradually began to tune the salesman out, not because he was being rude, it was just that he couldn't tell him something he didn't already know.

Now Kaisty and Neil do own a home but technically it is a town-home actually more in line with a condominium. None of this bothers Neil but all of it bothers Kaisty, she expected to be further along by now. The salesman offers Neil a seat in the new S500. Neil steps in with a gentle manner reserved for fine automobiles as the salesman gives the door a good swift close. Neil likes the feel of the door closing, it felt like a vault being shut. The salesman knew he would like that. Neil powers down the window to ask a question, the salesman answers and Neil powers the window back up again.

Kaisty reaches into her purse while throwing a fake smile and nod Neil's way as he checks to see how she is doing. She pulls out a small prescription bottle of the anti-depressant Paxil with only a few tablets left. She places the odd shaped pill on her tongue, rolls her eyes at another childish "Wow!" as Neil settles in behind the wheel then guzzles down her salvation with an eight ounce bottle of Perrier as she sweeps a languid, uninspired eye over the auto show.

This couple here, Kaisty and Neil, are a main focus of this story, the story of Newport, and to a lesser degree so is this fledgling Mercedes dealership owned by Davis Rothman. And there are others.

That couple right over there drinking lemonade and laughing amongst themselves. Now that's Robin and Scott Mofford and their little girl Amy. They would not be considered players but the winds of power and consequence change quick and firm in Newport and they may soon shift in their favor. Scott owns and operates a modest yet successful (by rational standards) moulding and painting company. Robin received her real estate license six months ago at the urging and insistence of her grandmother. They are here because they simply wanted to enjoy the rich atmosphere and gaze at the beautiful cars. Now Scott is dreaming of that wild new SUV over there but in truth laying out sixty thousand dollars just isn't in the cards for Scott and Robin. Winds shift quick in Newport though. Amy holds Robin's hand as she runs her little fingers down the long grill slats of the new Rolls Royce and giggles.

Last but not too far least we have the Starbucks girls. They are referred to by one name because they are basically one entity and the names change every year anyway as they come and go from the group, similar to a professional sports team. And what they're up to could be considered a high stakes game easily and certainly.

The four girls standing close for support and conversing are looking, searching and mining for an up coming and not necessarily but preferred single man who has a firm footing in potential or realized wealth or has fairly easy access to it. They are named collectively 'The Starbucks Girls' because Macarthur Boulevard, south of Fashion Island an inch or two, spills into the Starbucks off Pacific Coast Highway. And this is central command for these young ladies.

Why here, one may ask? Easy, being that Macarthur Boulevard runs right up along Fashion Island, this road brings young executives in for their after work java of some kind or another. And these girls lay in wait. They are only worthy of mention because one of them, a twenty six year old girl by the name of Marty. And Marty feels she is overdue. She believes she may be too critical or not pretty enough or some god somewhere responsible for luck or good fortune just passes her by. This is her third trip to the Newport Auto Show and that is not good. She is dressed in a pink and green blouse and skirt that lengths to a silky rest two inches below her knees. Marty has a white sweater draped over her shoulders knotted just above her ample cleavage and her thin arms hang purposeless by her sides. She will wear the outfit today and return it tomorrow. It is thought of as woman's right.

Marty is holding her shoulders a bit tense but since she does it a lot she does not realize it. Her hair is long, styled modestly and brown. She knows this is serious business yet her friends seem to giggle at everything. They don't understand, due to this being their first or, god forbid, maybe second auto show. But Marty feels the pressure and she has seriously considered moving back to Tennessee. She loves southern California or maybe she loves merely the idea, the dream of it.

"Hi there!" A handsome gentleman in his late twenties says to Marty, which startles her.

People who are somewhat introverted are usually startled at such advancements by people who are rather extroverted. The ones that are chronically introverted don't react at all, Marty is not there yet.

"Oh, oh hi." Marty responds a bit flustered.

"Beautiful cars aren't they?"

"Yes, yes they are." Marty replies as she guards the sun from her eyes with her thin pale fingers.

"Do you come to this show every year?"

"No, this is my first."

"What's your favorite?" The well dressed but casually well dressed young man glances around smiling.

"Oh, oh I don't know." Marty squints hard and glances around. "Maybe that one." She points.

"Ah!" The young man laughs lightly. "Well, that's great, nice little Porsche but that is in the parking lot my dear."

Marty laughs out loud, turns red, covers her mouth.

"Oh well how about that one." Marty points to a 1928 burgundy Dusenburg masterpiece with dark cream fenders, standing dominant even decades out of its era.

"Yes, nice selection." The young gentleman nods his head and smiles.

On that note he places his open palm on the buttons of his dark blue blazer elbow protruded Marty's way. The offer for a stroll is accepted as Marty slips her delicate thin forearm in the slot provided within the tightly knit tweed. Marty's expression shifts quick to a look of cheerfulness and ease. But the guarded optimism lurks there as well just under the surface.

The No Shows

The first of the notable no shows is Jack Harton, the number one real estate developer in Newport Beach.

Mr. Harton upon review of the gorgeous woman lying face down on the deck of his 123 foot Palmer Johnson yacht has decided to skip this year's auto show. In the fairness of full disclosure the only time you would spot him there is to find a new girlfriend anyway. They usually last six to nine months upon first meeting. This girl, this 'situation' as Jack refers to a relationship has lasted a phenomenal twelve months.

Mr. Harton is not at the Newport Auto Show as he is inspecting every curve and exposed tan line of the reasons why. A breeze relays a sample of her tantalizing feminine chemistry to his utter delight as he sits just above on the second deck with a circling finger in his scotch.

Jack Harton is the owner of Real Corporation and again it would not be over the top to say he is the number one developer in Newport. It is a constant arm wrestle over a chess game and winds of conquer and momentum shift quick and fierce. As absorbing as the goddess is on this warm dreamy southern California afternoon, Jack's mind wanders to the property. The last piece of undeveloped property in Newport Beach.

A quick wind swirls about and attacks gently his black and gray hair as he reaches for his captain's cap. He sinks a bit in his tan leather chair and takes a quick deep breath.

Jack closes his eyes and launches off the bow toward the coast five miles off over the lazy swells as seagull. Once he

reaches Newport he is at the property within seconds after a
wide northerly turn. He hovers over the twenty acres then
dives in an earthly lust to within and inch of the soil then
scampers over the soil like a rodent might. The soil is
intoxicating as he burrows under like an earthworm's dynamic
dictates. He squirms along under the rich soil then juts out and
up as bird again baring his breast to the warm and generous sun
holding its position bright and mightily in the sky. The seagull
appears to sit on a warm thick updraft and peers out over land
and sea as his sweet ardor.

Mr. Jack Harton of the Real Corporation wants this land
and in bad way. And a lady by the name of Mrs. Claire Binsent
wants him *not* to have it.

The second notable no show is Mrs. Claire Delane
Binsent, the General Motors heir to fortune and the true
reason for this story. She is not present today, in fact the last
time Claire attended a Newport Auto show was, well, the very
first one in 1974. Sure, Claire appreciates a fine automobile like
the rest of us but not enough to spend a gorgeous July day
revolved around them.

Claire sits peacefully on her veranda overlooking the
great Newport harbor. And she does so with her favorite
companion and most recent favorite companion on her lap,
Bruty. Most recent because a woman of her age and passion
for animals leaves the dilemma of having a new creature to love
every ten years or so. Today and now her blessing is Bruty a
seven year old gray Tabby cat. Of course he was a stray like all

the others over the years. Like Muffy Wuffy, asleep and blissfully so, on her very own chair right next to them.

Claire pets Bruty with a tender gentleness only a woman can assemble, a rather old and fabulously wealthy woman. She sips her Vermouth with the other.

There are about a hundred widowed and wonderful old ladies of Newport, but only one that posses exclusive ownership to the last parcel of undeveloped land in the heart of Newport Beach, California. And substantial a parcel it is at near twenty acres. One may say twenty acres is nothing more than a square inch seen from an airliner by a coveted tourist flying into John Wayne Airport. Yet very few places on earth can the natives boast that land is sold for more or is truly worth it, with or without the right business model or home built upon it.

At a mere three miles from Fashion Island between streets by the names of Macarthur and Newport Boulevard and butted up against Pacific Coast Highway sits one huge plot of dirt. In Newport's one hundred and fifty year history the only buildings that have rested on its back have been those to house tractors, horses and other farming equipment of all sorts. The last crop it produced was a peculiar combination of pomegranates, strawberries and about six fig trees. All Mr. Binsent favorites but this was in the late fifties and Mr. Binsent is long since gone.

Amazingly some of the humped soil rows still remain and Claire would probably have something planted there currently if she had the energy to oversee the cultivation and nurturing. Mr. Binsent bought the property from Mr. Wrigley of 'Wrigley Gum' fame and fortune in 1951, who had quite the ranch on Catalina island, twenty six miles off the coast. Who himself bought it from an old tired farmer back in 1938. In 1949 Claire and Edward moved to Newport Beach from Detroit where Edward ran the General Motors Empire for the better part of twenty years.

Her eyes are gray blue and they smile. Her lips still possess a small measure of sensuality to them but she never wears lip stick anymore, maybe just a little lip balm. Her skin is old and weathered but well cared for. Her smiles are genuine and her angers few.

Claire Binsent is not at the Newport Auto Show simply because she does not need to be or desire to be there.

......FOUR

Morning after the Newport Auto Show

The day upon which we meet again shall be glorious
as you were once my sunshine as for now you have
become a stranger.

Braston Livingston
Newport Beach Poet
1881

Living room of Neil and Kaisty Landitt

7:38 am Monday morning

Neil sat there and took it. Kaisty tore into him
unmercifully mainly because he knew he couldn't possibly be
the reason for so much anger being spewed at him. And
because he read somewhere that people on drugs, of the
psychiatric variety, can bring on violent and irrational reactions

in some people. So there was no point in Neil trying to make a point until she had simmered down, which in her case could be a day or two.

Without being obvious, if Neil leans back in the couch and looks hard to his right, over his shoulder, he can see his new silvery gold Mercedes with the pearlesant slippery gloss depth quality that Neil marvels at through the French doors. "Oh what a machine and oh what a bitch," Neil mutters under his breath. "She was so sweet a few years ago, what the hell happened?" Kaisty's eyes bug with anger as two large veins bulge from her sweet silky neck.

After a solid eight minute tirade Kaisty ran out of gas and shuffled back in a huff to the bedroom in her slippers and bathrobe then slammed the door while certainly putting her whole body into it.

"I wonder if my gold beauty out there needs a wash." Neil speaks to himself. "I know I just got her yesterday but it was sitting at the show all day and out in the driveway all night—ya, I think so. Sure, it could get a little dirty in one day." Neil sits there in his heavily starched dress shirt and blue-stripped boxers with only one sock on. He sits there for a minute or two with a dull stupor to his eyes. Kaisty slams the toilet seat down and Neil cringes, strains to look over his shoulder at his new Mercedes again.

Conference call to Real Corp. from Harton's yacht
Three miles off the coast of Catalina

8:51 am Monday morning

"I want that land! I pay you son's a bitches to get me what I want, what I need, and what I need is that frickin piece of property. I can build fifty homes worth three and a half million each on that land. And if some other son of a bitch builds fifty homes you two are so fired! Got it, damn it?"

Neil sat there and took it as Roger Harton spewed evil sparks at Neil and his partner Alec Grendale. Mr. Harton built his development company from the ground up in 1963 in the city closest south to Newport Beach by the name of Corona Del Mar. And as legend has it Mr. Harton could have bought the property from Mr. Binsent before his death in 1975. Mr. Harton could not come up with the cash in 1975 but he surely could now and *Mrs.* Binsent is not interested or amused by his yearly offers and covert ploys. Although Mr. Harton claims he only has a hand in the business these days—that hand is enough to stir the pot and cause ulcers across the board.

Mr. Harton smashes the disconnect button on the conference call console, throws his Bloody Mary across the deck of his yacht like a shot over the bow then rants and raves his way to the captain's bathroom. He yells at the deck hand before slamming the door. Jack stands there furious, clutching his fists hard against his thighs while still in his pajamas—the pajamas with the little embroidered gold anchors. The Captain standing stoic all in white pays no attention; his eyes in squinting grins are fixed out at sea. His face weathered leathery and dark tan, expresses no interest and is only mildly amused by Harton's outburst. Occasionally Roger will watch his

Captain with the wonder of a young boy. Sometimes he wishes he could simplify his life to the graceful almost romantic plane of his Captain's. The chiseled, weathered face of the Captain looks at his navigation instruments and his happy with that. He puts his eyes, the grinning eyes, back out to sea then takes the bill of his cap with his thumb and forefinger and pulls it further down to just above his eyebrows.

Neil and Alec look at each other stunned. In business there are two ways to motivate: constantly encourage or constantly stun. Roger Harton likes to stun people.

Imports of Newport Auto Dealership
Conference room

9:27 am Monday morning

"Now listen, listen to my words, very carefully to my words. If you men and I use that term loosely, if you men don't sell seventeen more Mercedes by the end of the month I'm going to fire every one of you milk toast bastards. You lazy suntanned pricks with your stupid Armani suits. Wipe that look off your face you son of a bitch!"

Davis Rothman's arm is stretched out rigid with his index finger shaking from anger at the smirking salesman. He lowers his voice but the anger broadens and deepens, his face contorts and grimaces as his next comment comes out as pure resentment and envy.

"We—are not going to let those bastards at Fletcher Jones keep selling five times the Mercedes we do every damn month. That piece of shit must have moved fifteen/twenty Mercedes to our four yesterday." A salesman interrupts. "Actually it's three, my guy backed out this morning." Davis slams both hands opened palmed on his desk. "Now if you losers can't pull it off I'll—god damn it, I'll do it myself!"

Davis throws a Styrofoam cup half full of coffee in the general direction of the salesmen, coffee splatters hitting the shoes and pant legs of two.

"Now get the hell out of my office and sell some fuckin cars and don't forget to smile you bastards!"

The salesmen walk sheepishly out onto the show room floor and in that show room one could hear a pin drop on cotton as no one buys Mercedes Monday morning at 9:30 am. So you have nervous sheepish salesmen pacing and ducking out of the way whenever Davis pokes his head out of his office door every twenty minutes or so.

There are only two things worse than death: A
dream that was not passed on or an entrepreneur
who sank into profound apathy.
                        Charles Wrightwood 1923
                        Newport's first resident
                        Millionaire

The kitchen of Robin, Scott and Amy Mofford

8:05 Monday morning

The aroma of pancakes, bacon, eggs, coffee and syrup
saturate the air of their little neatly appointed kitchen. Amy
groggily wipes her eyes and reaches slowly and carefully for her
orange juice. Robin looks over her shoulder and gives Amy a
gentle smile that she doesn't see as she lifts the orange juice to
her lips with both hands. Robin opens the freezer reaches in
for the two and a half quart plastic container full of frozen
water, a contractor favorite. The night before Robin prepares
this simple urban frozen marvel and adds a dash of lemonade
powder as a sweet touch. Ok, here is how it works: Robin
makes Scott's lunch which usually consists of ham or baloney
with a slice of cheese on each side. Mustard on one slice of
bread and mayonnaise on the other. Maybe some chips,
definitely something homemade like cookies or cake. Here is
where the frozen jug comes into play, it keeps everything cool
even on a hot day then as it melts it becomes his drink for the
day, all contractors do it. Scott learned this trick from a buddy
of his in Arizona.

Scott enters the kitchen, Robin quickly greets him with a
kiss, Amy looks up with an orange smile. He is ready to go, no
breakfast, although Robin tries to insist but he rarely ever eats
breakfast, most men do not, the ones who really work for a
living. God gave that edge to man, he must produce first,
keeps him light for the hunt. Robin is mildly annoyed, he is

wearing one of his better shirts to work, blames herself somehow.

"Honey bunch we're starting Mrs. Binsent's moulding install today. I'm hoping to give it a good milking, Ha!" Scott laughs.

Robin cover Amy's ears with both hands.

"Hush sweetie that's horrible, I know we need the money but Amy—honey." Robin gives Scott the nicest chastising he has ever or will ever receive as she tilts her head to one side, grits her teeth gently and forms her eyes into smiles all hovering over her deep well of love for the man.
"Ha! Give me that little button nose pumpkin shmumpkin." Scott reaches for Amy's nose. She closes her eyes and scrunches her face in anticipation. "Gotta go girls." Scott takes a bite out of Amy's pancake, gives her a wink, tousles her hair, kisses Robin on the forehead cheek and nose.

Robin eyes are closed, she melts.

Mrs. Binsent's Veranda

Early Monday morning, sun just coming up.

A Woman in her late seventies relaxes on her veranda as the sun breaches the, seldom considered, eastern horizon. The sudden gentle burst of sunrise sends a tranquil shot of warmth and light to Claire's glorious back yard and her own frail shoulders. She is grateful for such earthly blessings. Miniature brilliant white butterflies with tiny lavender spots imported from Brazil flutter about a gooseberry bush as a spider snips away at his dew drenched web like a camper cleaning up his site after a night under the stars. And very fine particles of dust not motivated by life are caught in the seduction of first light, a little way off to her left. There is a gradual aliveness so delicate that only a keen desire to sense and discover may be perceived. Claire takes it all in deeply.

The bay ninety feet away is illuminated as well in the subtle gush of sunrays where Claire's yacht glows enormous in its slip. Roaring up the harbor in relative silence are fourteen powerfully graceful oars at the hands of Coast Crew, in a mere strip of a vessel. Eight young men held firm by the promise of intercollegiate dominance. The mere mention of which, Orange Coast College, striking fear in ivy-league hearts, three thousand miles to the east. The crew slips into a low-slung mist and is lost. "Go get um boys" breaks furtive from Claire's breath. She sits there without a want unfulfilled, she sits quietly, eyes closed with her cat Bruty lying very contently on her lap. She is awake, fully conscious.

So, being that she is rich in a rather ridiculous way and the envy of every land developer this side of the high Sierra mountain range and has lived in Newport for fifty years, what is she looking at with her minds eye? To answer or take a shot at answering that one would have to understand the history of Newport to a degree.

The forties and fifties were Newport's golden era. Hollywood's best kept secret. John Wayne use to live a short three minute walk from where Claire is sitting this very moment. And if you have the Duke you have them all with either a home near by or at least visiting frequently. Gary Cooper spent a lot of time hanging around, he even owned an enormous ranch seven miles to the east. Vivian Leigh, Katherine Hepburn, Olivia de Havilland teased and conquered their way through the leading men of Newport on many occasions. Bogart and Becall could be seen sailing their craft 'Santana' all around the harbor often. Even Clark Gable road his old bicycle right along that path over there and show up at party or two when he would grace the locals with his presence. And the parties, oh the parties, very laid back and very entertaining. Most of the time they were thrown by guess who? Claire.

Mrs. Binsent lives for three reasons these days. She could have cashed her chips in several years back when her husband Edward died. She considered following him into the afterlife but simply decided not to. The phone rang or something else came up as she would tell her close friends over the years. When Fluffy Muffin passed on she again considered a similar fate for her herself but again simply decided against it. Six months later Claire adopted Muffy Wuffy. She discovered the difference between a survivor and someone a bit weaker is that the survivor decides and manages to hang on a little tighter and also manages to somehow to cheer *themselves* up a little and find something to live for.

Claire Binsent lives for three reasons. She supports the local Humane Society doggedly. She lives for her remaining friends from old Newport and Mrs. Binsent lives for the game.

Her eyes remain closed as she recalls vividly Clark Gable riding his rickety bicycle up the path -which is flanked by mansions now- for a party at the Binsent's. 'It was a lousy old bike,' she grins to herself. She also recalls later that same evening when she and Mr. Gable slow danced and laughing softly as her husband lay passed out on the veranda after several scotches.

Bruty figgets some and Claire begins to caress gently. A breeze lightly ruffles her gray locks as she takes in a deep breath, as deep a breath as an old woman can take. She smiles, eyes remain closed.

The game, if she sells the property the games is over. The first offer she received was in 1966. That Tuesday late November she understood where Newport was headed and decided to have some fun with it, throw in a wrench now and then. When one is very rich, the very rich play big and sometimes dangerous games. She never needs the money, never has, never will, but she needs the game. Mrs. Binsent has received 617 offers during the forty-three years since the first offer. Each offer is met with a polite and sometimes not so polite letter of refusal. The City of Newport officials over the political generations have attempted to force her to give up the property but General Motors bottomless well of resources and Detroit (where Claire spent her formative years) savvy have kept them hopelessly at bay.

She begins to nod off into a wistful semi-sleep and as she does she sees in her dreamy state John Wayne and his wife Pilar dropping by for drinks and good conversation. 'Down the hatch with the latest batch' was the battle cry as the sun melted into the pacific like frosting on one of Claire's warm butter rum cakes.

Marty and her new friend

Very early Monday morning, still dark.

Marty is wide awake. The young man sleeping next to her is not. "Was it Rob or Bob? Damn I can't remember." Marty wonders quietly to herself. She shakes her head in disgust at herself for being so accommodating so soon. She searches under the covers for her panties and slips them on while giving the young man next to her a 'don't wake up look.'

After all, meeting someone at the Newport Auto Show then spending time with them from that point on isn't really considered a first date. But she likes him, she may even like him a lot. Marty lights up a cigarette in the dark and looks out the large window at the foot of Rob or Bob's king size Benton Falmour bed with sculpted mahogany posts. The delicate brilliance of Newport sparkles and shimmers in the early morning moonlight.

Karen's place

Karen calls John, leaves message.

"It's ok—I think I like the prologue better though. And I *love* the Taste of Newport, what was that all about? I like the morning after the show, that was cool, call me."

Karen takes a shower. John calls—leaves message.

"Get over the prologue it's not about them. I had to introduce the characters somewhere and I like the Auto Show better.……..more chapters coming, it is moving good……I think. I might e-mail them to you. See ya."

Karen turns off the shower, thinks she hears her phone.

......FIVE

Ten Days Later, Early Morning

Newport Coast Golf Course

The long rolling greens stood like frozen ocean swells. The sun is bright and generous with warm light wind wisps throwing the pin flag to and fro. And the clouds, the clouds are giant towering puffs of fluff and brilliance in lofty grandeur and sharp contrast to the exquisite purplish blue back drop that is sky—quite a sight. And there are trees, tall, fully expressed indigenous red oaks lining the fairway. As frail as a nervous golfer's swing is, the red oaks stood as confident pillars in a somewhat mocking stance. All of this set graciously on the coast of the great Pacific Ocean. High up in the early morning sky a faint three quarter moon remained across the low heavens from the morning's mighty sun.

A golf ball awaits, Titleist by name, at the feet of Neil Landitt, driver resting against his waist. Perfectly creased, tight at the waist lose fitting in the leg, green plaid pants flutter in the breeze. And he is hard to miss with his bright yellow Callaway golf shirt. Neil has a pair of binoculars pressed tightly to his sockets.

"What the hell are you looking at, we have a foursome breathing down our neck." Alec blurts.
"Motion them to play on through." Neil calmly replies.
"Not that damn property again."

Neil does not respond for a moment.

"Seventh tee is the best, I can just see it down through that gully, that damn bluff is in the way a bit though."
"She will never sell."
"You never know."
"You're obsessed."

Again Neil is silent for a moment.

"Do you have any idea what Kaisty would do if I delivered that property to the old man. I tell you one thing we would move into Big Canyon (wealthy residential community connected at the hip to Fashion Island) the next day. She's always wanted to live there. Right across the street from Fashion Island, imagine that."

"Oh lord, just hit the damn ball." Alec blurts in laughing disgust.

Neil folds the strap around the binoculars neatly and places them in the pocket of his golf bag. He walks over to the ball already teed up with the driver over his shoulder like a lumberjack prepared for a big whack. Neil plants his feet, fidgets some, sets the club behind the ball while slumping his shoulders, head down. His nervousness comes out as easy as a flipped switch from a hundred fathoms down in a man's soul. As though, implanted at birth, the phrase 'hit the ball straight or die' is a standard of existence that must be met and seldom is........

Neil fidgets, again, actually it is more of a streaming current of fidget. He looks to his left down the fairway, looks back down at the ball, looks down the fairway again, looks down at the ball. An urgent focused anxiety takes over, the shot must be taken. A numbed confidence also takes over without any realistic basis for that confidence.

Neil raises the club high remembering to keep his left elbow in to his ribs, tries to slow the motion of the club on its downward arch. He cannot resist a quick powerful stroke, ball soars. It soars some more then begins to slice. The ball is still gaining altitude as it flies over the trees as the true wickedness of the slice is brought to bear. Neil screams "Four!" which means run for your life as the ball lands in the adjacent fairway, golfers scramble for cover.

"Shit." Neil cracks under his breath.
"She will never sell Neil."
"You never know."

Neil and Alec carry their bags across the parking lot to the trunk of Neil's Mercedes Benz an hour later after three hours of frustration and an occasional laugh.

"When are you letting loose of that ten year old Infinity and buying a Mercedes, you tight ass." Neil bites.

"Ah, you know, Jenny and the kids, you know how the money goes." Alec defends while cleaning his cleats.

"That's a bad plan—you know what Mr. Horton says."

"I know, I know, 'conservation of energies and resources brings and demands contraction, something like that."

"Well, he's right."

"Come on, not again, you know little Bradley needs a new wooden leg and Jenny, Jenny's eyes, you know they don't match."

Neil gives him that look, the look a friend gives you when it's your turn to jump when you were the first one to dare in the first place.

"Ok, ok we'll just stop by for a look." Alec caves in.

Imports of Newport is a twenty minute drive up the coast from the golf course and Neil uses every micro moment to extol the virtues and features of his new S500. Surprisingly Alec takes moderate yet guarded interest this time, this time maybe because he knows Neil will never, ever shut up about it.

......SIX

Davis Rothman stands at the front of his dealership trying to figure out if that is a little dog or a cat walking on the sidewalk across Pacific Coast Highway, seventy-five-feet away. He squints and leans into his interest with his hands in his pockets. He is doing this because there is no one stopping in with even the slightest increment of interest in the nine Mercedes he has lined up for viewing.

At that moment when Davis is convinced that what he sees is a cat and turns to go into the small showroom a large American sedan -the model is of no importance in a exclusively foreign car market- with blacked out windows pulls into his entrance way. Davis stops, pulls his hands out of his pockets. The car comes to a stop in front of Davis, there is a ten second pause that feels like forty five before the back window is lowered half way.

"Mr. Rothman, you are Mr. Rothman we were told." A Ukrainian man about forty says.

"Yes, ah, yes." Davis replies.

"We were told you don't sell lot of the Mercedes here."

"Well, well that's getting fixed I assure you." Davis stiffens and begins to walk away. Through clinched teeth he mutters "That son of a bitch."

"It doesn't matter, stop, doesn't matter. You will never sell as many Mercedes as the big dealer up road, you will be out of business in year, two year tops."

Davis stops clinches his fists and turns around.

"Who the hell are you? I don't need this shit we have two Mercedes going out later today.

"Fletcher Jones has probably twenty going out today."

"Alright, ok, what's your damn point, you have obviously done your home work but I have a business to run here."

"We can fix it all for you."

The Ukrainian man gets out and another man hands him a brief case. He lays the brief case down on the hood hard without regard for the paint job and Davis is the only one concerned for the black gloss finish. He opens the brief case and $100,000.00 cash delivers a shot of its magic to Davis' eyes and heart. He unclenches his fists and involuntarily holds his breath. His cheeks flex and ridge into a fixed smile.

"Do—do you want to buy a Mercedes?" Davis composes himself to ask.

"No, no, we need this cleaned for us through your business every few weeks." The Ukrainian says brazenly.

"Screw you, I'm not going to prison for you, get the fuck out of here!" Davis blasts.

The man, the one in charge, takes a $10,000.00 bundle and slips it into the fledgling Mercedes dealer's blazer pocket.

"We are back tomorrow, for you to think about it, yes?"

The only chance Davis Rothman had if he honestly did not want any part of this was to give the Ukrainian back his $10,000.00 right then and there. Unfortunately he did not, they never do.

11:15 PM   Rothman's office

"They are right Imports of Newport, meaning me, will be out of business in less than two years." Davis moans under his breath, thinks maybe he can do this for them for just a few months then they could simply find someone else.

The bundle of hundred dollar bills sits directly in front of him, it has a power over him, a presence greater than his own. It speaks to him like it speaks to all men. It tells him 'I am the answer to every thing' and 'easy money is the best money.' Once a man acquires money in an easy manner his mindset is altered instantly, he cannot easily escape its gravity. Light cannot escape a Black Hole even at 186,000 miles per second. Davis Rothman is unable or unwilling to muster a speed of escape anywhere near that fast, the money is his master and he its grateful, obedient servant.

The Ukrainian will be back tomorrow and Davis Rothman will hand over his soul and the Ukrainian will hand over their laundry with exact instructions on how to clean it. The fight with Fletcher Jones Motor Cars is over. The struggle to regain his soul has begun.

What the Ukrainian's really desire is land, a lot of it, this being the ultimate motive. And they will be sure to make good use of Davis Rothman.

.....SEVEN

It's not that Robin was not aware of or did not know about the property or would not have loved to be the one to deliver it. But this was all new to her. No question she wanted to do something right by her broker but seemed just as concerned about keeping the mistakes to a minimum. The fact that she is standing in the middle of Mrs. Binsent's impressive maple riddled study was by sheer accident. You see her husband Scott just happens to be installing twelve inch wide crown and base mouldings in that very room. Robin just stopped by to drop off Scott's lunch, which she swears sometimes he forgets on purpose.

"Hi honey, did you forget this." Robin waves Scott's lunch in the air with a wowed smile on her face.

Robin stands there, her golden hair with faint red highlights held up tight in the back and the rest framing her face and gently curling in toward her chin. Her brown eyes excite as Scott notices her presence. This is one of those rare breed of women especially in Newport who really don't know how beautiful they are. She is wearing a dark shimmery green business skirt and coat, an ivory white blouse with a high collar and a ruffly kind of ascot/scarf. Typical attire for a female real estate agent. She doesn't look comfortable with the business woman persona but Scott thinks she looks damn cute. Her left heel falls inward and Robin flips it back before she loses balance.

There is a sweet but brief embrace and Scott kisses her forehead.

"Well, what do you think my sweet?" Scott asks in that somewhat mumbled drawl, exclusive to career contractors.

"Wow this is amazing!" Robin cheerfully replies.

"Someday baby girl—someday."

Robin eyes twinkle and she smiles broadly at the prospect. But Scott knows full well Robin would be happy if they were together on Mars in a leaky tent.

"Is this your helper?" Mrs. Binsent speaks as she creeps into the study with the help of her walker.

Robin and Scott respond with embarrassed chuckles.

"No ma'am, no ma'am this is my wife Robin.

"You're lucky she is a beauty."

"Oh, thank you, I'm so embarrassed, I........."

"Enjoy it while you've got it my dear."

"Scott will you be done by the end of the week?" Mrs. Binsent changed her tone somewhat but it remained friendly.

"No problem."

"Good in that case I will take your wife with *me* as ladies have to stick together and keep each other informed of the latest fashions and such.

Mrs. Binsent pushed the walker aside and took hold of Robin's left forearm.

"Let's go honey."

Mrs. Binsent led Robin to her, as she would say, 'understated' parlor. Understated to the fabulously wealthy is still rather rich to the senses. Norwegian antiques, Claire's favorite, are placed meticulously about. The high ceilings with stained class windows just under the roofline give the room an ethereal, cathedral feel when the light pours down in the early afternoon. They have a seat and right on cue Marisah, Claire's maid and general hostess offers drinks. Robin says no thanks but Claire raises two fingers anyway and says "Honey, my mango tea is to die for."
Robins grins agreeably. They chat.
Mrs. Binsent likes Robin instantly, you can see it unmistakingly in her eyes. Robin sees the sparkle in her intensely alive, pale green eyes and the serene crooked grin the lady exudes but is unaware that it is in response to her own beauty and demeanor.

"Robin honey, I have and idea, you and your husband are invited to spend the day on my yacht—this weekend."
"I—oh—ah—ok!"

.....EIGHT

A VISIT TO THE PROPERTY

One hour ago the blazing summer sun dissolved gracefully and dutifully into a cobalt blue aqueous dream that of the Pacific Ocean. And the sea speaks to the San Bernardino mountains standing sentry to southern California, seventy miles to the east. The sea says to the mountains 'You are strong and still, yet I am ambient and I have strength as well'. Yet the mountains are silent as they feel no need to utter a sound. The sun does speak as it rolls below the horizon saying 'My strength is broken for the day, enjoy the heavens of night.' And the royalty of Newport are nourished by it all as all have settled in for the evening except for one, one man.

Neil sat in his Mercedes and clinched his eyes closed hard trying to stop Kaisty's voice from playing over and over and over. "She won't stop riding me until I give her a chunk of the moon and a star." He grumbles to himself. Right out side his door lay the property. Yet he stayed in his metal cocoon with a white knuckled firm grip on the steering wheel. With his eyes closed and fighting to relax he flew above the land like a bird. He imaged crawling along its rough tilled texture quick like a rodent. He got underneath it as would a worm. "This would go far with the old man too, you pull off something like this and you're basically the right hand man from then on." He spoke softly.

Neil opens the door and takes his shoes off, then socks. He presses his white, sun deprived feet in the moist rich soil. He wanted to feel a part of it. He wanted it to feel a part of him. An intoxicating shiver raced up his legs. He laughs quietly. It was dark now except for his headlights. The European blue hue of the light gave the property a ghostly yet inviting feel. There was only a delicate sliver of moon slipping in and out of the clouds this late July night.

Neil walks out to where he thinks the center is, rolls up his pant legs and digs his feet in as deep as he can. A cool dense coastal breeze rich with the oceans fragrance ignites goose bumps on the skin of Neil's bare forearms and neck. There was only one problem Claire Binsent won't even accept offers any more, she won't even converse at all about the property. "The only undeveloped parcel of land in Newport and the bitch won't build on it, sell, or talk about it," Neil grumbles again.

Neil thinks that's fine though he's a smart guy. He will think of something, people change their minds every day his father once told him. He worms through the soil quick then pops out as bird lunging up powerfully and flew above it hovering in wistful circles. "The old man was right, about fifty very custom homes would be just about right at around three a and half million each, with upgrades, lots of upgrades." Neil as bird spoke. "They could be built and sold in two years, easy. I've got to come up with a plan, I've got to think," Neil as bird added.

Back at home, Kaisty wrestles with the cap of a Zoloft bottle. She angrily smashes at it with the heal of Neil's Fathonric dress shoe. She picks up three tablets and leaves the rest on the floor. She strips off her robe and sits on the toilet, leans against the sink top, mutters something incoherent, then falls asleep.

Neil closes his eyes and extends his arms. He projects himself to all seven corners at once. He squirms his toes down a little deeper. Neil asks the heavens for a spiritual and physical marriage of convenience. A hundred years ago this was not considered a large piece of land, but in 2008 it was a major prize in *the* major coastal city. Neil opens his eyes and breaths in deep. This is church for a developer and 'the deal' is a spiritual experience, a conformation of devotion, a gift to their Deus.

In the long southern shadow of Los Angles abides a relatively small coastal town. Do not let it fool you and do not fool with it for some of this worlds most powerful people reside there.

Margery Winnlit
Newport Socialite

Karen's place

Karen is at her computer reading. Her cheekbone is cupped in her left palm, smallest finger folded under against her soft cheek. Right hand holds mouse loosely. She fidgets occasionally, drinks some coffee. The glow from the monitor enhances the casual interest that cultivates in her eyes.

......NINE

SUNDAY MORNING

Robin just makes sure Scott does not make any major mistakes, which can easily happen to a man getting ready for church. Mismatched socks would be considered capitol error, everybody notices that. Robin tries to lay his clothes out the night before but it is something one would not want to set their clock by due to the attention eater—Amy. So keeping an eye out for Scott selecting a tie, shirt and socks that don't clash too much is all a loving wife can hope to accomplish on an expeditiously paced Sunday morning. This endeavor can be put in percentages. Twenty five percent of Robin's attention is on Scott, fifteen on her self and the remaining one hundred percent is on, around and within the realm of sweet little Amy.

Amy fans helpless, as she loves her mother to create her princess. Amy herself at six could probably pull off most of the effort after several years of the routine. But she loves the ceremony beyond all others and to study Robin's faces of expression during and through each stage of creation.

"Now honey, the white leotards not the blue." Robin directs and Amy already knows as the ceremony of creation has also become a game.

Amy steps up to the mirror, blonde hair entangled and in all directions after eight hours of dreaming.

"Ok, first let's brush out all these knots."
"Ouch."
"Sorry my sweet."

Robin goes on automatic, curlers, curling iron, blow dryer, spray bottle of water with conditioner mixed in. All sorts of clips to hold this and that up. Amy's activity is in the mirror, she observes and files away everything, all women do, even six year old women—especially six year old women. And she studies her mother, her intensity, her focus, her attempts to make Amy laugh, her compliments, the way she scrunches her face in concentration.

"Ok, hop down missy and put your dress on and shoes, they're all laid out on your bed. We will take the curlers out in fifteen minutes, right before we leave."

Amy knows this already as she runs down the hall smiling broadly.

Robin gets ready herself at break neck speed with occasional quick glances at Scott making sure those major mistakes are not being made. Scott takes his time. Puts on one sock, takes a break. Puts on his slacks and a shirt, then dillydallies. Puts both shoes on then slips out to the back patio for a smoke.

Robin converges on Amy for a final whirlwind of primping. Robin steps back quick for a fast intense inspection. Amy's eyes widen and her lips part in wait for the words she has heard every Sunday morning, well, since she understood the words.

"Perfect, just perfect."

St. James Church

The Moffords arrive in the parking lot of St. James church on this warm and generous morning god has graced upon them. They greet their friends genuinely; Amy's cheeks are pink from her marathon smile. The families begin their way up the old brick stairs as families have since the 20's in hopes of salvation or something less dramatic as merely a nourishing communion with their savior. Pastor Donaldson greets them kindly.

The fourth aisle is Amy's favorite and she has tried them all. Amy takes Robin's hand and hurries to the center, she loves the center, isle four. Scott takes up the slack in groggy toe. They sit on the worn heavily varnished pews. Smiles and laughs all around the Moffords as seats are taken. Some mask their pain well enough and others not so well and others are honestly in high grace of spirit. Today is the day of sacrament. And Amy takes sacrament very seriously.

Across town at Boag Hospital—Emergency

At Boag Emergency there is a holy gathering of another sort as Dr. G. Perry Osland gives out the tablet and injected sacrament to his flock after a night of fervent excess. Neil brought Kaisty in an hour ago.

Neil sat in the emergency room in dead silence, only the soft 'hursh murr' of the central air breached the otherwise utter silence. The nurse manning the desk behind a five foot high wall was completely without sound. Neil sucks his lips in, make a 'fwip pop' noise then got up and tells the attendant nurse he would be back in a few minutes. She looks up and gives him an approving grin, says nothing then goes back to her crossword puzzle. Neil's shoes make an annoying 'squirsh squirsh squirsh' sound on the large white industrial tiles as he exits the facility.

As in all great fairy tales and as oblivious as Neil may seem at times he is keenly aware (if only metaphorically) of the tiny little golden key that opens the first little cottage style door that leads to the big fifteen feet high, two foot solid oak door with steel reinforcements that will take much more to navigate through to a women's knighting of him as her prince of hearts.

Chocolate and flowers, this is the tiny little key that opens the little cottage style door, chocolate and flowers. But there is an ogre there as well, seven feet tall with a steel battle grid over his face and he is armed. He must be maneuvered around on tiptoes.

Just about any great looking dozen roses will do as long as a man doesn't choose the wrong color. But the chocolate is a whole nether deal, story and situation. In fact, one cannot consider themselves truly Newport if one does not know where to find the finest chocolate. Most mistakes of men, if truth be told, are in the chocolate arena. Basically to make a short story shorter Neil once bought something for Kaisty that simply said chocolate on the wrappings in her valentine arrangement a few years ago. Maybe that will fly in Nebraska but you don't get away with that if the girl is born and bred Newport.

Neil knows the best chocolate and the best for all occasions, redemption or otherwise, is the Godiva chocolate store on Pacific Coast highway as Neil rushes in and grabs Kaisty's usual favorites. Now usually he will linger on the verge of loiter to enjoy the utter sense consuming chocolate scents of the quaint shop but this time Neil hustled back out to the Mercedes. He makes a b-line to the harbor where their twenty-four-foot, twenty-year old sail boat is docked.

"When I get Kaisty out of there we are going to spend some quality time around this harbor here, maybe even head out to Catalina for a day or two. Good, great plan." Neil mutters under his breath as he cleans up and places the flowers and chocolates around. He stands back with his hands on his hips.

"That will do, that's just fine."

Neil drove back up to the hospital and hustles into the emergency room with that tight knotted aire about him that suggest he is on the verge of being in trouble. He walks that way a lot around Kaisty lately. Shoulders up tense, jaw tight, clinched teeth smile, weary eyes. Kaisty's doctor comes out of the observation area with a grin on the verge of a smirk and mildly shaking his head.

"Mr. Landitt your wife is fine, mean, but fine. Maybe just and extra sleeping pill or two in her that's all." The Doctor laughs in pitiable little chuckles.

"I couldn't wake her—I tried." Neil defended knowing down deep he did not try that hard for fear of having her wake up and snap at him. Neil has learned the hard way to tread lightly around Kaisty especially recently.

"Hey Doc—are those anti-depressants she's taking really that safe and well—effective, she seems so—so unstable since she's been taking them?" Neil sheepishly asks.

The doctor conditioned from birth by the American Board of Psychiatry does not bat an eye. "Mr. Landitt let me assure you, people have dedicated their lives in research of these chemical imbalances and in your wife's case, bipolar state caused by chemical imbalances and have the right medication or will have it soon. Not to worry Mr. Landitt, we are the authorities in such matters, years of research."

"Yes sir I—I know we've been told pretty much that exact same thing a few times but, and I don't mean to assert that I know how the biology of the mind works, but couldn't there be something from the past bothering her, you know—all knotted up and hidden driving her a little crazy? Something she can't quite put her finger on? Maybe several things you know I'm just thinking about it. I mean, and again I'm just a real estate developer, but isn't the mind a fairly rugged and—and brilliant thing, can it really go out of whack that easily with the chemical imbalance idea—I mean, you know? Again, I almost feel like apologizing before I even say it but isn't depression an emotional response to life? I mean something must of happened, right? I—I know I'm rambling here sir but………."

The doctor may very well have considered Neil was rambling on if he had been listening.

Right on that note Kaisty storms out of the observation room past the doctor, past Neil and out the double automatic glass doors that give out a 'quish whash' audible as the sensors are tripped then quick angry steps out to the Mercedes.

"Good luck young fella." The doctor smirks on the verge of a frown, having no interest in nor did he even listen to what Neil had to say, for he is the authority in such matters.

Neil in sinking to a new depth of sheepishness walks stiff, slow and sullen to the driver side door of the Mercedes. Kaisty and Neil sat in the parking lot in absolute silence at Boag Memorial Hospital right outside the emergency room. Neil held tight by the emotion of anxiety as Kaisty is fixed by resentment, each staring ahead. Boag is the national model for health care, inpatient or out. The facility is expertly managed and local wealth fund it to perfection but with all of its brilliance and towering respect it could not help to ease the tension within the silvery gold Mercedes where Neil and Kaisty sat miles apart. As handsome, rich and confident as the hospital and surroundings are it is equally bankrupt of emotion and barren of endearment within the confines of the automobiles interior.

Kaisty sat coiled, working which angle to take with her verbal attack, Neil sat waiting for it. Then, inexplicably, Neil in a rare show of assertiveness with regard to Kaisty took sudden and sweeping control, which surprises them both.

"We are going to spend the rest of the day and evening on the boat, maybe head out to Catalina and we are going to have a wonderful time and I'm sorry, things like this happen when you love someone and I love you and—here we go."

Kaisty was so shocked all she could muster was a flabbergasted "Ok!" Neil started the big duel over head cam V-8 and found himself suddenly kindred to its power, flips his sunglasses from his forehead to his nose in a quick gesture with his index finger. Neil sits up perfectly straight and speeds off to the marina holding his newfound confident demeanor for nearly the entire two mile drive.

Kaisty carefully walks down the dock ramp and Neil is wondering if she is still harboring resentment from the hospital fiasco. Kaisty lets out quick little laughs as she stumbles and grabs hold of his arm. If she was really that mad she would not of done that. Neil is relieved.

Neil's sailboat is slipped not too far from some of the magnificent yachts of the harbor. Kaisty smiles with the twinge of embarrassment as they step on their Gulfstream 37. Neil is a proud yachtsmen, the boat is immaculate. One of the most therapeutic processes a man can perform is to work on his boat, alone. Neil has done that many times and many times he has dug himself out of what can churn a man up into quite a knot. Kaisty steps below holding the handrail tight.

"Neil it smells like—oh honey!"

The cabin is filled with roses, white and peach with scattered red ones. Kaisty's eyes moisten, she is rarely touched or at least rarely displays much of such a sloppy emotion. And this is definitely how to catch her off guard.

"Oh my god, oh my god, oh my god! This is soooooo sweet—and what is that over there Neil?"

Kaisty points to the bag on the bed. She knows full well what it is. She opens the gold and white bag, breaths in deep.

"My favorite chocolate in the whole world!"

Neil is feeling pretty damn good about his efforts, arms folded, leaning against the cabin doorway. He stands there with that damn stupid smile men have on their faces when they seldom get it right. The sun is well into its fiery plunge as a chilled mist rumbles into the harbor at a laggard pace bringing with it the rich bouquet of the ocean.

Kaisty's excitement has relaxed into a sweet serenity as she nestles up under Neil's arm and tight to his side on the cabin bed, held lightly by a dreamy bliss. The right combination of chocolate, flowers and nautical seduction can do that for a woman. Neil is thoroughly at ease and utterly content.

A boat down the way is playing some jazz and by sheer accident it's just the right volume for repose. The pressures are never too far off from Neil though. Like a harpoon from the heavens it finds him.

"Honey—Neil, you see that yacht through the port hole?"
"Which port hole, port or starboard?"
"Oh I don't know, that one."

Neil still feeling rather in control of the situation, presses further.

"Come on sweetheart I've told you at least ten times."
"I don't know and I don't care. That yacht right over there."

Neil strains to look over Kaisty's head.

"We can have something like that for us someday, don't you think?"

Kaisty prods with her stun gun on low as she circles Neil's belly button with her moistened forefinger. The only thought Neil's mind would or could entertain was delivering Mrs. Binsent's property to Harton. That is the only viable way he could ever imagine buying something like that for Kaisty.
"Someday honey—you bet."
Kaisty dives her finger into Neil's belly button for a well intended emphasis.

The Jazz played in delicate lively tones and the pressures where manageable. Kaisty's instabilities where rarely and synthetically stabilized and Neil enjoyed his boat, his wife, and his relative peace.

That Same Evening

"I'll be there in a moment my sweetness." Scott says as he rummages through the hall closet. "Ah here it is." Scott whispers to himself. Amy is fast asleep into the dreamland of her choosing as Scott races down the hallway in last years Halloween costume and pieces from the year before, his black Dracula cape with his Zorro mask and Star Wars light saber. Scott is not wearing anything else. He flies into the room and Robin bursts with laughter. Scott has left his senses being in the moment running around the room quoting something that Shakespeare never wrote. He smacks his knee on a long antique bench at the end of the bed, he hops around holding his knee in pain. Robin is now crying with laughter. Scott falls on the bed.

"Oh my Dracula/Zorro/Jedi knight super hero! Are you ok my sweet husband?"

"Ouch, shit, kiss it quick!" Scott replies seizing the opportunity.

"Yes my dear even Superman needs a little first aid now and then."

"It hurts here, too."

"Oh—honey."

The Following Morning

The face is that of a woman in her early thirties. Her eyes are open, her expression calm, serene. Her mouth is parted slightly. Her hair under water swirls delicately over her face now, a peaceful face. Her sandy blond hair retreats over her forehead and gathers above her head obeying the water's gentle force delightfully which exposes a large dark purple bruise to her temple.

Her loose lifeless body bumps up against the hull of a boat over and over and over again in sympathy with the rocking of the harbor waters.

'Whirp! Whirp!' Two short high-pitched blasts from the siren of the harbor patrol. They have come upon another 'floater.' Every other year or so, one or two women are found in the bay all about the same age, so tragic. They are rarely identified or claimed. The boat she is up against is Neil and Kaisty's and they are sound asleep inside as the retrieval begins. Such an indignity, as the seven-foot aluminum pole with a large hooked end takes hold under her arm pit and pulls her over to the side of the patrol boat.

Her face breaks the surface of the water and the sunlight exposes in grim realism, a bloated and bruised woman's face. They drag her limp body over the side, both men show no emotion, they do not dare. Both men have worked the harbor for over ten years, recovered seventeen bodies, almost all women. They do not allow themselves to feel, if they did they would not continue in this line of work very long. Neil and Kaisty are fifteen feet away in a kind of apathy all their own, sound asleep.

......TEN

A Few Days Later

"Oh honey, guess what?" Neil casually mentions as he leans against the counter top with the heal of his left foot propped up to the cabinet and his right hand over the corner of the counters edge waiting for his toast...........to toast.

"What?" Kaisty replies as she sits at the half-inch thick glass table in her plush white bathrobe, hair wrapped up tight in a towel nibbling on a strawberry while sipping on some coffee.

"Mr. Harton sent us all a memo stating that whoever has the top sales for the month may have his tickets for the party at the Ritz this year." Neil nonchalantly mentions as he takes a big bite of his seven-grain toast.

Neil has no idea that what he just said is what Kaisty has waited for and needed from Neil since their marriage in 1997.

If the eyes are the windows to the soul, then Kaisty's eyes just screamed this was *the* event they needed to be part and parcel to if they want to get any where near to and touch the nucleus of phenomenal wealth that embodies Newport Beach.

Kaisty sets down the small leafy green top of the strawberry and finishes chewing slowly without comment. She tightens her robe, checks the towel that wraps her hair then stands up. Neil is now leaning over the sink eating his toast and doesn't realize Kaisty is standing directly behind him.

"Honey isn't that great?" Neil says as he turns with a surprise in his eyes to find her a foot away from him. "Hey sneaky, you've wanted to go since I can remember."

"You're going to do it right—you're going to win right?" Kaisty says with the look deep in her eyes of someone stuck in a hole pleading to the only person within a hundred miles to please get help.

"Oh—oh sure I'll do my best, you know I always do." Neil shakes his head in affirmation then turns back to the sink with a twinge of uneasiness in his eyes.

"Promise me, promise me that we are going." Kaisty pleads with a desperate tone in her voice, nearly a wince.

"Geez honey ok—ok!"

Kaisty hurries from the kitchen to the retreat and sanctuary of her bathroom and shuts the door behind her. Neil looks over his shoulder still chewing and says "What's got into her." Neil rinses the crumbs out of the sink and wonders what on earth he did this time. Kaisty sits on the toilet with a death grip on a Kleenex. She is not crying. She understands the parts they must play and of course Neil does not. Getting Neil to understand is not important. Riding him hard to get the tickets is.

Kaisty has seven different little plastic bottles on the counter, most of the psychiatric variety. She grabs the two bottles she thinks was the latest and best combination. "Which one is the shot and which one is the chaser?" Kaisty half heartily ponders.

Neil lightly taps on the door and asks her if she is ok. Kaisty replies with a semi antagonistic "Uh…..huh."

Kaisty is not well, she has not been for some time. Her doctor tells Neil she has a chemical imbalance but truth be told Kaisty's mind is not deficient of Paxil, Ativan, Risperadol, Effexor, Depakote or any other synthetic chemical. Her doctor has said Kaisty is border line schizophrenic but the truth is there is a lot of Kaisty balled up and snarled tight in past experiences and incidents, which in present time does give the impression of someone being torn in two as the condition of schizophrenia would suggest. Some would say these incidents must be addressed. But her doctor's latest and greatest assessment and diagnosis is the condition of bipolar. The greatest marketing scheme yet to push an avalanche of pills onto and into Americans—by force if necessary. And there is not a chemical on earth synthetic or otherwise that can bring it all back together for Kaisty. Kaisty is not well, as she sets a little green and white tablet on her tongue.
Kaisty sees the shadow of Neil's shoes under the door.

"Neil, my friend locked herself in her bathroom with a gun to her head the other day. She went cold turkey trying to get off Ativan."

"Oh?"

"Her husband had to kick the door in."

"Wow."

"This will never happen to us Neil—because I will never stop taking them…..."

Neil is standing sentry on the other side of the door as bemused as always. But his resolve is set. One way or the other he will have tickets to the party at the Ritz.

......ELEVEN

Mrs. Binsent's Yacht—The Nordic Star

Crash! Crack! The apparent open, direly clean glass door of Mrs. Binsent's 140 foot yacht built by Hargrave, was apparently closed. Scott did not break stride as he crashed into it nose first. Robin drops her purse and rushes to him as he falls to his knees holding his nose with both hands.

"Honey! Honey, honey are you ok?" Robin bursts.
"Ouch, shit, fudge!" Scott rips.
"Try not to swear honey—I don't want Mrs. Binsent to think we are trailer park trash."
"I said fudge."
"Not to worry honey, father was a truck driver in the nineteen thirties." Mrs. Binsent says with a smile as she creeps along with her walker designed specifically for the yacht.
"Oh he's fine." Robin nervously says with only a cursory examination. She is always the first on the scene of any accident and always takes some responsibility out of fault or not.

Scott looks up at Robin with a disapproving glare as the areas beneath both eyes begin to turn black and purple.

"I think its broken Robin." Scott says with a pained grimace.

"Don't worry Scotty I can get you any nose you desire, Kostner, Pitt, Depp, you name it. I'm up on all the stars even in my decrepit old age. Hell, I can even get you a Cooper or Gable nose for that matter." Mrs. Binsent tenders.

"What's a Cooper or Gable nose Mrs. Binsent?" Robin asks.

"Never mind sweetie."

Scott pulls himself up then the blood starts. Robin runs for a towel without any idea where one might be found. Mrs. Binsent yells to the steward and Marisah for wet towels and Marisah is there before she can finish the sentence.

Twenty Minutes Later

Mrs. Binsent has finished tending to Scott in the stern of the massive yacht. A blurry combination of black lacquer, brass, thickly varnished teak and port holes is all Scott can make out as Mrs. Binsent gives Scott a kiss on the forehead. Robin is mesmerized by the light cream tan leather couches with black piping, nicer than any she has ever seen in a home. Scott has two huge oversized Q Tips -that were only on the market for a little while and Claire bought about fifty boxes of them- sticking out of his nose. The black and purple just under the surface below Scott's eyes are darkening now and spreading.

The Steward pushes up a stainless steel cart next to Scott with large bottles of several alcohols of choice and juices for mixing, Vodka and cranberry being Scott's favorite. Within fifteen minutes Scott feels no pain, due in large part the four Vicodin tablets Mrs. Binsent has so graciously stashed for him under a napkin. Scott looks at the pills then at Mrs. Binsent. She returns with a devilish grin to insinuate even the devil himself may need an escape now and then.

Three Hours Later

Scott and Robin emerge from Boag Memorial with Scott in a wheelchair and a larger than life nose splint and Robin pushing and laughing. Yet Scott is under the influence of the finest pharmaceutical grade-A narcotic painkillers in the land and a large white bag of same in his lap. Scott tries to smile but it pains him greatly so he manages a glassy-eyed grin of glee at Robin's jokes as she leans over his shoulder and laughs lovingly into his ear.

"First I told him Brad Pitt, then I changed my mind to Johnny Depp but I'm afraid it turned out like Harrison Ford's. I hope it turns out ok honey bunch."

"Owe—owe! Don't make me laugh!" Scott pleads.

A light breeze kicks up as the sun begins its slow dive.

Robin's cell phone rings.

"Oh, hello De De, oh I'm sorry we won't be able to make it, I forgot to call you, Scott broke his sweet little nose." Robin converses while helping a sluggish rubbery Scott into the Chrysler.

Scott shakes his head trying to snap out of it but fails miserably.

"You guys are lucky!" De De blurts in envy.

"How's that?" Robin puzzles.

"Come on girl you're kidding me, Boag has the best candy in town, Scott is going to be one happy boy for a while, hence my envy and jealously. Hey, what did they give you Percodan? Darvocet? Vicodin? Oxycodine? You've got to hook me up girl!"

"Oh come on—you're kidding right?" Robin naively returns.

"Ya sweet pea, you bet."

"I'll talk to you later, ok, Scott is drooling all over himself."

"No..........I am mi nima na no not..........not." Scott slurs, drools and grins as blood trickles out the bottom of the bandage.

"Maybe I'll stop by later Robin, ya know, check in on your old man."

"Oh, no, not tonight I've got to take care of my baby."

"Lord knows, believe me, he's being taken care of, say what's the strength and how many tablets per bottle and how many bottles?"

"I'll talk to you later De De."

"Wa—Wa—Well my sweet back to Costa Mesa, someday we will be making a ra—rabla—right turn to Newport Beach but today it's left to Costa Mesa." Scott manages to get out slowly with a minimum of stammer. Even in his blood shot glazed over eyes you can see the dreamy longing.

"There is nothing wrong with that honey bug." Robin replies without the faintest urge to budge from their current station in life.

"I—I just, well, I just feel better when I lo—look towards Newport as opposed to...........well you know." Scott struggles. The heavy sedation begins to win out once again.

"Oh that is just a dream having its way with you, it couldn't be that much better—maybe it's worse. Robin says in prophecy.

Scott tries to smile then winces in pain as he looks back at Newport in his rear view mirror heading up the street. Maybe it is just a fools dream but it is real enough to burn deep and resolute in Scott's heart, mind and soul, as blood trickles down from under the bandage.

Robin's cell phone rings again.

"Hello Mrs. Mofford, I will be at your house in ten to fix your computer. If it wasn't for your *six* year old computer crashing all the time my children would starve, ha!"

"Oh lord Bill, I forgot, we will be right there, Scott

broke his nose, he had to have emergency surgery."

"Ya know—Uncle Bill sure would like some of what Scott has right now."
"What do you mean, 'Uncle' Bill."
"Oh I think Scott knows what I mean. Did the good doc hook him up with the candy?"

Robin takes a napkin out of the glove box and wipes some drool trickling down the corner of Scott's mouth.

"What?"
"Never mind miss gem slippers of innocents, I'll see you in ten."
"What?"

Newport bathed in the late afternoon's malleable sweet warmth, which precedes by about an hour the final westerly decent for the day of the massive white fireball that is sun. That which collapses somberly, into a striking ambered orange blushing with smoky lavender accents exploding out subtly across the horizon. Typical for late July. Scott kept his eyes on the reflection of Newport Beach as he drove deeper and deeper into Costa Mesa.

As the intoxication of the dream slightly waned in the near impossibility of it, Scott's attention shifted to the sunshine that rode next to him. When she is at her sweetest and most magnificent he feels the —as most men do- the dull pulsation of undeserving. But he has no plans of climbing down from her, it's merely a humbling design flaw Scott resolves, "It's all god's fault," he grins, as he listens serenely to Robin tell him about

Amy's up-coming play.

    As Scott pulls in the driveway there is no pain anywhere in the world, anywhere in him, anywhere in the furthest reaches of anywhere. Life is perfect, broken nose and all, sustained and balanced if somewhat synthetically derived out of the sortilege little white bag on his lap. Little Amy is sitting on the porch waving with enthusiasm along with Barbara, a fourteen year old girl from four houses down there to baby sit. As Scott and Robin get out of their car, the computer repairmen pulls up and about a hundred yards down the road Robin's father is headed their way in his big white Ford truck. Robin takes it all in and says sweetly yet under her breath "Never a dull moment."

    Bill the computer repairmen heads up the drive in a slow stride and hunched over shoulders with tool kit in hand. He alters his direction Scott's way sporting a wicked grin. He pretends to punch Scott in the nose with his free hand. Scott smiles with a painful contortion.

    "Where's the candy bitch?" He leans towards Scott and says quietly.

    "It is right here in this little bag where it is going to stay. If you are a real computer fixer or whatever you call your— yourself I'll give you a couple Vicodin when you finish— bitch."

    "Oh you tease—deal."

    Robin's father jumps out of his truck, broad smile heightened by a big laugh.

    "It's about time my little girl smacked you one."

Laughs all around.

"So, did the doc hook you up my favorite son-in-law?"
"Dad!" Robin replies, embarrassed.
"Come on Scott, every one knows you never leave Boag without a little white bag full of candy."
"Dad!" Robin duplicates earlier response.

Robin's dad puts his arm around Scott's shoulder and walks him to the door.

"Your guy sure is popular." Bill whispers to Robin.
"The computer is where it always is Bill." Robin points with a flustered grin.

Amy runs to Robin, wraps her arms around her waist while looking up at her with a wide smile and quick giggles. And all is right in Robin Mofford's world.

"Hello, my sweet little love button."

Aside from the drama of the day Robin and Mrs. Binsent had wonderful conversations while touring the harbor and Mrs. Binsent likes Robin—a lot.

......TWELVE

Amy's Room

"Mama, mama, mama!" Amy calls to Robin, her mother, as she passes Amy's room.

"What is it honey? And aren't you supposed to be at least trying to go to sleep?"

"Ya, but I can't. Please read me the story about the Golden and Crystal Kingdom with all the princesses and princes and kings and the one and only queen they all don't like very much." Amy says while applying a little six-year-old emphasis on 'much'.

"That is *yes* not *ya* and didn't we just finish that?"

"Ya—I mean yes but please, please mommy it helps me dream!" Amy replies with a moist glisten of plea in her pearl blue eyes.

"Alright, alright but only a little bit tonight and most little girls go to sleep *to* sleep and not specifically to dream by the way."

"What does sp-speci-fic-al-ly mean?"

"Never mind, give me a minute and assume the position missy."

"Yippy, yippy, oh yippy!" Amy exults as she sits up and rustles her little self up against the back board and draws the comforter up neatly over her lap and smoothes it out with the palms of her hands then folds her hands into each other and waits patiently, eyes closed, broadly grinning.

Why she wants to hear that story again is beyond Robin. 'It's not really for kids.' She thinks as the skin on her forehead tightens while waking down the hallway. 'A gift from Uncle Tim and god only knows where his head is at.' Robin mutters under her breath as she goes into the living room to tell her husband Scott she will be in a little later.

"I'm going to be with you know who. Honey—if you would not mind pausing the movie and putting the Daiquiris back in the fridge. I'll be a few minutes with our princess."

Scott does not say a word just shakes his head, runs his fingers through his sandy blonde hair and adds a faint smile then presses pause on the remote. He sets the control in his lap and folds his arms over his chest and the smile grows. As this is par for the course in the Mofford home.

The Mofford home is immaculate and unassuming or maybe better put, unpretentious. Robin would not have it any other way and that trait is the only real unpliable trait in her for she is truly an angel. Of course if they had money the DNA of desire would most likely change the décor and square footage of their cozy home. But for now they appreciate what they have and it is in superb condition, Robin would not have it any other way.

The floors are oak, original 1940's style, the narrow two-inch wide plank type. And before they moved in Robin and Scott and even Uncle Tim sanded every square inch by hand while on their hands and knees. Which became the prelude for four coats of Varnish, also applied by hand. The walls are plaster, not that cheap gypsum stuff. And the windows are the same old sash ones that were installed sixty some odd years ago. Scott wants new ones, Robin loves the 'sometimes they work, sometimes they don't' old ones.

This entire track of homes was built right about the time the GI's invaded America -after invading Germany of course- and there was a tremendous hope and abundant production for many years to follow. Well, this particular track on the east side of Costa Mesa was parcel of that expansion and is the pride of the up and coming and promising Republican thirty something, minor leaguers.

Every single home up and down the block adorns a window or two with a flower box beneath it. And if there ever was a city ordinance to enforce beauty it would surely begin with that. White picket fences are 'out' for the most part as homeowners have declared a benign and fun loving war against each other to see who can come up with the best design using any and all building materials. Although, as one might guess the Mofford's dream and desire extends to, and ends, with a white picket fence.

Robin strolls down the hallway and looks down at the hard wood floor each time it creaks then makes a left turn into Amy's room. Amy happens to be looking up at the ceiling.

"What is up there honey?" Robin asks with no true interest as she thumbs through the book case for the story Amy desires.

"Oh, just god and stuff." Amy replies matter of factly.

Robin has minimal response, just an "Ah," mostly because how do you respond to an answer like that, she thinks to herself.

"Alright, let's see, is this the one? She shows the book to Amy and Amy nods approvingly. "Here we go. Once upon a time of times in a magical land far far away...... "

Amy begins to laugh.

"Why are you laughing honey doll."

"I'm laughing because the story is r-e-a-l-l-y good."

"Relax honey, ok, where were we, The Golden and Crystal Kingdom was run by a queen yet there were so many former kings still around people found it a little confusing. There were quite a few princes and princesses in the kingdom as well. But the queen of all *was* queen because she had to her sole ownership and rule, the last plot of virgin land right in the heart of the Golden and Crystal Kingdom."

"Mommy—why does she keep it like that, you know just dirt and stuff?" Amy asks as she asked the last time Robin read her the story, a couple weeks ago.

"Well my dumpling, it is like when Georgia Frontiere took the Rams to St. Louis." Robin replies in recalling a conversation her husband and Uncle Tim had about football.

"Momma, why did she take some animals to St. Louis.?"

"I mean, who is she without the Rams, you see that is the point, that's like the queen and the last piece of land, every body wants it, honey bunch, it keeps the spotlight on her. You know what I mean sweetheart?"

"Mommy, can we just skip that part."

"Good idea pumpkin, ok, all the royalty in the land wanted to buy the land from the queen but she would never sell it and every prince in the land knew he would become king if he could acquire it. And all the princesses dreamed she would be at his side when......"

Amy closes her eyes and smiles, her whole body sank a little from the tranquility of her favorite story being told by her favorite person in the whole world.

Amy's eyes snap open with concern. "Mommy, what's wrong with that princess?"

"Which—which one honey bugs?"

"The one who doesn't seem very happy, I thought all princesses are suppose to be happy."

Robin in rubbing her right temple thinks to herself why Uncle Tim gave this book to Amy for her birthday says simply in an apathetic tone. "Well, maybe things will get better for her."

"But mama, you *just* read this fairy tale to me and things got worser for her." Amy states, eyes wide with question.

"I know honey—well—but—I......" Robin fumbles and searches for an answer she will never find."

The Polo Match

5:00 am Saturday morning. Outside the night's sky is placid and tranquil by the promise of first light. Inside Kaisty sits in front of her vanity mirror in her posh thick white bath robe clutching with both hands a cup of coffee. Today is a great Saturday because Kaisty and Neil were invited to a significant event, a Polo match. Basically, if you are seen there good things may come. This is why Kaisty is up at 5:00 am looking with keen focus and planning at her face. With a few accents Kaisty could be considered beautiful and she knows this. So today she will go for striking as she continues to drag and prod Neil for a richer and finer lifestyle he neither truly desires or finds necessary.

If the woman is striking they notice the man. And to the man may come opportunity. Very simple process and very effective.

Kaisty has a small prescription size bottle in her hand now. She considers it medication. She was told it corrects a chemical imbalance within her brain. A once considered 'miracle of design and ruggedness' by scientists the world over, the mind today is considered as going out of whack at the drop of a hat. She twists the cap off slowly while leaving her eyes on her own eyes in the mirror.

Her doctor says they may try a new combination in a week or two because the admixture she is currently taking gives her suicidal thoughts. Kaisty has not told her doctor this quite in those terms only that she feels kind of crazy and weird while she is on it. Her doctor tells her *not* to stop taking her dosage abruptly because it would be worse than continuing which is the vicious cycle she is riding or which is riding her.

Kaisty sets two tablets on her tongue and swallows them without drink. She begins her craft, her art, with a primer, a liquid foundation, and then a dusting powder. She leans back a little and looks to her left into the bedroom to see if Neil is awake yet, he is not. Next to Neil is Kaisty's riding outfit. Kasty basically stole the outfit while filming a feminine hygiene commercial which she plays once or twice a year to remind Neil the career she gave up to marry him.

Kaisty is pleased with her creation and she will wonder intently the rest of the day what people think or thought of her appearance as she practices smiling to and from her reflection in the mirror. She tries a sly mysterious grin at one end of the spectrum all the way to a big bright smile with glassy twinkles gleaming from her brown eyes at the other. She imagines different situations where she may use them all. Neil sleepily appears behind her wearing only his pajama bottoms. He gently rests both of his wide palmed hands on her thin silky shoulders then kisses her neck and says "You look beautiful my sweet ."

"Would you say I look striking?"

"Yes—sure my love."

Neil rubs his eyes and yawns as he continues his journey to the shower, slips off his pajamas as Kaisty spies his thick flesh danglings with a quick glance.

Kaisty places her attention back in the mirror where it belongs. Kaisty is pleased with her work, her art, her creation.

7:30 AM

The road that leads up to Squires Stables in the very exclusive Newport Coast is nestled between Newport Beach and Laguna. It meanders on up to the stables within an exquisite landscape of gorgeous flowers of all sorts and towering eucalyptus tree branches canopy over the road. All within a well conceived back drop of epicurean greenery.

Kaisty sits as a princess, perfect posture, chin up and out, ruling the moment. She is of such wondrous spirit and generosity that she grants Neil his fumbling explanation on how the in-dash satellite mapping works.

"See honey—um—it shows us exactly—see right there! I mean if we did not already know where we were going it would show us how to get there."

Neil explains and unexplains as Kaisty offers a sweet tolerant smile as any gracious princess would as long as the peasants behave.

Kaisty's eyes excite as they approach the handsome New England style entrance. Three consecutive twenty-five feet high ornately carved wood and stone structures mark the gateway to a rich man's sport. The entrance leads to another road which winds through an even thicker lush forest then breaks suddenly into a wide open meadow with an immaculate and rather dazzling equestrian center placed right in the center of the grassland. A handsome old thick wood fence frames the center beautifully as it follows the contour of the gently sloping field. A ways off to the left the southern tip of a vineyard is visible. Large healthy pale green leaves and thick rough stalk envelop and entwine row upon row of weathered wood palings about four feet high. The vineyard rolls back and up into the hills where a large all wooden winery sits with a rusted metal roof. A soft and sublime 'Wow' breaks from their lips in perfect unison although entirely sovereign of each other.

Kaisty knows this is the place to be and be seen if one ever wanted to climb in status. As Kaisty ensnared herself in scheming into that hopeful ascension, she and many who have come before her never quite realize until it is much too late that it can be for many, a viscous downward spiral if one is not bred into it properly.

Maybe Neil always knew this, because his attention was riveted to the majesty and sheer muscular strength and stance of the Polo horses and that was just about all he was interested in. Neil was lost in the moment, for once he parked and got out of the Mercedes he fell into an enthralled focus as the power as sculpted beauty of the six horses nearest to him held him in their allure. The elegance and strength touch him profoundly. Neil was amazed and surprised at his own unusual response. He stopped gently and respectfully, hand extended to the closest horse. There was a magical quality to the air as the horse took a quick jab at the soil with his left hoof as the muscles shivered then firmed fast in his leg. That froze Neil but deep inside he took the gesture as a show of affinity towards him, not a threat.

In fact Neil was *so* into the moment he was not aware he had left Kaisty in the Mercedes alone and not bothering to open the door for her or even acknowledge her existence.

Kaisty fumed. "What the hell, I have to open my own god damn door! How embarrassing."

A caretaker hands Neil a cube of sugar and Neil begins to inch closer, his eyes wide, smile broad. "It's ok sweet boy." Neil has not been this close to a horse in twenty years and never really thought that much about them at any point in his life as this was very out of character for him. Kaisty goes off on her own. "God I hope he doesn't embarrass me." She says quiet but harsh. "Forget him, concentrate on your walk, act like you belong here." Kaisty adds.

Kaisty walks about the horse trailers and engages in small talk. A little ways off a woman steps her black calf high riding boot out of a brand new Rolls Royce with equally new and magnificent horse trailer attached. Kaisty does not pay much attention to the splashy show of wealth, initially. She continues with what superficial if not artificial conversationing she can conjure to impress. Something only a woman can sense in a battle of identity draws her attention back to the woman and the Rolls Royce. A woman about Kaisty's age exits the automobile with a striking figure of her own, also in full riding gear, as her beauty radiates to all corners of the equestrian center. Kaisty cocks her head slightly and squints which may mean she recognizes her or instantly hates her or— who knows. But never the less Kaisty feels threatened.

Kaisty begins to feel the twinge and pull of jealously but tears herself away and continues to work the crowd. After about twenty seconds she takes another quick look at the woman, this time her husband is standing next to her. A rather handsome figure in his own right in full riding regalia. His dress is for one purpose, to play Polo. Kaisty tears herself away again, she knows if she does not she will be paralyzed by that same jealousy. Kaisty cannot afford to fail, she continues her business.

Now the woman spots Kaisty and recognizes her immediately. The woman covers the forty yards that separates them in swift confident strides. "Kaisty, oh my god Kaisty, is that you?" Kaisty turns quick. And she has a quick reaction. Here's what happened. Kaisty recognized her, realized she must be filthy rich, became paralyzed with jealousy. The fluidity of her determination to conquer stops cold. Every vital function within her body and mind ridge into the solidity of envy. Hate was next.

Although Kaisty may have liked her in the High School they attended together, she hated her these many years later, this morning. The jealousy and hatred synthesized into an evil stone glare. Kaisty knew, she just knew all the attention she had garnered for herself was now to be placed upon the stunning and striking woman standing three inches taller and few inches fuller in the right places and thinner in other right places in front of her.

All during this reaction to this woman Kaisty did not utter a word and she certainly did not say goodbye as she turned stiffly in search of Neil, her day was finished.

By now Neil has asked just about every trainer or care taker for sugar cubes and apples; he displays no shame in his own behavior. Neil now has a pocket full of sugar cubes while he is captivated as the enormous head from the enormous beast lowers its huge streamlined and muscular neck to Neil's palm. Both man and animal exhibit serenity and gratefulness.

Both of their eyes display a mutual affinity. The mighty Polo breed horse licks Neil's palm in thanks which sends shivers down both of his legs.

Kaisty comes fast like the devil's own tornado and says quickly and sharply. "I hate this fuckin Bonanza bullshit, that bitch ass whore—whore—slut—bitch.........let's get the fuck out of here." Neil replies tranquilly. "You won't believe how gentle these amazing giants are Kaisty and honey you know I hate it when you swear like that."

Kaisty is ten feet from Neil and gaining speed in her angry gait as she responds. "I don't give a flying Polo fuck about those wretched creatures, I just want to go home—fuckin, fuck!"

Nothing Kaisty said or ranted about or even raged about the rest of the day had any affect on Neil's serene wonder and respect he garnered from his thirty minutes of feeding the grand Polo horses sugar cubes.

Karen's place

Karen sends text message to John: "I love the sag-way from Amy's room to the polo match. That is, if, the forlorn princess is Kaisty. It's her right? Call me. Kind of waiting for it to get rolling though."

No response from John as John is writing, deep into the evening.

......THIRTEEN

A NOTE ON MARTY

"Are you depressed often?"

"Yes."

"Do you wish you were someone else?"

"Sometimes......maybe."

"Is that a yes?"

"Yes."

"Any fantasizing about death."

"Not really."

"Is that a no?"

"Yes—I mean no—I mean Ugh! I don't know."

"Do you lay awake at night worrying?"

"Yes."

"Does it all feel hopeless?"

Long pause, little tear rolls off the far edge of Marty's right eye.

"I suppose."
"Any suicidal thoughts?"
"Not really."
"Is that a no?"
"Can I go now?"
"Yes and I will see you next week."
"Ok—I—ok."

"Alright young lady just have a seat in the waiting room and my nurse will have your prescription in a few minutes and you keep your chin up."

Marty feels limp and pathetic as she takes a seat. She is the only one in the waiting room. She takes solace in that. She will not have to pretend she is ok. She would feel compelled to do that. If Marty had grown up in Newport of course she would not care if people thought she was a little messed up. But she did not.

She sits with her knees tight together, her hands pale and folded into each other resting on her lap. She is slumped over some, her hair falling over her cheeks. Marty looks in apathetic stare at her shoes, the right toe is on top of the left toe. She recalls her mother saying "Don't do that honey shoes do not grow on trees." Marty misses her mother terribly that instant.

Marty's eyes draw tight in concentration. She thinks she hears a church bell. It is faint and distant. "But it's Thursday." Marty mutters softly to no one. Marty takes fleeting relief in the strong mellow 'bongs' of the ringing bell. A tiny little grin emerges out the side of her mouth recalling her youth and church on Sunday mornings.

In the office behind closed doors the doctor is in a high state of agitation. He hates that bell even though he can barely hear it. He gnashes his teeth in disgust. His facial features become gaunt and rigid, his pupils dilate and blacken. They take on an unholy black tone and depth.

The bell stops ringing and Marty's relief stops with it. And the uncertainty over her new boyfriend and her worries and her desperation creep back. The three headed monster that rides Marty.

The doctor rubs his temples and sighs heavily, "That son of a bitch, that damn bell." He curses under his breath.

Marty was just a few minutes ago diagnosed as bipolar—after only fifteen minutes with her doctor. He said she had a chemical imbalance within her brain—all in fifteen minutes.

"Here you go Ms. Humphrey." The nurse says as she pops her head up from behind the nurse station then slips out of sight again.

"You can call me Miss, I don't mind." Marty says in a thin somber tone.

Marty labors to her feet, she feels numb, pathetic.

"I have to take both of these?"
"Yes honey."

Marty forces a strained smile then shuffles out, eyes glazed over, very close to crying, miserable. She mopes down the hall staying to one side, eyes lowered. She thinks about going back to Tennessee. She wonders if Rob really likes her like he says he does—again. Marty clutches the prescription with one hand and a handkerchief with the other. Life feels misty gray, murky and unreal to her as she stands in the elevator, all talking around her seems muffled, distant. The color has drained from her face; she can barely hold herself up let alone go back to work. She knows the girls she meets at Starbucks tonight will cheer her up, she tries to focus on that. Marty can't tell if he really likes her, she has lost that keen sense she use to have, she feels numb, pathetic.

"Fifteen minutes—how could he tell what is going on with me in fifteen minutes, chemical imbalance?—screw him." She barely mouths the words it was more thought than anything. But she does take the pills, many of them, and never really sorting through anything, never really gaining an ability to handle life, confront life, understand life. Marty exits the elevator.

Passing Marty in the hallway on her way to the doctor is Kaisty Landitt. She walks with a caved in look about her, she needs to talk to her doctor. The latest drug he has given her has brought on suicidal thoughts and that has never happened before. Kaisty's jaw tightens as Marty walks by her. Her bottom lip quivering, even though her lips are crammed together. They do not speak to each other, they never will.

......FOURTEEN

She ran haplessly through woods of trees and yellows, greens, and reds as magenta and scarlet. All these as cream of the earth, home of the bugs and rabbits and bugs and deer. She ran frantic, pedantic, her eyes wide with fear and desperate. Her blouse torn and hanging lose, clutching to keep what was left over her sumptuous breasts. Wonder plunder, worried wonder, terrified wonder. She weeps in bursts, running reckless, frightful crazed panic. No certain direction but deeper into the dense woods for hiding. "Why, why is he doing this to me?" The young gorgeous girl cries in muffled sobs.

The sun has tried all afternoon to penetrate the dense canopy of trees and brush. Only small dots and slices and slivers of light play through and shift location as the branches and leaves breeze here and there, to and fro. She collapses in exhaustion still clutching her blouse, still looking fast over her shoulder, still terrified. He is somewhere, he must be close. She cannot run anymore, her castle is too far. The young voluptuous girl crawls under an old dry rotten log. Creatures of all sorts chirp, quip, rankle and click at the sudden thrusting of her supple body onto their world. She balls up whimpering. She now understands men can be monsters, apparent monsters and real monsters.........The End

Claire Binsent gently lays down the Danielle Steele novel on her delicate teak coffee table.

At her feet is a wooden box the size a couple of shoes could fit in. This is a wooden box ornately decorated by Claire's own frail hands. Painted flowers and real gems glued to it with a solid gold latch. She reaches down for it, lifts to her lap and sets it there. This would be more difficult for her if it had not happened so many times in the past.

Claire places her left toe behind the right heel, knocks off her Ferragamos and reaches down to slide them under the chair. She stands up with the box under her arm and bracing with her left hand on the arm of the sturdy solid teak lounge chair. She does not need her walker this morning for loss as in love can at times give one a strength. She walks down some steps leading to her sprawling *work in progress* garden. That is the way she likes it, always changing, never really finished. "Finished, where is the challenge in that?" She would tell her friends. She looks around for a good spot while clutching the box to her chest. She heads toward the south west corner and picks up a little shovel along the way.

Claire stops. She kneels down and very delicately places the wooden box to her left. She begins to dig. Muffy Wuffy died last night. Claire knew she was old but it's always tough. Muffy was lying on her usual elegant Prachnun antique chair, a little maple piece built in Norway circa 1841, when her little heart that graced Claire's life for so many years just gave out.

She sets the box in the shallow grave she wishes she could of dug deeper but her shoulders are old and tire easily. Claire does not shed tears anymore for she knows life is short and fragile for every one, every thing. She packs the dirt with the palms of her hands then kisses her fingers and presses them into the cool soil. "Good bye Muffy Wuffy, thank you, I love you, let's do it again sometime." Claire softly and sweetly spoke.

Now she struggles, she struggles to stand but the day is warm and generous upon her. She walks with effort over to a bench in the middle of the yard and sits. The air is calm and sympathetic to the old woman. Claire looks up, her attention drawn to two birds in chase for the thrill of it. She shields her eyes from the sun with her frail trembling hand and marvels at the massive ashen clouds with soft gray underbellies. She is saddened that most people don't understand that animals live for pleasure and sensation just as we do. She chuckles softly at her own sensitivity.

Sometimes when people lose animals they want to die themselves, they really do. One does not hear about such impulses much. Claire thinks and has thought if she did that to herself, a lot of animals would not be cared for. So she will visit several shelters over the next few weeks even though she already does and make sure any needed repairs or expansions are covered, which she already does. She will visit and calm their rattled nerves as she reaches through the metal bars with her thin shaky hands to pet them. And she will bring them treats that she will cook herself. Her chauffeur Clifford, in his Robin's egg blue suit with matching short brim hat, will hold the tray of treats for her and roll his eyes whenever Claire tells him how sweet they are and how sad that not enough people adopt animals. "Yes Mrs. B., I know, I know, I'm sad too, very sad." He would say while inspecting the clouds. This ritual began in 1956 with little Buck, a frazzled, mottled pooch that Gary Cooper found hiding under his custom Packard on a rainy night. He walked into Claire and Edward's back entrance which leads to the poker room with two bottles of liquor under one arm and this wet dog under the other. Claire took care of the dog and Gary and the boys played poker all night.

Then one day not too long from now Claire will bring home a cat or dog or if a stray anything is fortunate enough to even dip a toe in her back yard she will treat them as royalty. Mrs. Binsent lives for three reasons and one of them is for the love and care of animals.

......FIFTEEN

"I will lock up, got a proposal to work on for tomorrow." Neil says while shuffling papers for effect.

"Get the lights, you forgot the lights last time." An office secretary reminds.

"Got the lights." Neil returns.

"Neil I can't believe Jeff won the tickets to the Ritz party—you have been here longer and worked harder, *I* think."

"Ok, now I feel worse. Tough luck I guess."

Neil lost by less that $1.700.00. Neil is sick as he roams around the office with his right hand on his hip and his left rubbing his chin wondering how he is going to break it to Kaisty. A business that handles millions of dollars in transactions a day; how could he lose by a lousy $1,700.00? Neil stands in the middle of the sprawling office and rubs his face hard and slow. Then he begins to scheme. He looks around quick just in case a straggler is working late in a cubicle somewhere. There is no one else in the office. Neil knows the cleaning people are down stairs, he has about fifteen minutes.

Neil quickly makes his way over to Jeff's office. To his delight it is unlocked. He races over to his desk and finds nothing. He walks behind the desk where Jeff would sit, notices he standing right in front of a window. Neil drops to his knees. He crawls to the drawers and opens one. Neil's eyes bug, lips ridge into a fiendish smile. "I'll just take this attractive and colorful little ticket and run over to our Hewlitt Packard and run me off a copy. "What the hell—who will notice? Well the paper is a little thicker than ours. Ah hell it'll work." Neil narrates in a sly whisper.

Neil runs over to the color printer as the tension and excitement of the moment mount in him. It is safe to say Neil has never done anything quite like this before. He stands in front of the copier and opens the lid and sees his stretched to the maximum grinning face in the glass, Neil freezes. He becomes instantly paranoid and irrational and well a bit stupid. "What if someone can tell I used the copier to copy this, maybe it has memory somewhere in there?" He mumbles to himself and peers into the inner working of the machine under the glass. "Kinkos—I'll go to Kinkos, hell I'll even drive to the one in Costa Mesa, that will cover my tracks."

Neil rushes out with his coat over his shoulder, the ticket in his breast pocket and the lights on. "There will be one happy Mrs. Landitt to go home to." He ponders gleefully. Neil zips down Pacific Coast Highway to Newport Boulevard. He bolts up to Seventeenth Street running all applicable traffic lights then creeps into the Kinko's parking lot. He slithers into the copy store and veers away shyly from the copiers and into the stationary section to regain his composure and nerve.

The last customer leaves, that leaves Neil and one employee. "He'll have to be killed." Neil jokes to himself under his breath. Neil stiffly walks to the color copier. Opens the lid and places the invitation face up then closes the lid. He pushes the copy button and a blank copy emerges. Neil lets out a muffled "Shit!" He lifts the lid and turns the invitation over.

"May I help you—sir?"

A shot of adrenaline and panic race through Neil, his posture stiffens, face flushes.

"No—no, got er done, got it goin on, it's all good, looks like we're good to go." Neil turns four different shades of red in eight seconds.

Neil pushes the copy button with the lid up in his excitement and sudden anxiety. The flash blinds himself and the store attendant.

"Oh lordy, lordy—let me get this." The attendant blurts.
"No—I, ah—I........." Neil responds flustered.
"I insist, ok, what do we have here. Hey, I recognize this, I made these last week. I usually work in the Newport store but a gal called in sick today in the Costa Mesa store here—so here I am. How come you need a copy?"

By now Neil is near critical mass with trepidation after that little enlightenment. His body reacts rigid and frozen, his mind is nowhere to be found for a quick reasonable answer as his eyes are fixed to the ticket in the attendants hands.

"Ah—I lost mine."
"Oh, well whose is this one?"
"Mine."
"Oh—ok, well here's what you do. Set it right here, you were on the wrong side upside down and everything, set it right in the corner here. Alright I will set the color for the best reproduction, now I will scan it and give it a second to process."

That second was a brutal expanse of time for Neil.

"Ok, alright here you go sir, not bad, excellent."

Neil sat in his Mercedes and dabbed the sweat from his sideburns and forehead. He took a deep breath and let it out fluttering his lips. He smiles, presses his console phone speed dial for home.

"Hello my sweet, daddies got good news for his baby girl."
"Quick, the Sopranos are on." Kaisty says in an irritated exhale.
"Well, do you have any plans, let's see here, for August twelfth—oh let's say at 8:00 PM?"
"Why aren't you home?"
"Honey, my sweet honey doll face, what starts with R and ends in Z?"

There is a stunned silence. Yes, are different types of
silences. Neil is able to hear the stunned silence on all six
speakers. Then in the highest pitch shrilled scream ever
registered on earth, Kaisty shrieks, "Oh my god! Oh my god!
We're going to the Ritz party!" He can hear her now running
through the house in full stereo screaming as though she is
under full attack by her exhilaration. Neil laughs and smiles
broadly and performs a quick hard drum beat on the steering
wheel.

"I will be right home honey, I've got to run by the office
real quick."
"Ok, ok, honey Yippy! I love you, I love you, I love you,
I love you soooooo much!"
"I love you too baby girl, you have no idea."
"I do, I do, I do!"
"It says here you have to write a poem, ok honey?"
"I will, I will, I will!"
"I'll be home in a few minutes."
"Yippy, I'll be waiting you for my wonderful, wonderful
husband."

Neil races down Newport Boulevard to Pacific Coast
Highway, he makes a quick left. "La! La! La! There'll be peace
in the valley, hero's and villain's, hero's and villain's, la, la, la,!"
Neil sings mightily as every star in the sky winks approvingly at
him through his moon roof. Neil engulfs the thick coastal air,
which permeates the entirety of his flesh and soul as his new
silvery gold Mercedes holds him up a notch above mere mortal

men. "Rock rock, roll, Plymouth rock roll overrrrrr oh, oh, oh!" Neil picks up steam singing along with Brian Wilson's 'Smile'.

Neil flies down PCH to Newport Center drive. Fashion Island appears bright and inviting to Neil even at 10:00 o'clock at night. He turns left and on up the grand entrance flanked in quarters circles on either side by forty palm trees, imposing lush palm trees. Each with its own set of lights to set it off. Union bank stands tall and unapologetic in its fiscal dominance and Real Corp. is wedged in between it all on the thirteenth floor. Neil peers up at it through his moon roof with a devilish grin. He pulls into the desolate parking lot.

Kaisty has not stopped running through the house in an all out eruption of thrill. Finally the break she knows they desperately need even if Neil did not. In one final exhausted pirouette of ecstasy she collapses on the couch. The screaming is over, heavy pants of depletion ensue. Her smile is big and beaming, her hands are clinched fists of excitement and in one last burst of energy she scissors her legs up and down and hard into the couch. "He did it! he did it!" She screams in a high pitched shrill. "My prince!"

Neil dashes up to floor thirteen and quietly in stealth slips the ticket back in Jeff's drawer. "My princess, for you my princess." He sings as he hustles out of the office flicking the lights off in a rare gesture, as his senses and awareness are heightened by his covert mission—accomplished. He was a little devil tonight and he likes the sensation of it. He runs out to his Mercedes and rips out of the parking lot. With CD blasting "We'll find a meadow filled with grain there, I'll give you a home on the rangeeeeeee!" Neil sings out.

A few minutes later Neil pulls into the driveway. The only light he can see are enticing candles in the window sill of the master bedroom. "Oh this is good." Neil sighs to himself. Neil opens the front door with authority. "I'll be right up princess."

"My prince," Breaks softly from Kaisty's lips as she lights the floating candles in the honeysuckle scented bath she has prepared.

......SIXTEEN

Imports of Newport

"You know—you know you do well for yourself and for, of course, us Mr. Rothman." The Ukrainian in charge with eyes glaring dominant says as he runs his large calloused hand through his greasy jet-black hair.

"Oh—yes, yes." Davis smiles deviled, he is always nervous no matter how well things are going with these guys.

The Ukrainian folds his arms across his chest and nods his head up and down slowly, sporting a demonic grin.

"We have something else to mind Mr. Rothman. And we need the help from you—our business partner." The Ukrainian watching the window chuckles under his breath, the one watching the door just smiles and wipes his mouth.

Davis' stomach tightens. He knew something else would come of this—it always does in dealing with the devil.

"We want some land, a lot of it, Mr. Rothman." The man's face, which was fairly amiable a moment ago turns to stone, his eyes in ridged focus to Davis.'

"Oh?" Davis replies with a tight grin.

"Yah—yah we heard about some old bitch with twenty acres she had since around the year of 1950. Oh think of big Mercedes dealership we could build together.

The Ukrainian looking out the window bites the inside of his cheek to suppress his laugh, knowing full well the true intentions.

Davis grinds his teeth, nods in sympathy with a gaunt look of regret.

"We need to appear le-giti-mate. Right word—legitimate?" He looks at the other men standing near the door and window who shrug their shoulders with blank faces as a reply. "And we think to look like local businessmen, so we thought of our friend Davis Rothman. We want to make offer through you our partner, yes?"

Davis has difficulty catching a breath and felt faint all at the same moment as he loosened his tie and blotted his temples with his handkerchief.

"Oh—oh how interesting," Davis manages.

The Ukrainian reaches into the inner pocket of his black leather coat.

"Relax Mr. Rothman, here take cigar." The Man in charge stuffs a fine Habana in Rothman's breast pocket. "Give time to think about."

The Ukrainians leave.

Davis puts his elbows on his desk and places his head in his hands and mutters "Oh how bad could it get, we make her an offer, if she accepts great, it she does not that's the end of it, right?"

In full disclosure—the offer was tendered. And here is what basically transpired. You see, Mrs. Binsent's lawyers tend to field offers as sort of a sport nowadays, because they know she will never sell. It is more of a hobby to them in that they enjoy finding out who is in front, behind or on the side of offers. Large amounts of money have a history and sometimes it can be a bit shady. So Claire's Lawyers, Max and Gene, let it run to a certain point. The point where the party making the offer gives up enough information for maximum transparency. The kind of transparency that can sink a ship. That is pretty much all they care about, that nothing got by them. Humans like to have a game and that happens to be theirs. In fact Claire's lawyers will know more about the Ukrainian's money than they do themselves, before the day is out. They discarded Rothman as the principal within the first thirty minutes. They even toyed with the idea of reporting the Ukrainian's and their mob money to the INS but a lunch date or an earlier tee time became available so a simple decline of offer sufficed.

Davis has taken to pacing his office in recent days and that is what he is doing at this moment, occasionally rubbing his face hard, staring at the floor, then hands on his hips looking out the window. The salesmen are gone for the day, the showroom is dark. The palm trees outside the big windows stand rich and exotic with drowsy leaves that ruffle in the breeze up high. They stand thin and tall against the sunset with clouds of all sorts, some streaming, some puffy and others simply scattered wisps. The sun's blonde yellow rays reaching defiant and mightily through them all, descending seemingly against its will as the sun begins the journey to become morning for the world beneath.

Yet Davis paces uneasy. He is not quite sure the source of is anxiety, he just knows he is in a bit deeper now.

Karens' place

Karen and John are down the street having dinner. Karen nibbles her thumbnail, makes reluctant eye contact with John.

"It's kind of airy fairy John, I don't think it happened like that. And what is with those two flying around?"

"Don't worry it gets worse."

"I recall it being more brutal than that."

"Let's go over this again, you said 'Write it like a fairy tale.'

"I know but……"

"I'm all ears Karen, what do you suggest?"

"And what about all the scandalous affairs, where are those?"

"That was in the spring, I'm writing about what happened that summer, remember how you said it haunts you still? And if you want Fitzgerald, read Fitzgerald."

"Oh you're no fun. Just write about what happened then."

"I was getting to it Karen."

......SEVENTEEN

Morning of, the party at the Ritz

Kaisty wakes up with a concept or better put within a concept, likely it had the power to stir her out of her slumber. The concept is that of creation, a womanly design if you will, beauty. The dress will just have to work she cannot worry any longer about that. Kaisty understands beauty. The presence must be more grand than the sum of its parts an all must be in place or all is lost for the evening, the opportunity. She knows this.

Kaisty's skin must be radiant naturally. She knows what to consume to make this happen. The ingestion of 25 mg of niacin at around five o'clock this evening will bring about the necessary flush she needs to build on. Kaisty scoots up against the backboard, eyes closed, in deep reverie of visualization. Neil is spread out seemingly to all corners of the bed. She usually hates that but not this morning, not the morning before the party at the Ritz.

Kaisty goes over the process like an athlete before a championship game. She will condition her hair most of the day in an egg yoke/beer formulation. Manicure at 11:30 am, always the same day of any event. Full massage at 1:30 pm also the day of allows a woman to walk less rigid in a fine fitting dress. Fluid movements, within her vision she must think in fluid movements.

Kaisty will read aloud from 'Alice in Wonderland' to smooth out any daily bad habits in her communication. She must speak smoothly and smartly. She expects Neil to be a bit of a dope around such wealth. She will have to make up for this. He will be granted forgiveness if his woman is wonderful.

Kaisty drifts into dreams of silvery pastel shimmerings, deep within crystal cascades of opulence as cavernous bellows. She bows and kneels to the Deity who resides there that beauty may be bestowed upon her, through her. Lace as rose petals suppeled tender, flutter in swirls across her reverie. Early morning dreams are not enslaved by time though as the setting sun paints the clouds with a brush of iridescent pink copper. Golden sapphire tides rush over her as the sun plays delicately upon her skin as children's whispers. Off at a distance the slumbering gray mist of lost beauty, times ravagings, will be held back today as would Satan's howling roar at the gates of heaven may be held at bay—for now.

Kaisty understands beauty. The day is planned; she can sleep a little while longer. Kaisty clutches her comforter and pulls it tight under her chin. She smiles dreamily, her right eye twitches mildy.

Two Hours Later

Saturday morning at Fashion Island is quite an experience to behold as women are held firm by their focus—albeit dreamy and glazed over. Their husbands on the other hand if they were unsuccessful at sneaking out early for a golf game tag along—sometimes. And if one could pinpoint the idea from which they operate off of, it may be along this line: 'Sure, ok, let's hang out at Fashion Island for awhile and why did they move Starbucks to the other side again honey?' Any real interest would have to be cultivated by something nifty they stumble across out of shear accident in utter boredom. For women though it is quite different, quite another idea entirely.

Fashion Island is Kaisty Landitt's world, it defines her existence and she is why it exists and creatures like her. Whatever it wants her to be this year she will strive and toil to become it regardless of personal costs or financial considerations. That is just the way it is in Newport Beach. The standard of existence must be met and Fashion Island must define it. A woman feels a pressure and desire as one emotion upon arrival to the parking area. Newport standards of existence are alive, they breathe, its demands are simple—total compliance of mind, body and soul. Once the mind is seduced into believing that god's own laziness in human design is transformable, the soul will yearn for it and follow without protest. Total compliance, absolute submission, endless self scrutiny. A thick coastal breeze appears in its drowsy playful serenity through the open air mall setting. Those who shop early this Saturday morning are of a pleasant nature. The complexion may change though throughout the day but the atmosphere is usually quite wonderful as one might find in the eye of a storm. Laughing children, live music are the thin veneer that covers the master game played by the adept and those who must comply to what the Island defines as beauty, they simply must.

'Sally Lane' is the best store to find that special evening gown. And it is also the best place to empty ones wallet. The store is separated into three sections. Paris designers take up the eastern end of the store. New York designers the northern area of the store and all other designers are scattered throughout.

Neil Landitt lifts the tag for a quick glance. He is relieved to find the garment at a reasonable price of $250.00. Then a few moments later after sipping at his coffee in hopes of jolting himself out of his groggy state he realizes the price was $2,500.00. "Holy shit!' He grumbles under his breath.

"What's that honey?" Kaisty asks sweetly.
"Oh—the coffee sure is hot."
"I'm sorry honey, want me to blow it cool for you?"
Kaisty perks her lips and winks.

Kaisty has bought four dresses from this store in the last seven days and returned three of them. One she has hidden from Neil and when he says in 'Leave it to Beaver' prose "Hey—I've never seen that one before." This comment on their way to a dinner party Kaisty will reply with a smart, "Oh this? I've had it for years." The dress she is going to wear tonight at the Ritz is near finished in its altering. Neil has no idea why he had to be here this morning, as his golf clubs send him subliminal messages from the trunk of his Mercedes.

Maybe it is because Kaisty really loves him this morning.

Neil spots a woman and finds her a compelling if not a perplexing sight. He figures with quick stealth glances that she is in her mid fifties. But every god given allotment of flesh head to toe has been altered and reconfigured to sell her as a rather attractive thirty-five year old. But Neil, in knowing the truth by keen observation as he hides behind a rack of dresses finds this creature hard to process in his mind. His filing procedure for every person met protests that she's much younger. She's fifty-five but she's not. She's thirty-five but she isn't. So Neil stands there, takes a sip of coffee, shakes his head but the process is stuck. The simple process of encountering a stranger and processing her image is stalled. He tries again to shake the calculation through but it won't budge.

The woman has spent $117,000.00 to create beauty and the illusion of youth and she is still unhappy with her bottom lip.

"All set honey bun, don't worry about a Christmas present, this dress is all I need for the *whole* year."

But Neil will worry about a Christmas present, he had better, If you're a man and your wife is born and bred Newport, you had better.

On the way out to the Mercedes they window shop, arm in arm. They stop in front of a very fine watch store.

"Oh honey that's that watch I was telling you about, it would look so handsome on you. A. Lange & Sohne, see that one right there."

Neil dips down and looks inside the wrist ban and spots the price. And the price is $25,000.00.

"Neil I really want to get that for you someday."

And Neil really wants to go home.

The pain came down in a dreary thud—
unannounced, unwelcome. The pressure sickening,
the days joy smashed and darkened. Past and future
vanish, only stark cold hardness of present. I tip
heavy, the boy who pours my coffee, usually I do
not. The cheerfulness and chatter around me just
make it worse. I am alone, so alone.
Alone in an avalanche of the past but not the past
that I understand. It is the past in which the events
are occluded, dark shadows prowling in blackness. I
sip my coffee, today I will have my cheek bones
enhanced, today my surgeon will lay out a plan, my
beauty must survive, it must.

Note found in the hand of
Natalie Bausett—Socialite
by paramedics following
failed attempt to resuscitate her

......EIGHTEEN

The great orchestration of sunset employs as its Maestro a lone seagull hovering seemingly devoid of motion some two hundred feet above the beach sand. Only an occasional slight list from side to side reveals but never spoils the magic as a warm, thick updraft generates the loft necessary for the pearlescent white bird with black tipped wings to hover in the air and which at times appears to sit on the wind as he peers dreamily out into the immense Pacific ocean.

The western horizon is on fire with a thousand mile wide golden amber blaze streamed with burnt orange smolderings. And shimmering pulses of translucent crimson radiate through. The clement and slumbering evening's blue sky is a willing and languid backdrop, for the gradual upon gradual decent of the mighty sun into the sea that prompts no sound or splash, as the ancient chorused plunge commences.

The buildings in and around Fashion Island empty except for the obsessed and the perfectionist, for they do not obey the intrinsic laws that govern the quickly diminishing workday. They toil. Still others have left early as their visions of wealth tend to be overwhelmed by their scarcity of discipline to achieve it.

The rest and remaining of Newport Beach fall to the sacred ritual brought to bear by the order and seductive charm of the ever churning Cosmos. People arrange to meet somewhere for a drink and good conversation as others go home alone out of desire or dimly lit social necessity.

The day maids and nannies sit in apathetic expression at the bus stops waiting for the slow certain ride back to Santa Ana—fifteen miles to the east.

Gardeners finish loading their trucks and begin their own track back to the same town and many stop off at a liquor store along the way in hopes of whatever numb solace it may provide. The Mexican workers that keep Newport in its manicured splendor are done for the day and some are even thankful, thankful as the slaves of the south were that they remained alive, if only to pray.

The Seagull draws his wings in tight and dives forty feet then on instant opens his feathers full as the dense saltin air lifts him back high as god would one's spirit in joy. The hues of the sunset begin to lose their distinction in what has become the final casts, from golden amber to butterscotch. And what was a burnt orange blush just ten minutes ago has melted into breathtaking ghostly copper inlays. The crimson flames are now faint scarlet as they ignite in a burst of blending, becoming the first note to the overture that is evening.

Many of the older wealth have timed their bourbon and tonics with an occasional Valium in perfect unison with the glorious extinguishing of the blazing sunset. And many younger Newporters lean heavily on their anti-depressants. The gentle pulling westward on the raphe nuclei within the inner most sanctum of the brain by the descending sun, releases an increased measured dose of serotonin, a natural chemical in the brain that soothes. Of which, they plan on using to its ultimate benefit regardless of future consequences. The psychiatric drugs they consume work their magic and weave their damage among the trusting and desperate.

Old money, new money, is not at issue. Having money *is* the issue. And if you do not please pretend as though you may if only and merely for us to gape upon as one would a landscape, however derived.

                    Newport Eccentric
                    Randolph Galsboro

_____

Emerald Bay is exclusive and this word which is clearly meant to separate a particular thing from another, by force if necessary, will be defined as follows:

1. Limited to that which is designated.
2. Excluding all others from a part of or share in.
3. Disposed to resist the admission of outsiders to
   membership, association, intimacy, etc.

4. One better have a substantial amount of liquid
    assets.

Every home has a stunning ocean view, every single home. The homes are beautiful but the location is exquisite—meaning:

1. Of peculiar refinement or elegance.
2. Carefully sought out, ascertained, devised.
3. Of delicate balance in refinement as sensed, intense or keen, as pleasure, pain, etc.
4. Again—lots and lots of cash, actually gobs of the stuff.

Within the grandiose confines of Emerald Bay an older gentleman is waiting for his wife with a bowtie in his left hand so his wife may extend the courtesy as she has for forty-seven years. He holds a bourbon with a slight tremor in his right hand. He is wealthy, phenomenally wealthy. He begins to doze as his wife fuses with her outfit. This will be his thirtieth party at the Ritz and of course many at the Fours Seasons but the Ritz is by far his favorite. One of his first exceptional deals was struck and launched there one winter evening is 1967.

He drifts off and passes through a thin veil of separation, that of analytical thought and dreamy reminiscence. At the moment of passage he is reliving *the* deal that turned the corner from just making ends meet to and in the direction of, and towards fabulous wealth. His bourbon begins to tilt in his lap as he is barely holding it now. His wife reaches to upright the pure crystal glass with gold brim which brings him back from his deep rumination. She is a goddess to him, whether 25—45—or 75 years young. Their driver motions that the Bentley is out front as she helps her frail old husband to his feet and fastens his bow tie neatly all the while receiving his loving gaze. Tonight will be wonderful as the old man will dream up sweet things to whisper in her ear, he always does.

The driver waits for the tall gates of Emerald Bay to open. He slowly drives the big Bentley out and onto Pacific Coast Highway towards Fashion Island and the Ritz three miles North. And there are others in steeled chariot, about a hundred or so converging on the same location as the sun melts in dissolving as a fiery splendor to the beholder.

......NINETEEN

The headlights pour cool luminous beams from the steel and leathered chariots into Fashion Island. The conversations within are as varied as there are roads to riches. And the Ritz welcomes and sparkles to all in its stately grandeur. Eyes come alive regardless of age as the drivers round the last curve and begin their clamber up the magnificent entrance. Adipose palm trees flank the way dressed in tightly wound little white lights that sculpt up the exotic husk to and including the first layer of the fully expressed, lavish palm leaves.

The night's air is alive and electric, as the stars wink at the accomplished like diamonds on black velvet. They accept their blessing no matter by what means achieved or at what cost to their immortal soul. Bentley after Rolls Royce after Maybach come to a graceful rest at the entrance of the Ritz. Neil and Kaisty arrive at the entrance, Kaisty has planned her exit style from their Mercedes and her first ten steps over and over in her mind.

Neil motors down his window, he flashes a big greeting smile for the valet. Neil hands him the invitation.

"Hello young man, here you go." Neil gives Kaisty a quick glance and she returns with a beaming coiled thrill to her eyes.

The valet has physically handled many of the invitations as this one feels odd to his senses; it feels a bit slick and thin. If that had not caught his attention he may not have bothered to check the number to the master list. He thumbs through the list. Neil and Kaisty take in the luscious atmosphere with the reflection of the big, brightly lit Ritz letters bathing in their mesmerized eyes as Neil squeezes gently, the top of Kaisty's hand.

"I'm sorry the number on this invitation meaning *this* invitation has already been accounted for, you see right here— NR1945483. The valets left eye wanders as it slowly oscillates left to right."

"Oh—sure—I see that, must be an oversight on your end. Where do I park?"

"I am sorry sir I will have to confiscate this invitation, please move along." The now reddening valet says in an escalating pitch, quick wiggle of his wandering eye darts to the low heavens and is fixed there.

Neil's eyes glaze over into a rage but he says nothing. He motors up the window and slowly rolls toward the exit. Kaisty, biting her lower lip hard, sits stunning in appearance yet stunned by incident, her poem neatly squared in her lap.

Neil is not happy with himself to say the least as they drive out of the Ritz. And he has to think fast. He knows enough about women not to defend himself too quick, it would only heat up the tension and Kaisty may shut him out for days. Silence is Neil's best option for the moment. He decides to to drive to Corona Del Mar to the exact spot he asked Kaisty for her hand in marriage from one knee and over looking the deep turquoise watery expanse of the Pacific Ocean. Neil grins out of the left side of his mouth for the plan he has in mind within this difficult pressured moment.

After three minutes of dead silence.

"Boy—I screwed up babe." Neil says, followed by a nervous smile and solitary anxious laugh.

Kaisty does not respond at first. She is looking out the window into the lightly misted dreamy twinkle of the Newport evening which seems suddenly out of reach to her. The headlights that pass them on up to the Ritz are torturous to her, she must look away. Yet she considers just letting it go as she cocks her head in surprise that she would even consider the notion. In all her pain and disappointment she sees an opportunity and seize it she will.

"How much did you loose by?" Kaisty swivels her whole body toward Neil with a cold but interested glare.
"$1,700.00 stinkin dollars, can you believe it?" Neil speaks solemnly but feels a measure of relief in that Kaisty appears relatively in control of her emotions.
"I saw a tennis bracelet for $1,900.00 I liked yesterday— I think it is only fair."
Kaisty pushes out her lower lip then draws it back for a well-placed emphasis. Neil not too concerned whether her reasoning makes sense, jumps at the offer for a peaceful and

equitable arrangement. They continue on and out humiliated.

The thin and neatly groomed valets scurry to attend to the wealth of Newport. Most of which are happy and in good spirit by natural or synthetic means. They make their way to the masterly engraved thick teak doors. Ornate by a nautical theme of the seas fury and a hopelessly ensnarled boatsman by the tentacles of a giant octopus. A trained observer even with carbon dating employed would be hard pressed to ascertain the true ages of some of these glisteningly jeweled Newport natives.

They make their way down the hallway adorn with heavily varnished teak paneling and nautical brass fixtures. The dim chandeliers give the procession an eerie ghostly feel. Laughter from anticipation glitters through the cortege. The haunting glow of the ballrooms entrance is inviting and hypnotic. A few begin to trickle in, eyes brighten, smiles widen for the ballroom is festoon gorgeously with white roses and every other rose known accenting throughout. Bright somniferous chandeliers tantalize, hung velvet pearl white satin ribbons breeze about delicately. Stewards of all shapes and sizes stand sentry next to each table. A childlike valence of wonder takes over the wealth as they look for their names on the exquisitely decorated dining tables. Each with its own carved ice sculpture in the center, in a nautical theme of course. Some sit, some stand as they converse with acquaintances they have known for decades. Others find a way to be alone even in this close setting as they are so hopelessly in life.

The ballroom begins to fill now and all spirits are raised a notch by the inherent nature of social grouping, fabulously wealthy social grouping. The kind hearted, those who have sold their souls, those whose integrity remains relatively intact, the lonely and desperate, those who clamor insatiably for attention and approval and even the borderline evil. No one is spared in being lifted in spirit to some degree.

A wonderfully dressed woman in her early seventies wearing a sapphire blue dress with shimmering white lapels and a high collar by French designer Rutone commands attention. Her smile is confident and mischievous as she stands perfectly erect with her hands together at the fingertips at her waist. Her fingers are parted as they must be to accommodate the five gem studded rings she is wearing.

"Welcome, welcome! Welcome ladies and your filthy rich bastard husbands." The host gleams.

The lustrous congregation roars in laughter.

"Have I got an evening planned for you, everybody got their poems?"

The room engulfs with a disjointed chorus of "Yes—yep—oh yes I do—I sure do—damn it I forgot mine—I spent a month on mine!" Rings through the ballroom.

"Fantastic but let us toast and eat first you lascivious poets!"

Fifteen chefs deliver the cuisine personally on cue, it is tradition. The ballroom gently bursts with hushed as well as raucous conversations and laughter, plenty of laughter.

A chapter could be written alone on the menu for the evening. So just the best of the evening will be listed. Filet of Lake Superior white fish with a bourbon cream sauce and a sprits of lemon is of most worthy mention. The Alaskan King Salmon also is a favorite of the night. The Maryland crab cakes are always thoroughly enjoyed along with the Ritz Gazpacho which consists of fresh tomato, rock shrimp, avocado pearls and hearts of palm with six different fatally sumptuous sauces to choose from. Wonderful cuisine but just a sampling, just a sampling.

Neil pulls up to the very point of the bluff over looking Big Corona beach where he proposed to Kaisty seven years earlier. They sit quiet and stare out at the sea and the inlet to Newport harbor. There is only a very faint horizon left to illuminate, very faint. Lights from the pier extend out into the final minutes of dusk. Neil experiences the expanse of the Pacific Ocean as hopeful, Kaisty perceives it as desperate.

"What's that in your lap?" Neil sheepishly asks.

"My poem."

"Oh right, right." Neil feels even worse. "Let me hear it."

"No—no forget about it."

"No I truly want to hear it."

"It's about my cat I lost, you don't like cats, remember right before we were married—I lost my cat?"

"Oh—cats, little tigers they're neat—really."

"You don't like cats, you'll just laugh."

"No I promise."

"Alright, fine!" Kaisty blurts in a huff.

"Honey look, seagulls at night, I didn't know they flew at night."

"You mean flying rats."

Kaisty reaches into her purse, pauses, lets out a little cough, wipes away moisture from under her eye with the palm side of her index finger delicately, then reaches again. She pulls out some lip-gloss that she barely touches to her lips out of nervous compulsion. She lifts the paper folded tightly into eights from her lap. Kaisty unfolds it as her shoulders tighten with apprehension. She clears her throat.

Swell of Spring's Night Sweet Sadness

Evening's glow falls upon gathered stones
As night's silver shimmer unveils by sun's
 warmed moon
Shallow breath, quick glance
Bristle winds blow through leaves of many
I sit and wait patient no more
Cool night's silk embrace myself as soul
While he runs phantom on fences of light and
 crystal tunnels, with whispered roar
My mind races with fear and loss
 then numbed in despair
For not cut of brow by viscous brawl quells
 the spirit of tigers call

For love of night and lure of scent......
As the night shown bright by sun's warmed
    moon
And crystal tunnels under fences of light fall
    silent
With swells of spring's night sweet sadness

Neil is silent, he says nothing, no apparent reaction at all because what he just heard was the most beautiful collection of words and sweet idea he had ever heard. He has the faint traumatized flinch in his eyes that befalls someone when he sees or hears something almost incomprehensively beautiful. He shakes his head mildly trying to collect his thoughts but stalls.

"You hated it, I knew it, you hate it and you're not saying anything."
"I—I—I."
"I hate you, I tried so hard, you have no idea how hard it is to lose an animal."

The now critical necessity to respond sobers Neil up to muster a comment.

"Kaisty—that was the sweetest most wonderful thing I have ever heard."
"R-E-A-L-L-Y?"
"Yes, really."

Neil saw in a movie once where the leading man found himself in a similar situation. Neil opens the door and gets out without a word. He walks over with a confident gait and opens Kaisty's door. "May I have this dance my dear?" Neil extends his hand and dips his shoulders. What Neil is doing is so out of character for him that Kaisty does not protest or question. She lifts her thin arm up and out and it hangs in the air weak and limp but willing. Neil gently and gracefully pulls her out and up close to him. Kaisty in a rare show of affection nestles her head into and between Neil's chest and upper arm. But before she does, Kaisty looks up at Neil with a rare look where all the defenses are down and the usual rigid features are replaced with soft pliable ones. And while she looks at him, he gently wipes a tear away from under her eye with his thumb. She whimpers softly, vulnerably. Neil leads her to the front of the Mercedes. The headlights are still on. Kaisty's pale gold dress gives off satin pearlessent shimmerings in the light. Kaisty's earrings dangle down long from her earlobes. They ignite in a soft brilliance with an illuminating glow just under her jaw line and next to her slender silky neck. The glow continues into her hair, Kaisty's face framed heavenly. Neil is held captive by her beauty. Neil rests his chin on the top of her head. They dance with very little motion sweetly but upon mountains of entangled emotion. There is sorrow and discontent, inescapable sorrow and discontent.

The Ritz Ballroom

'Tap, tap, tap, klink, tap, klink.'

The hostess in her empearled eloquence raps on a pure Christofle crystal glass with a solid gold teaspoon.

"There is always a catch isn't there?"

Affirming grins and nods, hushed laughs and smiles all around.

"Yes, you may read your poems for all to enjoy!"

Bright eyes and wide glistening smiles throughout.

"But you must do it naked."

Grumbling and cursing under breaths erupt, for they all know Margaret and they all know she is not kidding. Paper begins to crumple, fold, wad up and tear and even some become projectiles.

"No, no wait we may have a customer, over there, yes over near the entrance."

All eyes jockey for a look, standing thin in the door way bathing in the effulgence of the hallways dimly lit chandeliers stands a blonde goddess which no one recognizes.

"Come over here sweetheart, yes honey, you may hug the wall if you must."

The robed gorgeous creature steps onto the platform.

"And your name honey."
"Vicky."
"Yes, yes and your poem my dear?"

Whispering and chuckles resonate through the ballroom.

"Ah, no—I."

The hostess covers the microphone and speaks into Vicky's ear. "Didn't Robert give you a poem?" Vicky responds. "No, he just said if I stand up her naked for five minutes he would give me two hundred dollars—I don't think I really want to do this now." Margaret responds. "Damn him, that idiot!" She uncovers the microphone. "Ha! Yes, alright, small snafu."

She steps down and grabs a poem out of a man's hand before he has a chance to stuff it in his blazer pocket. Margaret quickly shoves it in the girls quavering hand. "Disrobe, read it then get the hell out of here, comprenda?" Margaret looks out to the restless, animate congregation with her trademark million dollar smile. "Alright! Enjoy!"
No one is prepared for the beauty that unveils. The girl eases her left shoulder out of the black silk robe with pale

lavender lapels as it drops in slow fluid ruffles to the floor. Howls, gasps, suppressed gasps, bad whistles, good whistles, hard clapping, covered eyes, bugged eyes ensue. Her voluptuous curves are on the order of overwhelming.

A very old man not terribly interested in this display mainly because he cannot see that far pulls out a piece of paper from his old paisley vest pocket. He unfolds it as his bony and bruised hands tremble. It is a poem he slaved over, many nights perfecting. He reads it very quietly to himself with an old man's crackle in his voice.

Night Walk

Telephone lines crackle and run as the late night
    conversations zip over head
Skies black splendor, stars flicker as fragments of sun
On a sidewalk I stroll, head down
Crack after crack cements only fear
Souled humans asleep in rows of castles, left and right
Faint glow of television seen through breezing silk
    Curtains
2:00 am—deep night calms myself as restless being
Cat's tale wisps back of my leg, startled I greet and kneel
For he is restless soul as well, calmed only by
    adventures of night
Purrs as passion, he welcomes scratches under chin
We walk together for a block or so then creature of
    night slithers up over fence leaving myself to
    thoughts that churn as they churn under and over

Lazy swooping wind blow leaves about—another
    uneasy soul as mine
Solitary call makes line above crackle then quick silence
    as I head back, now malleable in mind and body—
    thankful.........

The silk robe removed reveals skin of creamy tan illumination which finds its genesis deep within the mysteries of a young woman, merely accented by the sun's blessing as golden tan lines. She stutters some, clears her throat. Her natural and ample breasts arouse the fascination of one and all causing glazed-eyed wonder in heart and mind for the beholder. A light from behind shows soft and radiant through the half inch gap of her upper thigh and blonde furred splendor. With near critical mass of seductive lure, some find this too much to bear as men grasp their freshly kicked shins under the table. The older the wife the less the concern for even they are enamored if only by dreamy reminiscence of their own supple youth.

The young lady has gathered herself now, she is ready. Her nipples draw tight and perk outward. She starts with a quiver to her voice.

New Money

A guest of and to wealth
Misty fogged morning, stirring of soul
Suns power slow burn

Hearts of relief, minds of regret
Coffeed nectar pours in goblets on veranda of
    gold and leaves since yesterdays fall
Ready haven morning breach of night
As sails ripple and snap at journeys end
I see my son walk with the effort of infancy
Robed wife appears, sparkles of bright and ease
The sun wins war of mist and fog, suns delicate
    warmth, welcome
Yet I stir uneasy
For I am a guest of and to wealth
Oh simple time and more of like mornings may
silence the decades of pasts loss and losing

Wild clapping, standing ovations of all sorts. The girl picks up the robe, holds it to her breasts, covers her crotch with her left hand as she runs out of the ballroom.

"I am going to assume we are all sufficiently aroused to dance!" Margaret beams gleefully.

A chorus of "Yes! Yes! Absolutely! Oh yes!" erupts. As the men and women stand the ballroom is awash in glimmering shimmer of fine gowns and jewelry. The dance floor fills quick as the oldest rock and roll known to man blares from the speakers. Confetti falls from the ceiling with colors that for an instant appear as flaming pastels followed by an avalanche of iridescent silver and pink balloons.

Across town on Claire's veranda

The night wind is warm and welcome upon Claire's face. She sips her Vermouth of which she has had three. The stars flicker to her but burn steady for their distant worlds. A moonbeam fell on the bay an hour ago and Claire is held serene by its seduction. A ghostly figure arrives on his rickety bicycle. He is wearing a plantation tuxedo, the one she always envisioned him wearing no matter what attire he would show up in. She has no concern whether this is real or imagined or if it is even in its proper time. The figure steps onto the veranda, Claire can see through him into the moonlit ripples of the bay. "I could always see right through you Clark Gable." Claire says playfully. "Dance my dear?" Mr. Gable extends his ghostly hand.

Two miles out at sea

Two miles out at sea on his yacht Jack Harton is relaxed but intently focused. His palms are spread wide with fingers touching left hand to right. He gently bounces his thumbs to his lips. As the party roars into the evening, Jack sits quietly on the upper captain's deck. He gives a quick glance down the stairs and spots his girlfriend painting her toenails and watching Biography. He sips from his scotch and looks out to the faint glow of the Newport coast. At two miles out it seems so manageable. But he knows better. You see the rich, the very rich need to continually expand. People with nothing do not understand this. They think 'boy' if I had all that money I would just relax and enjoy it. What they don't get is that once you begin to expand in a big way the dynamic is to continue beyond any personal or reasonable need for so much money. If one does not obey the dynamic one begins to contract, which is a death of sorts. Jack sits uneasy now.

A cool saltin mist rolls over the bow and Mr. Harton takes another sip. Thirty years of conquering leaves one on a 125 foot yacht agonizing over how he is going to acquire those last remaining twenty acres of prime virgin real estate that would cap his career very nicely. Jack Harton knows the whole story back to front, inside and out as he closes his eyes and goes over it once again. Mr. Wrigley of Wrigley's gum fame buys land in 1938 from an tired old farmer, sells to General Motors top man in 1951. Edward Binsent dies leaving the property to his wife Claire Delane Binsent. Mrs. Binsent does nothing but continue to grow pomegranates and figs on the property. Jack Harton whispers to himself the joke about the last important use of the property was for buffalo to graze upon a hundred years ago. He knows the story of Mrs. Binsent being chauffered around the property having conversations with her late husband. Jack knows all about the land.

As his girlfriend walks up the stairs wearing only those little white spongy separations between her freshly painted toes, he takes one last hard gaze at the coastline and the lights from the homes up on Spyglass hill and all of it in its slow burn sparkle.

The Mofford's kitchen

As Scott and Amy dance Robin writes out a shopping list for the following morning but the moment pulls her in and she is inspired to put the tenderness and fun of the sight to paper and poetry.

Shopping list:
    Celery
    Milk
    Eggs
    Baloney

And behold a child's dance
Treasures to the eyes and heart
His warm gaze is upon her now
As she spins with glimmers of sweetness, a
    youthful spin
Her eyes wide with delight
Wide thrilled smile looking up at him
The blessed rewards are rich and wondrous
A dreams creator, loves such wondrous
Tenderness as beams of light, warm light
A peaceful evening pores over as joy
She steps on her father's shoes and he reaches for
    her hands
They dance

Sugar
7 grain bread
Dish soap
Cat and dog food............

Quick note on Marty

Marty is not doing well on her medication. She is standing outside the back door of Rob's home in the dark with a steak knife in one hand and a credit card in the other. Both hands are shaking. Rob is away on a business trip. She knows this. Marty is trying to unlock the door with her tools. She is driven by an intense compulsion to rearrange Rob's furniture. She must be quiet, she must get in, she must rearrange. She has a plan. Marty is not doing very well on her medication.

ICU, Boag Hospital—Guarded

The three young men from Ohio are resting peacefully in the coma of their choosing. A guard sits outside the door; he is dozing off. His head slumps to his chest which startles him out of his groggy state. His posture stiffens quick as he slaps his left hand to his side arm in reflex. He dozes off again.

Newport's slow burn into the late evening continues yet goes unnoticed and is of little concern to a lone seagull atop lifeguard tower 32. His passion is the moonlit coastline. Once a month the moon stands just high enough above the horizon for the best exposure. His only care being whether the moon is in the right spot for the show. The seagull squints his eyes into smiles of anticipation. His attention fixes on the upcoming swell. It is a good one, he knows. The swell waves up a good eight feet, as it does the light from the moon shows through the back strongly, igniting the blue green phosphorous that bursts in a blaze, illuminating the wave's contents. Swirling and tumbling within are three seals. The seagull squawks his approval, quick flutters excite his wings.

The wave crashes, silver mist exploding skyward. The seagull juts up intoxicated by the spectacle as he hovers for a brief moment then dives through the silver and blue green phosphorous mist as his thrill. His passion fulfilled.

Surf's Up

A diamond necklace played the pawn
Hand and hand, some drummed along
    to a handsome man and baton
A blind class aristocracy
Back through the opera glass you see
    the pit and pendulum drawn

Hung velvet over taken me

Dim chandelier awaken me
To a song dissolved in the dawn

The music—A costly bow
The music all is lost for now
    to a muted trumpeter swan
The glass was raised, the fired-roast
The fullness of the wine
A dim last toasting...........
While aport adieu or die
A loss and grief, heart-hardened eye beyond
    belief, a broken man too tough to cry

Surfs Up! Aboard a tidal wave
Come about hard and join the young and
    often spring you gave, I heard a voice.
Wonderful thing! A children's song......

Poem found in the shoe
of Van Dyke Parks.
Poet found dead under
Newport pier—1967

Karen's place

Karen is reading. John is sitting, nervous with his hands, puts them in different places every ten seconds.

"I'll make coffee." John releases himself from the tension.

"Well—John we've been friends along time, ever since the blind date my sister set up. So, that said, I don't like it. Or, should I say it like an editor might: 'I love it—but I just don't love it enough.'

John slows his motions while making coffee. His face flushes with a suppressed exasperation.

"What's the problem? And that was a good date, our only date by the way and it's not my fault you're blind."

Karen laughs in little feminine huffs.

"It jumps from scene to scene, you're driving me crazy! And weren't adjectives outlawed or something? Last but not least, if you want to write poetry………. "

"Your exact words were 'Write it as though your looking through a kaleidoscope' remember? That means image to image and I thought you liked poetry."

"I know but………don't give a girl what she wants—give her what she doesn't expect."

"I'm going home. You said kaleidoscope."

PART TWO

If a microscope were more like a kaleidoscope, everything you may examine in Newport possibly fantastic is most likely illusion.

Newport's Favorite Humorist
Gilbert Sullivan 1905-1961

Newport

In 1918 it snowed in Newport Beach, in the surrounding towns of what are now Corona Del Mar, Costa Mesa and Huntington Beach. Children were described in local newspapers as 'cheerful lunatics' slipping and sloshing all over town. It has happened only once in seventy-eight years so a casual mention will suffice. Merely and interesting side note. It all melted by 2:00 pm.

If one were to drive down to Balboa Island which happens to be only two hundred feet off the shore of Newport, there is a Pavillion's market to your right before you go over the bridge. It is a wonderful market as it has everything a millionaire or billionaire might desire. In fact Warren Buffet was seen in swim trunks and a tank top last summer buying grapefruit and vodka. It is safe to say his leisure was not found in the next morning's newspapers.

This market has everything, the finest of everything that is. The bakery emits smells that even ones own mother may toil in vain to produce. The wines seem to be almost exclusively from the eighties and that is apparently very good. Now something which is of most worthy mention is the size of the strawberries not to mention all the other succulent fruits and vegetables. Someone has even set out a tray with those massive strawberries dipped in white and milk chocolate.

A girl in her late twenties or a lady in her early forties who's cosmetic surgeries have taken well reaches for one of the dipped strawberries and takes a small bit. As she backs up she notices a little sign underneath the chocolate clinched gems that reads $6.75 each. Her eyes grow wide as she looks to her left and right quick. She sets the luscious berry down the size of a small fist and walks away wiping the chocolate off the corners of her mouth.

This market here is not extraordinarily worthy of mention for its own sake but the location under and around the area of the store is. As we make our way outside and through the picket line –the Union decided to strike this week- this specific parcel of land has a grand history. Before there were seven million dollar homes with private docks about three hundred feet away, over the bridge on Balboa Island, there use to be a small dirt landing strip for barnstormers and your casual pilots of the time. If one closes his eyes and lets his imagination walk he can hear the clatter of those ancient Curtiss 0x-5 engines and he could see those canvas and wooden marvels. Engines spit and rumble, smoke swirling back fast by the thrust of the wooden propellers, the auspicious leer of a pilot standing near. And if you let go completely one can see an altogether different time. If you're able to shut out the angry dull chanting of the picketers which appear as one nebulous entity, one can make out the Model A's and Stutz Bearcat coexisting effortlessly, for the love of flight connected all and had no social structure to burden and separate. Men stand virile with hands on hip in their handsome leather flight outfits as their girls sport the latest fashion under umbrellas held with a delicate grasp. Laughs, cool breeze and joy. Blankets sprawled picnics prepared. Wine, cheese and bread. More laughs, easy conversations and the thirst for flight. No large buildings to speak of, only a few homes and garages scattered about. And they all would look forward to the great parties of the evening, 1920's style.

That is what you can see with your minds eye if you care to but it has been gone for a good seventy five years, only photos scattered around city hall as whispers of the past speak to those few who bother to look. Newport is all about power, wealth and beauty exclusively though nowadays. And a social structure has been laid in masterfully and without mercy the likes of which the great Roman Empire would blush in veneration over.

Newport, formally a true shipping port, is not really Newport at all—well let's just say it should not be. All the way up until 1868 Newport was in fact Pueblo De Santa Ana, which translates roughly to 'home on the warm wind.' The agricultural Mecca of the long and beloved Spanish coastline. The people were proud an honorable, life was simple and fulfilled in all respects. All that ended with the white man's conquest and encroachment of the west all the way to and including this massive California coastline. Ninety percent of the native Mexicans eventually moved south which leaves the remaining ten percent, which exist through generations to present day.

Of course the question must arise as to why for they have methodically and over the numbing of time and steady coercion have become no more than a slave. The once finely cultured humanity has been reduced to a manageable and necessary sub human level as perceived, with a contemptuous low brow. Some have said in hushed privacy Newport is no more than a sprawling twenty first century plantation and the Mexicans -chronically stripped of their dignity- keep it beautiful. Harsh comment. Of course they may occasionally take pride in their work as it just happens to be human nature, even if one is not paid well. And even less occasionally the elite of Newport appreciate them as one would appreciate any vassaled servant and even that is rare and fleeting.

Marisah Lopez is cleaning Mrs. Binsent's bathroom but in fact not really, as she fakes slow cleaning strokes. Mrs.

Binsent fumbles with the lock to the safe mounted in the closet, she forgets and starts over, she remembers then goes right past the number, starts over. Marisah can see the tumbler of the safe if she moves to a particular corner of the bathroom where the door is hinged and through the space made by the door next to the door way. Marisah squints and strains to see, then writes down a number and begins to clean the toilet. She has three numbers so far but she is not sure of the sequence but she will be, eventually.

Claire Binsent slips on with little abash an enormous diamond ring over her finger of which makes four now displayed. She tilts her head from side to side and turns her hand to the best light for the one that captures her fancy for the day. In the safe there are five or six, more equally stunning rings she does not bring out for the recital, perched next to several diamond and gem studded necklaces.

"Marisah!" Claire yells.

Marisah stops cleaning, thinks she is caught spying.

"Yes ma'am." Marisah responds cheerfully as all vital functions within her tighten.
"What do you think? Come here."
"Yes ma'am."
"Here—try this on."

Claire pulls out a necklace worth in the neighborhood of seventy-five thousand dollars and throws it over Marisah's head. Marisah reactively stands a little straighter and a shot of excitement gleams from her eyes.

"What do you think honey, is that a Tuesday necklace?"

Marisah cannot speak, she can not think, she cannot answer, especially a lofty stratospheric question like that. She is looking down at twenty seven of the earth's most precious stones. Claire slowly steps toward her, takes two fingers and lifts her chin.

"Is that a Tuesday necklace or not?"

......TWENTY

Nurse's office, Amy's school

Amy has a severe disorder. She gets a little nervous before tests at her elementary school. Sometimes she gets really nervous other times just a little. And other times she is caught daydreaming, especially when birds are chasing each other outside the window of her classroom. Other times she has so much energy to burn she's not quite sure what to do with herself and is occasionally disruptive. Amy casually mentioned the nervous part to her teacher, the teacher not so casually told the school nurse about all of it. And in turn the nurse recommends moderate sedation. Ritalin is the candy coated hell she has in mind—to start with.

Robin, Scott and Amy Mofford sit across from the nurse—Ms. Connors.

"Oh yes, yes the Moffords, hello, yes, hello, glad you could make it."

"Hello Ms. Connors." Robin extends her hand. Scott's hands are folded tight in his lap, his mind is on an installation job in Newport.

"Ok good, let's get right to it, Amy look at this scale here honey. Just how much anxiety do you have before a test." Nurse Connors says while holding up a placard with different contorted faces escalating with corresponding numbers that rise up to near frightening appearance of severe anxiety.

Amy squints a little, bites her bottom lip then takes a little stifled breath.

"Well—sometimes it's forty with that face and sometimes it's seventy with that face." Amy says while drawing her shoulders up, she smiles gently, then drops them.

Scott looks out the window towards his truck in the parking lot to make sure the contents in the bed are safe and secure.

"Oh—really Amy—well Mr. And Mrs. Mofford I'll cut to the cause her. Amy is suffering from attention deficit/hyperactivity disorder and aggravated by a generalized anxiety disorder, which stems out of a chemical imbalance. She will need a full battery of tests for formal diagnosis though. We are lucky to catch this early. Now—ha! I'm not saying she is defective, no, no. Millions, about ten million children across this great country of ours are finally being diagnosed and treated for various and similar symptoms. You are very fortunate.

Scott squirms a little in his chair as this is an awkward situation he begins to notice. He has no real thoughts of agreement or dispute though. He just squirms. Robin is calm and intense. For unknown reasons she senses something cold and dark. Robin takes a quick glance around the room, she can't tell if it is in the room or that it is something within herself. Robin can't tell what it is or where it is coming from. Not yet.

"Yes, little Amy has an attention deficit disorder—oh yes, plus—hyperactivity disorder, which we call ADHD, according to a cursory evaluation I gave her last week, very common. Psychiatry has made great strides in this area with regard to children."

Robin did not give permission for any evaluation like that. Robin has pieces of information enter her mind in a murky and inconclusive manner. Just bits of information, something she read but only part of, something she saw on television about the wide spread drugging of children in schools while she was ironing one day. She turned it off halfway through because she had to pick up Amy from school or go grocery shopping. Robin also heard something about children committing suicide and murder after taking psychiatric drugs but can't remember where she heard it. Even stories about permanent brain damage caused by the drugs not to mention future dependencies—but there were always things to get done. Bits of data she filed away over the years without any real inspection, though she always found it disturbing then was swept away by the busyness of her life.

Robin's sense of a dark presence intensifies, the room seems to chill further.

"We have a doctor that will write a prescription for Adderall or Ritalin—that will correct the imbalance. Mr. and Mrs. Mofford, with all due respect in a year or two we wouldn't even be having this conversation.

"What do you mean?"
"Well I'm referring to 'Mandatory mental health screening' for all children for mental illness. And mandatory drugging of all children diagnosed. Isn't that wonderful—takes the problem right out of parent's hands and into ours."

Robin's heart stopped but her mind raced, even this happy homemaker from Costa Mesa, California knew that would be a very bad thing and quite possibly the end of civilization as the family unit,` all together. Even she knew that would mark the beginning of a new dark age for mankind.

"Oh, did I forget to mention the 'Mandatory mental health screening' and drugging is for all Americans, man, woman and child?"

Robin's eyes take on a steel resolute quality to them as she begins to form an opinion about psychiatry and this nurse in front of her. One day on Oprah, Robin, while folding clothes, listened intently to a man speak about how his child was taken from him for not forcing the child to take psychiatric drugs and that it was medical neglect and child endangerment by not doing so.

That piece of data was also entered into her forming opinion. Ten million children sedated at public schools are taken into consideration. The dark vacant eeriness of the nurse's eyes are taken to heart.

"Critical new discoveries, very exciting, did you know we can diagnose mental illness before a child is even born, while still in the womb? You might find this interesting, a mother takes a mental health screening test and if it is positive for any of a wide range of mental illnesses we can begin treating them *both* right away. You see whatever is going on with the mother is transferred through the genes to the unborn baby. So—we start medicating immediately, before the child is even born." The nurse says with a gaunt detached smirk.

Robin receives a sudden sick anxiety and a closing grip of fear tightens around her, she realizes that she is in the presence of a vile spirit.

Off in the distance the bellowing chime of a church bell rings. Being quite some distance away it is faintly heard yet it reaches all in the nurse's office. Amy hops a little in her seat and pats her mother's thigh. Robin gains strength from it. Scott is puzzled though, he wonders why it is ringing on a Tuesday. He notices an agitation emerge and quickly intensify in the nurse's eyes. Scott is transfixed on them as her knuckles turn white from the death grip applied to the pen in hand. Scott looks out the window in the general direction of the church bell then his attention darts back to her eyes. He gasps just under his breath; he can see her dilated pupils darken.

Bong.............Bong.............Bong.............Bong

They blacken to an unearthly tone and depth. A chill rolls up Scott's spine, he must look away.

"We should begin the medication for Amy immediately. About a quarter of the students here are medicated so don't worry about safety or effectiveness. Oh—don't look so pained, your number just happened to be up. If this were, let's say, Silicon Valley instead of Costa Mesa I would be diagnosing little Amy with high functioning Autism. Autism was a wonderful coup for us in Silicon Valley, we just rolled on in that city of tech nerds and said 'Oh my, what an alarming increase in cases' and started diagnosing and treating on the spot. We just, with slight of hand, opened the perimeters of diagnosis. Tell me, what profession can get away with that? That has been a very successful operation for us across the U.S. The field of psychiatry has big plans for children over the next decade or so, you have to get a handle on this *new* mental health crisis we are having, or about to have, or whatever, ha!"

Robin is startled by that comment. Her lips become ridged, her jaw tense. Her eyes widen and focus intently on the Nurse's pale ghostly face. She wondered why it was so quiet recently when she visited the school for functions; many of the students were sedated and silenced into highly controllable stimulus response mechanisms. The spirit buried deep by narcotic suppression.

"You may have heard that some of us, mostly doctors, are deputized by the sheriff to handle such matters on the spot."

"What? What the hell are you talking about? But you're a nurse!"

"Ho—yes but can't let you get away, medical neglect is a serious matter."

"When on earth did mental health become a *medical* issue anyway. I'll—I'll say probably the day you decided it to be you bitch!"

Something, a force of nature only a mother possesses came surging up from a seldom tapped stalwart source. Robin understood clearly her daughter was in danger. Scott looks out at the truck, sees some boys eyeing his tools.

"It is amazing how Christians just let us waltz on in, diagnose half the congregation, ha! Great place to drum up business let me tell you."

Nurse Connors did not say that. Robin heard her say that in her mind. The same mind that tries to push that very fact out of her head every Sunday service. She has seen it gradually happen over the last few years. And that was the breaking point, it all came together quick. Robin attacked within clasp of fury.

"If you ever come near my Amy or even speak to her again I will kick your cunt up into your throat! You evil witch—you evil whore witch! Chemical imbalance, that's fucking ridiculous! It's just a little fear, she gets a little anxious, she daydreams a little—she's a kid! We will work through it! Families have worked through it for eons you fuckin whore, bitch, fuck!"

Scott was stunned, nurse Connors was stunned, Amy was stunned—but grinning. Robin sensed an evil presence.

171

Mothers have a quick intellect and strength for situations such as this.

Robin held Amy in a protective cocoon on the way home. Both mother and child were silent clutching each other close. Scott would look over about every ten seconds, he doesn't say a word as he remains rather stunned but more proud than anything. He had only seen the sweet loving side of his wife all these years. Scott saw the tiger today, it amazed him, he did not sense the danger that Robin did. He felt a little stupid.

The rest of the evening was the quietest of recent memory. Dinner, no television, Amy's bath, feed the dogs and cat. Robin and Amy go to bed. But Robin gives Scott a kiss on the cheek and says she will spend and hour or so in Amy's room then come in later.

They huddle close on Amy's bed, lights out. The little Pooh Bear night light soothes, the pink walls glow protectively. Scott heads out to the back yard for a cigarette and a beer still scratching his head, still baffled. Robin and Amy dose off.

Robin is held from any real depth of sleep. She is suspended in the thin veil, that of a wistful dreaminess hovering in sympathy over utter slumber. She is released from her fear and wrath. The old sash window is wide open, Robin flies out. She flaps up quick to the top of a telephone pole and sits momentarily. The property is four miles south, she leaps to flight. The evening is cold, dark and the rolling fog churns and tumbles in from the coast. Robin as bird climbs up through and above the fog.

The stars glimmer in approval for the stance against evil she took today, the sky is clear and enormous in its expanse. The moon is full and bright giving the aura that it just might be alive and watching her every move. Robin can see the towers of Fashion Island jut out of the murky fog. She dives down through the heavy mist. She is directly above the property as she draws her wings in tight and picks up speed, straight down. Robin casts her wings out hard inches above the rough tilled soil and runs along as rodent, a hundred feet in seconds. She dives under the soil as worm. The soil is rich and moist as she squirms around in bliss. She squirms and worms, worms and squirms.

Robin pops her worm head out of the luscious loam and launches out as bird, wings in furious lunging sweeps. She is two hundred feet above the property promptly, glides momentarily taking in the enormity of the twenty acres in stark contrast to the development around it. Robin as bird hears a soft cry from Amy in her sleep, she heads home.

Robin rushes in back through the window and becomes woman, mother, wife. She drifts peacefully into sleep now. Now she can.

Robin was in the presence of evil today, a psychiatric nightmare was averted by quick intellect and a gut feeling. A nightmare that looms and lurks in the shadows—for they are the mental and spiritual predators of Newport Beach.

This time -our time- must be won or a new dark
age begins. Satan, wearing a white coat to the
knees has a prescription for you and your children,
as he lies in wait at every other corner in a well
cared for office complex. He says to trust that he
is the authority, the doctor. That all your troubles
are no more than a chemical imbalance. And he is
here to help you and that you should thank god for
that. Eradicating these monsters falls upon our
shoulders. And we shall weep in joyous occasion
when our good lord blesses us for the stand we took.

Pastor Paul Donaldson
Saint James Church, Newport

......TWENTY ONE

Imports of Newport

The Ukrainian is leaned back in a red leather covered chair on its hind legs with his feet on Davis Rothman's desk. Another is standing near the door and still another is peering intently out the window with an embedded sneer to his expression. No businessman appreciates someone's feet -let alone this idiot's- on their desk, even as a joke. Of course if those feet belong to a woman with size seven high heels—well.

But Davis says nothing, does nothing. The Ukrainian studies Davis, rocks his head slowly from side to side. Davis is rambling with nervous comments on the verge of being incoherent. The man with his feet on Davis' desk with the dominant squint to his eyes offers yes nods acknowledging nothing in particular except for the fact that he owns him and Davis fears him now.

"We going to take old bitch out, kill old woman." Her daughter will sell property to us for fraction of value and all the heroin she can eat, ah ha ha!"

The other two Ukrainians laugh, one keeps a tight eye out the window for the shadows *they* fear. Davis does not laugh and his breath quickens as the color drains from his face.

The two watching the door and window have no affinity between them, whatsoever. Their was a Swedish girl involved but she is long gone. The dislike remains though. One punches the other hard every other day or so and they are on a short leash by the one in charge.

"She was so nice, oh my little Swed." Dragane, the one next to the window, chuckles under his breath as he forms his hands into a v-shape against his crouch.

"Fuck you." Yurrgi utters harshly adding a scathing glower.

"Shut up, both of you." The eldest Ukrainian barks.

"Ok, here is what we going to do and how you help..........." The Ukrainian says with a look on his face that suggests he has done this many times before which included someone like Rothman. He rocks back up putting the chair on all fours and places his forearms on Davis' desk. His eyes, which a moment ago glared dominant, now penetrate Rothman with total control. Davis' eyes are stunned to the observer, stunned numb. And the numbness reaches inward on him and consumes him.

An hour earlier Alec came into Imports of Newport to look at the Mercedes Neil has been nagging him about.

Alec is listening to a strange and disturbing conversation on the intercom to Davis' phone left on by accident in a salesman's office. Murder and treachery, terrible plans being laid. Alec sits hunched over wringing his hands, eyes bugged with shock. One of the Ukrainian's -the one watching the window- walks by the office Alec is sitting in on his way to the restroom. The man stops, backs up, understands quickly that Alec has heard everything.

Alec understanding the delicate situation he has stumbled into gives the look that, yes, he did hear but has know idea what they were talking about over the look of knowing full well that he knows precisely. The Ukrainian takes inventory of all the expressions and changes in color on Alec's face. Alec knows by the expression on the tough and rigid man's face that he is not buying the thin dumb expression over the knowing full well what is going on expression.

The Ukrainian gives Alec a look that communicates by its intensity and solidity that he is in grave trouble now. Alec's expression now has turned to fear and a pleading, hopeful request for mercy. The Ukrainian has no trace of mercy on his face, heart, mind, soul, past life, future life, anytime, anywhere.

Two Hours Later

Neil gets out of a taxi in front of Imports of Newport to pick up his Mercedes after its first service. If he had bought one up the street at Fletcher Jones they would have given him a Mercedes at least as nice as his to drive for the day. Neil does not know this and most likely would not care all that much. Neil tips the taxi driver handsomely and turns toward the dealership with and ear to ear grin. He places his hands on his hips and the grin is replaced with a searching smile.   He cocks his head from side to side and down shielding the sun from his eyes with his forehead to spot his S500. He locates it in bay two on its decent from the hydraulic lift. Neil's smile forms words. "There's my baby."

"Ok, she's good for you Mr. Landitt." The mechanic says in broken English while performing the chronic 'wiping of his hands' on a shop towel.

"Good, great!" Neil returns as he gets in with the ease and confidence that fine machinery bestows upon its owner.

As Neil creeps to the front of the dealership he spots Alec's Infinity tucked in a corner. "I'll be damned, that sneak, he is in there this minute striking a deal. Well, I won't spoil his surprise." Neil looks to his left then makes a right down Pacific Coast Highway. The new Ukrainian mechanic continues to wipe his hands with a cold blooded smirk on his face then throws a middle finger Neil's way and cursing something in Serbian under his breath.

> You never hear about a criminal saying they are
> *from* Newport Beach for Newport takes care of
> its own miss-wired and sick.

> Former Police Chief
> Edmond Rumhardt 1974

......TWENTY TWO

Starbucks Girls

The four girls at the local Starbucks in Corona Del Mar, the first city south of Newport, have a serious and specific routine. That is to secure the best table at 6:00 PM Tuesdays and Fridays and wait for prince charming to stroll in. No one sitting there can tell you why those days where chosen but like most rituals of a high order that's just the way it is. Now collectively and individually they have staked out this locale as to where the hard working and not so hard working young executives frequent. They roll down the hill from the Fashion Island business towers in search of nothing more than a Latte and a good chat with a buddy or two. Little do they know they are being stalked —so to speak- sized up, and become part of an endless dialogue stream of which there is no escape.

For this is the future pulse of Newport in its embryonic state. The future leaders and swindlers along with their female counterpart are hatched and incubated at this little Starbucks here. Of course the girls realize they never know what kind of prospect they really have but there are certain criteria they screen for to narrow the focus. First of all they do not look for a nice car. They know that will come easily enough with viable prospective earnings. It is the potential for viable future earnings they have their sites and sensors set for. This procedure of observation is a true science yet each girl sitting at this table has a slightly different technique they employ along with a different value along side each attribute observed. Very dry, technical stuff.

For instance: Is this, let's say, 'potential prince' a yes man? Does he just agree with what his friends talk about regarding current events and such because he is weak or does he honestly agree? This one is easy to detect and considered a serious flaw. Is he overly tense after a week in the towers? Is he trying to pretend as though he is not rattled? See here's the point on that one: Guys that are tense or look a bit haunted or hunted are the ones doing all the work. The load is dumped squarely on their shoulders. Funny thing with these guys, they allow it or simply cannot figure out a way to pass the work on. If Starbuck girl senses this design flaw he is considered weak and a little stupid. Stupid in that these young men are considered the mules of society. Newport girl will not tolerate a mule boyfriend. Fatal flaw. They go for the guy loading up the mule.

"Double mocha Latte, non fat," The barista blasts. One of the girls jumps up and shuffles over quick to get her drink.

That brings in Mr. Cool who is not necessarily a 'potential prince.' Now Mr. Cool is worthy of intense scrutinizing and dialogue streaming. The big question with *a* Mr. Cool: is he in truth just a mule and an expert at faking it or if he is a loader, does he really have the goods for proper wealth? Tough questions. The trick is simple targeted observation over time—like weeks before a contact is planned by Starbucks girl.

The guys that are in control at the office are also in control at Starbucks. That is the point. They continue to direct the flow and conversations and the mules let them do it. They cannot help it—they are mules. Once the separation is made Mr. Cool is put under a microscope as this is a solemn game for there are standards of existence in Newport and they must be met.

Before one gets too far into this mining expedition of sorts there is something that begs mention. Nearly every single one of these girls that have sat at this observation post over the years could easily create their own wealth and take care of themselves. They are at least as smart as and surely smarter than most of the young exec's observed. The problem is that even in this day and age it is still a matter of conditioning, or maybe better put, brainwashing. And safe to say no ones mind is getting cleansed. Those damn little fairy tale stories at bedtime of prince charming sweeping a girl off her feet and living happy ever after in the castle and movies pounding home the message and, and, ad infinitium. Then again the dirty little secret that flutters above women's liberation and independence, is that no matter what women are capable of they still have the misty dreamy urge for a man to lift them to the back of a pearl white stallion by a guy with a black cape and the long blonde hair and take control of their destiny.

Of course a women will take the control part away then give it back as part of a divine strategy, then take it back and, and, ad infinitium.

Then of course there are very basic questions and the most very basic question: Could I stand him touching me? "It's chemistry, everything else could be right but, well, it's chemistry," One of the girls said a couple weeks ago.

But all this flows over Marty tonight, she is held by a dreamy detachment, she is in love.

"Oh nice purse!" They all say to a girl who arrives late but only two really mean it, the other two really don't. "You're late girlfriend," Marty cheerfully adds.

The purse is predominately pink with a white poodle made using little white costume jewelry gems. There is a long black shoulder strap and other touches unworthy of mention.

"How's your man honey?" Karen, the girl with the purse asks.

Marty sinks a little down her chair taking pleasure in the thought of him. She places her hands in her lap and lifts her shoulders gently as she takes a deep breath. An easy grin emerges with twinkling eyes.

> "I'm a lucky girl, that's all I can say." Marty gleams.
> "God I need a frickin Latte!" Karen blurts.
> All five girls burst into laughter.

......TWENTY THREE

Late Evening

July 28th

Rolling and tumbling, fumbling and bumbling,
crying and dying, dying and crying. He is not
the one I am not the one. The rain falls on me,
the sky falls on me. The wind blows through
me, tearing at me. The earth swallows me, the
moon laughs at me. Rolling and tumbling,
fumbling and bumbling. He's wrong for me, I
see now, so dead wrong. Crying and dying, dying
and crying..............

Kaisty rips the diary from Neil's hands. It was actually
written in a notebook as its first incarnation meant to be
entered into her diary as she got around to it.

"You have no right!" Kaisty screams.

"Honey, but, uh." Neil defends.

"This is personal, very personal; it's *my* diary, *my* diary!"
Kaisty screams and cries.

"But it's good, really good!" Neil scrambles for any combination of positive words that may defuse the situation.

"That's not the point, you have no right! It is written by me, for me, about me!"

"I just needed some paper and it's a notebook and I..................."

"How could you," Kaisty exhausts her anger falls to her knees with the notebook resting on her lap and both hands holding it tight, head hung desperate, her hair converging over her face. Neil hurries over, arms extended, eyes bugged with concern. He gently sets his hands on her shoulders then places her hair back behind her ears and cups her face in his hands.

"Honey, Kaisty, it's good, really good. Is it a poem? Kind of sad but really, really good—let me help you."

"That's not the point—it has nothing to do with any of tha...tha....that." Kaisty sobs.

"I'm sorry sweetheart, I'm sorry." Neil kneels down and gently massages her shoulders. "I am *so* sorry, I'm sorry."

A couple of hours later Neil is sitting alone on the back patio. The night seems darker than most to his weary perceptions. Neil stares out without putting much attention on anything, his expression dull. He takes some solace in the faint hiss of silence as he rubs his temple and takes a sip from his beer. A motorcycle roars up the street cutting the cool night air as the sound travels out to the distance where Neil's eyes are transfixed, the faint contour of the San Bernardino Mountains seventy miles away.

Neil hears Kaisty break a glass in the kitchen. It sounded like she only dropped it. She curses quick and harsh. "At least she didn't throw it." Neil mutters under his breath. "Where are my damn sleeping pills," Kaisty grumbles.

Through his fence and down the slope Neil can see his neighbors swimming in their pool. Laughing and playful. He yearns for that easy connection with Kaisty again. Their amiable exchange and pleasure torments Neil and the steel bars of the fence between him and his neighbor's joy does not go unnoticed. The light from the pool lands on Neil's face in warbles of luminescent wakes. The diffused light ripples across his face tantalizing his solemn expression. He takes another drink of his beer, closes his eyes with more force than usual and rubs his temple again. He punctuates it all it with a heavy sigh.

......TWENTY FOUR

Claire rests uneasy, tossing and turning. If one is resting uneasy then one is not resting at all. Claire reaches over to her favorite antique lamp, pulls the delicate sterling silver chain. "Ah damn, I'd better do something with that land. Lord knows my daughter will screw it up and or the land will end up in the hands of those bastards when I keel over."

Claire rises from her bed with difficulty, Bruty hanging awkward under her arm. She walks over and opens the French doors to the veranda. The midnight air is brisk and welcome on the old women's senses. Crickets hush but just for a moment as she steps out. She slowly takes a seat and Bruty balls up on her lap, falling back to his purring reverie. "Hell I came from nothing, dusty little bare foot girl from Oklahoma."

The moon dances on the bays silver ripples in its crescent slumber, warmed by the sun unseen. Drowsy wisps of wind flutter the sails of the few remaining vessels owned by yachtsmen who still covet the discipline. The sailboats are flanked and dominated by an array of striking in appearance powered yachts of all shapes and sizes.

A possum runs along Claire's fence, up a telephone pole and zips down the line. Claire smiles tenderly at the sight. "Heck, I'd give it to someone if I liked them enough to trust them." The somewhat recently exposed little squiggly blue veins just under the surface of her skin can be seen around her temple. And extensive wrinkling with deep crow's feet off her eyes and her newly installed pacemaker for her heart are god's reminders to get ones house in order my mortal children. Claire's feels that pressure for the first time.

The first ten years of Claire Binsent's life was in the teeth of the depression. Life was tough sometimes unbearably tough. She closes her eyes and remembers her friends loading up their Model A Ford and heading for California. She counts on her fingers how many families she witnessed leaving the barren farmland for the promise of the west. She wonders about what happened to those families. As a child she figured everything would turn out ok for them, now as adult she wonders if it did. Every single one of them only wanted a piece of land that they could farm and call home. But the Oklahoma land became barren and the soil lost its strength from drought and depleting farming practices over the years. Hard times led to bank loans. Harder times led to foreclosures. Thousands of foreclosures.

Claire opens an old folder of hand written poems by her late husband. She runs her wrinkled calm hand over the one she wants to read, one of her favorites. Her mouth crooks into a soft grin, her eyes come to life. There is love in those eyes and a longing for a man who died a long time ago. She reads to herself with a tender quiver in her voice.

Carry Me Home

Fields of grain, stalks taller than myself as child
A breeze swoops down to play then laughs away
Yet I am old now
I recall a youthful game of chase through same
      fields with a girl
But I am old now, carry me home
Sky's stretch bold and blue as more cool wind
      falls on the plains from a distant sea
And I dreamed of pirates
My grand daughter looks at the field the way I do
      then places her hand on my cheek. Her tiny
      hand warm and soft.
She understands. Of any one she understands.
Yet I am old, so very old, carry me home.......

She closes the folder and holds it to her chest. A lone tear ambles down her face then meanders along her wrinkled features and comes to rest on her chin. She wipes it off with the tip of her finger.

"It does look a bit odd, all that undeveloped property just sitting in the heart of Newport. Lord, I am a stubborn woman. But the one I chose must be worthy of it."

She recalls her family moving the other direction to Chicago, her family abandoning farming for good. After much struggle they were able to mesh well enough into the hustle and bustle of big city life. They had no choice.

Claire's head droops as she falls asleep, finally. But before she fell asleep she came up with a nifty plan.

Karen's Place

Karen is sitting on her couch, watching television, both feet tucked under her thighs. Her cell phone is set loosely in her left hand. John has just left a text message for her. Karen does not open it. The phone rings, Karen does not answer it. Karen gives the manuscript a quick glance on the coffee table, curls the corners of her lips down momentarily. She turns her attention back to 'American Idol.'

"Boring.........." She utters in a whisper.

......TWENTY FIVE

Mrs. Binsent has a daughter and she has been slowly, painfully losing that motherly bond for a few years now. It is surely not of Claire's choosing as she has tried every conceivable then imaginable way to help her only child. Mothers do that and mothers become frustrated and some even sink into a deep apathy but not Claire. No deep apathy for her, not her. Unfortunately, it is a waiting game now. She still holds on to the hope her daughter may someday simply snap out of it. Claire will not let herself know how rare that is.

Gina Binsent is balled up in a tight fetal posture, stiff white linen and two blankets cover her entire body head to toe. She has tucked the covers underneath her where she could draw them in. She likes her cocoon. All desperate women do. An hour earlier she closed off all the light from entering the room although it is a beautiful midday, all in an attempt to shut out as many of her perceptions as possible. Another depressed and desperate female favorite. In her darkness and holding a pillow tight to her breast, Gina has some vague and obscure thoughts which pulsate over and over in aching nebulous procession. Nothing she can really put a clear idea to. But if one had to it would be the sickening pressure of failure churning and mobilizing itself through her mind as a permanent reminder.

All the sedatives and anti-depressants she has consumed and been encouraged to consume have not helped. Gina hates the dead feeling they cause but protests little. Maybe an occasional sedate smoothness has occurred, maybe a narcotic induced euphoria has sustained her hopes for a cure but with no lasting serenity. At best she is left with is an out of touch and anesthetized carelessness about her. At other times the drugs excite her into frenzied mental states where she wants to save all of the world one minute then a few hours later destroy all that it is and represents including and especially herself.

Gina's doctor gave no guarantees so here she lies in a tight ball in the dark, on a gorgeous southern California afternoon in the psychiatric unit of Boag Hospital. This afternoon she is not wholly depressed which consumes and permeate most days during her 28 day program—her fifth 28 day program. Today her doctor has given her hope. Today she will receive Electro Convulsive Therapy. She sees the reassuring smile on her doctor's face when he talked to her about it. She likes him, she will do what he asks her to do. She likes his smile.

Down the hall from Gina's room is the ECT unit. They are preparing for Gina. The machine was activated about an hour ago and ran through calibration and standard tests. The attendant smirks to himself and shakes his head in amazement that insurance companies pay for this procedure as therapy when he wouldn't even feel safe using it to jumpstart his car.

He laughs quietly under his breath. He looks around him quick, he knows better not to display such expression or attitudes around the doctors.

The ECT machine is ready with its souless dull hum and drowsy pulsating lights. The attendant sticks his head out the door and motions for the nurse. The nurse walks down the hall and gingerly taps on the doctor's office door. She continues further and quietly enters Gina's room and says "Honey we are going to get you ready now." Gina hears her but does not respond.

Gina has not met the expectations or the standards of existence of Newport royalty. She is a princess but has never acted like one or had the ability to behave like one. In fifteen minutes she will be punished terribly for that weakness and inability. Her doctor says it will help her, she likes his smile. She likes how he talks softly and confidently.

Gina unravels herself and crawls out from the bed linen, she strains to sit up.

"Today is a beautiful day isn't it—I mean outside, a wonderful day to be alive for almost everybody. Just not me. Doc says this is pretty much my last resort, ECT. It's the right thing to do isn't it nurse Ramlin."

"Oh yes honey, the doctor seems to think so," She has said this so many times she doesn't even realize she said it.

Gina slides over and onto the gurney then lays flat with a hopeful pale grin. She has seen this particular ceiling so many times over the years it is like that of a child knowing every variation of texture on their own bedroom ceiling.

She begins to roll.

The lights flip by as she senses them with her eyes closed on her way to the Electro Convulsion Therapy unit. Gina thinks of her mother, the first time she has thought of her mother in a long, long time. Gina blames her for nothing. She does not know when the dwindling spiral began, the slow boil. She wants to be happy again like when she was in her early teens. Gina drifts off to a memory as she relaxes the tight grip she has on the sheet next to her thigh and the aluminum railing her other hand holds. She use to love to walk to the end of the pier with her father early in the morning and feed the seagulls with little rolled up balls of bread. Her father would throw them high in the hazy mist of early morning and the birds would rush to it and snatch them out of the brisk saltin air. Gina would gush excitement. She feels the sweet sparkle of that very moment as she rolls down the corridor.

When her father died the pressures began, Newport style. Her mother Claire would tell her it meant nothing, not to worry about it and fifty other ways of saying don't worry about it. But Gina did. She never felt beautiful enough, smart enough, or cool enough, it was all awkward to her even with money to burn. The standards of existence in Newport must be met. And Gina could not even come close.

"If that is Gina we are ready for her—I don't want to make that mistake again. That's Gina right?"

Gina is rolled in and set in place. The attendant begins to explain to her what is going to happen as he binds her wrists and ankles with thick leather straps. He rubs an ointment on her temples for maximum electricity conduction and slips a metal harness over her head. Gina looks at him; he tries to avoid her eye contact.

"Try to relax, I've done this a lot or been attendant many times and the ones who resist tend to have quite a headache afterward."

"Ok—ok." Gina says in a thin quivering voice.

He tightens the band around her head making sure the receptors are placed exactly at the temples. Gina winces softly.

"Too tight honey?"

"Ya—a little."

"Now we don't want you to bite your tongue so I am going to place this rubber grommet in your mouth."

Then he injects her with the chemical Succinylcholine to keep her body from an intense writhing, which has been known to break bones caused by the jolts of electricity. In truth it is more for those watching than the patient.

The ECT machine clicks and hums in anticipation.

As Gina's doctor walks down the hall for the treatment, a Ukrainian man who admitted himself two weeks ago for depression (specifically to befriend Gina in hopes of acquiring the property from her after they kill her mother) stops him before he arrives at the ECT unit.

"Ah—hi doctor my name is Viga—ah, now Gina she will be able to think ok after your done—right? I mean, well let's just guess something. Let's just guess something like if she had some important documents to sign. I mean let's just guess."

The doctor does not say a word, he only gives a solemn side to side 'no' nod. The doctor follows with another nod to a nurse to get this idiot away from him. The nurse secures his upper arm gently but firm, spins him around in the direction of his room and says, "It is time for your medication Viga."

The doctor enters the ECT unit, every one stiffens some except Gina, she relaxes a marked degree. She tries to smile through the thick rubber grommet strapped tightly to her mouth.

The doctor flashes a reactive grin, his face now gaunt, his expression numbly menacing.

The warm concern he usually displays for Gina is gone. As cruel fate would have it he is not a man, he is not a doctor, he is a mental and spiritual predator. And he will use bursts of high voltage, which trigger seizures in the brain to ensnarl Gina's problems even tighter, out of reach even further. The ensuing electric shocks erase and eradicate a great portion of her ability to reason by giving loss to her memory. Then a final and brutal jolt to drive her down into a state of apathy she will never climb out of or have the presence of mind to even try.

Well, what is the sense of ruining my head and erasing my memory, which is my capitol and putting me out of business. It was a brilliant cure but we lost the patient.

Wrote in 1961 by
Ernest Hemingway who
committed suicide after
Electro Convulsive Therapy.
A fishing buddy of John
Wayne's for four days
one summer

......TWENTY SIX

A long breeze from a distant sea rushes and falls to Newport. A summer breeze, dancing and delicate upon faces of prince and princess. Unseen as a wind of change, a haunting breeze full of omen, sensed only as pleasure.

Wind Chimes

'Klinkle, tinkle, klink, klink, tink, tinkle, klinkle.' Kaisty's new wind chimes speak.

Kaisty's eyes are glazed, the synthetically induced grin has not left her face for two full hours. She lounges on her patio in the sun, rich blue sky and clouds stand great, light and towering. She succumbs to the benign compulsion of continuously stirring her strawberry daiquiri with her forefinger—and has been for two full hours. Kaisty thumbs through a *Homes for sale* magazine.

They are all nice to her as she turns from page to page. What catches her fancy and makes her stop and lay the magazine on her lap is the name of the street one house is located. 'Yacht Mischief.' She whispers to herself. 'I want to live on Yacht Mischief.' She got the combination right this time, Paxil with an Effexor chaser and a 600mg. tablet of Vicodin. All washed down with a 'Rock Star' beverage. She got it as right as she can without touching on what really is troubling her. A powerful breeze two miles above the earth begins to pull the clouds apart which now appear as cotton tearings to Kaisty. And much higher she spots the jet trail from an airliner. Kaisty frames the plane within her thumb and forefinger. She slips her sunglasses on and exhales gently.

'Klinkle, tink, tinkle, klink, klinkle.'

Davis Rothman locks the door to his office. Looks around even though he knows no one is there. He unlocks his bottom desk drawer. Davis stops quickly, he thinks he hears someone outside his door—there is no one there. He opens the large bulging dark yellow envelope. He pulls out a banded heap of hundred dollar bills. He slaps it on his desk with sly smirk. He pulls out another and another and sets them next to the first stack of hundreds. 'Thirty thousand dollars, sweet thirty.' Davis whispers. 'Man, I don't even remember giving them a key to my trunk.' He chuckles under his breath. He finds an envelope like this one in his trunk each month. Davis Rothman launders one hundred fifty thousand dollars every thirty days for the Ukrainians. Davis runs his forefinger lightly across each stack and grins widely, eyes twinkle deeply and his chin twitches in pleasure.

'Tinkle, klinkle, klinkle, tink.'

Robin and Scott watch Amy run, fun like the wind. Golden blonde pony tail flying. She struggles with her kite. It surges up, it dives down, juts up then nose first into the ground. Robin and Scott cheer her on. Amy tightens the determination on her face, runs as fast as she can. "Let out some line!" Scott screams. Amy fumbles with the spool but lets some out. The kite rockets up. Scott laughs. Amy keeps running, lets out more line. The kite rockets higher, higher. Scott applauds and cheers her on. Robin's eyes well up as it's all wonderful to her.

'Klinkle, tinkle, klinkle, tinkle.'

Mrs. Binsent is asleep on her back veranda. Bruty is balled up tight behind her feet. She dreams of a field she found in Oklahoma when she was twelve, summer of 1942. Every man or young man she knew of was either fighting in Europe or the watery battle fields off the coast of Japan. She sees the young boy of fourteen as she turns her head to the right who found the field with her. He is looking up at an expanse of Sooner sky, miraculous and blue with little white puffs of clouds. The dream is wispy and rich, the sunshine is warm and bountiful with leisurely wind currents crooking the tall grass from side to side. They lay on their backs in the tall grass laughing, holding hands. The sensation of first kiss will linger for days.

'Tink, tink, klinkle, klink.'

Early morning, at Newport Coast golf course. The sunrise to the east impels only a haze of light to the west where one star and a high jet stream wake the coast with a charming ease.

Neil sets the binoculars firmly to his sockets. He can make out just an acre or so from where he is standing of the property. He studies that acre. He stands perfectly straight with his left hand on his hip. His demeanor is that of one inspecting a great empire.

"Come on Mr. Gatsby! Hit the damn ball!" Alec rips. "We've got a foursome breathing down our necks!"

"Getting to it, old sport."

Neil calmly brings the binoculars down with an easy grin and places them in the hard leather case. He places the case in his golf bag and zips it closed. Neil draws out his three wood and places his feet about three feet from the ball. His anxiety creeps up on him, uniform for most men approaching a golf ball. But for some inexplicable reason he simply decides to hit it with minimal preparation or mental gyrations. The ball soars. Neil waits for the slice, the wicked dreaded slice to emerge and begin its errant arc. It never does. The ball lands in the middle of the fairway three hundred yards from its origin. Neil grins at

Alec and the grin stretches into a tight smile. Alec is equally amazed.

"Klinkle, klinkle, tinkle, klink, tink."

Mr. Harton has a dirty little secret. He has a soft spot for animals—even fish. He does not admit this and if pressed would deny it vigorously. The toughest men on earth have the most peculiar soft spots. Mr. Harton sits aft on the fishing deck. He takes a very small lead weight and wraps it tight with a ball of Velveta cheese. He looks over his shoulder to make sure the steward or his captain is not approaching as he would find it awkward to explain fishing without a hook.

Mr. Harton casts the line from his seven hundred dollar fishing pole with little effort or bother to go beyond the decks edge more than a foot or so. He looks over with his lips perched, eyes in squinting smiles of anticipation. The water gently ripples up to the boat and slaps the side with benign intent as the sun rays play hopscotch on the oceans surface. He feels a tug and looks over quick. He sees something large but what? The tug subsides. He winds the line up, the cheese is gone. Mr. Harton receives a shot of thorough enjoyment in feeding the oceans fish with Velveta cheese. He would deny this vigorously, he would say he was just a poor fisherman.

"Tinkle, tinkle, klink, klink, klink, tinkle."

Marty—Starbucks girl—is in love.............Klinkle, tink, tink.

......TWENTY SEVEN

Mrs. Binsent's Parlor

"Robin, I'm an old woman."
"No—no you're wonderful."

Mrs. Binsent scoots her chair over to Robin with slow laboring hops. She takes Robin's hands which are neatly bundled in her lap and wraps her own wrinkled and mildly trembling hands around Robin's young and beautiful ones.

"Let's have some fun."
"Oh, Mrs. Binsent, I'm sorry I have to pick up Amy then make dinner and........."

The old lady unwraps her hand and brings her index finger to Robin's lips and holds it there with a little quiver in the fingertip.

"Shuuuuu, I don't mean this minute."

"Oh—oh, I'm sorry—I."

"I want you to get rid of the idea of quitting the real estate business right this minute. Of course it's for you."

"Oh—well I know it's—well it's just that."

Claire places her finger back on Robin's lips.

"Let's do something with the land you and me."

Robin's eyes bug wide as those nine words just spoken expands the very essence of her actuality.

"I—I thought you would never sell, I mean I heard......"

"I am not my dear, I am giving it to you, conditionally of course. We will develop it together, have some fun, then it is all yours, simply as that.

"What about your children?"

"There is only one and let us just say she is out of touch and there is plenty for her anyway, so don't you worry about that."

Robin's toes went numb then she started to cry.

"Thank you sooooo much but why?"

Claire takes Robin's wrist and pulls her close to her and whispers "Because I like you and I came from absolutely nothing and I have never really gotten use to all this anyway.

And best of all there needs to be a new Queen around here when I am gone to fight off the bastards."

They both laugh, a rich feminine laugh with eyes forming to sly grins that only women in control can manage. Same eyes gleaming mischievous. Robin's tearing mascara making her cheeks a total mess. Everything from one end of the universe to the other was beautiful but it has been that way for quite some time. Then Claire decides to drops buckets of gold dust over it all and on Robin and maybe Claire picked Robin because Robin did not appear to need any of this to be happy and Claire likes that in a person—a lot.

Scott, who would never consider himself an eaves-dropper, was doing just that. He set the crown moulding down and sat on an overturned plastic bucket in the room he was working on—he has to sit. If Scott's jaw would of hung any lower with mouth agape, it would have unhinged and fell to the floor. He looks down at his hands which are large, calloused and rough from years of construction and they are trembling. His eyes glaze over and a twinkle begins deep, deep in the iris. An ear to ear grin snaps to attention on his rugged face. He lets out a little laugh burst then covers his mouth quick.

That is all there was to it, the transaction, the beginning of transfer of ownership of the most coveted parcel of property in the history of Newport Beach, California............."

......TWENTY EIGHT

28-5, Marisah has the last two numbers to Mrs. Binsent's safe. She slips a napkin on which the numbers are scribbled into her smock pocket without skipping a swipe in her cleaning of the master bathroom mirror. Tonight she will steal a hand full of Newport's finest jewels, then sell them one by one a month or two apart—she has it planned.

Marisah gazes at her reflection in the mirror with deep dreaminess to her brown eyes and a devious sneer. Her cleaning swipes slow to languid swirls. Her eyes well up with tears. She will enjoy some of Newport's wealth now, finally. She knows she is thought of as sub-human, she feels it every time the rich of Newport look through her as she walks to and from the bus stop. Marisah and her sisters have toiled in apathetic rhythm for sixteen years for the Newport elite. Marisah hates them.

At 4:30 she will pretend to leave. She will leave the laundry room door unlocked and slip around the south side of the mansion and re-enter, shoes off, and without a sound. Marisah will sneak into Mrs. Binsent's closest and hide. She will hide there until Mrs. Binsent is sound asleep, steal the jewels and slip out into the night never to be seen again. She believes this will bring her joy. She believes this act is no more criminal than their treatment of her and generations of her kind. She will risk and possibly lose her soul as so many of the wealthy of Newport have.

.......TWENTY NINE

Final note on Marty

It is the middle of the night, around three am. Marty is looking at her face and pale naked body in the bathroom mirror. But her thoughts are not desperate and solitary as they once were, like a woman making harsh judgments of her arrant curves, sagging shapes and less than stellar skin tones. Or, of course, the other desperate solitary thoughts of 'how could any man resist?'

Marty at this moment is propped up and sustained by love, all accepting, all confirming love. Love from this man. He knows her left breast is a little larger than her right—he laughs it off and kisses her nose. He notices, at Marty's insistence, her extra shapely hips. He grabs hold, says something to make her laugh and kisses her forehead.

A tear rolls down her cheek, Marty is in love. Marty can see her man balled up under the covers, she almost won't let herself believe it, accept it. She will be a Newport princess after all. Marty washes off her tears of joy and running mascara at the sink, watches it swirl dreamily down as she reaches for a towel. She looks around and sees through drippy wet eyes a towel thrown in the corner. Marty smiles. When they are married she will take care of this, all of this and the man balled up under the covers. She steps feeling light as heavens whispers over to the linen cabinet. She opens it. Marty takes out enough towels to stock the bathroom.

Marty begins to close the cabinet then stops, squints and cocks her head with an inquisitive surprise. She recognizes the color combination, style and shape of the purse, pink, gold and black with gobs of little rhinestones and a white poodle. Marty is too naïve to think anything other than it is a gift hidden for her. 'Oh, how sweet.' She says softly to herself. She is also a woman though and she cannot resist the temptation to sneak a peak as she reaches way back and pulls it out. 'That sweet, sweet man.'

It is much heavier than she expected. It is heavier because it is full of womanly things. Marty's breath quickens, her face begins to flush on instant. She pulls out lipstick, a cell phone, mirror, breath mints. Marty receives a shot of fury from that deep reservoir filled by god for this moment of scorn. She pours out the remaining contents on the counter, now frantic, her eyes bugged and crazed.

Marty knows whose purse it is but she will not let her self truly believe until she sees the identification. She opens the zip pocket in a quick hostile motion and pulls out plastic cards of all sorts. She drops them all except for the driver's license and holds it in her delicate trembling hands. Her bottom lip and chin quiver wildly, her forehead tightens and eyes well up fast as the little picture of Karen Vambert is smiling back at her, Marty's best friend.

Marty is too hurt to be angry, the breadth and depth of her sensitivity to life and living makes her respond this way. She grabs all of her things quick but not harshly like most women would. She is crying though, in tense whimpers, wet and messy. It is a restrained cry though in a hopeless, desperate way. The room is dark; she reaches for something to put on just so she can get to her car, it is Rob's shirt.

Marty's arms are full as she stands at the end of the bed. Rob is balled up under the covers, he hasn't moved since they made love. That was one of the things she liked about him, nothing bothered him. Apparently cheating on Marty with her best friend didn't bother him either.

'Shame on you—we—we—were in love.' Marty squeaks out between sobs.

Marty takes quick heart broken steps out of the room.

Marty was heavily medicated of the psychiatric type even before the events of the last ten minutes. She planned on weaning herself off the Lithium and Depakote like she had done with Paxil and Effexor against her doctor's wishes, because she really felt things were turning out for her now. The man, the dream she believed were hers to truly have.

Marty was not doing very well on her medication. Of course it does detach her from some pressing problems. But the drugs themselves diminish to a marked degree her ability to reason and use good judgment. The other day Rob showed up to find Marty straddling her fish tank pumping air into the

water with the tire pump from her bike. She said frantically
"The little air pump machine broke and my fish will die!" Rob
returned with "Honey, the fish store is three minutes from here
and they have lots of *new* air pumps there." Another time
Marty broke into Rob's apartment while he was away on
business to rearrange his furniture, she just had to—again. Or
the near crazed agitated states where menial tasks become
compulsions performed not out of any real necessity but used
as a needed and hopeful vent for her mounting anxiety brought
on by certain drugs. Like washing anything that she could cram
into a washing machine. Drapes—clothes—bedding—
pillows—shoes—jackets—throw rugs—purses. And then
wash them all again. If Rob pulls up and sees steam exhaust
billowing out the dryer vent, he turns around and goes home.
He knows. But the most dangerous lapse of reason occurred
last month when they were walking arm and arm down the
sidewalk one evening and Marty darts out into the busy street
to pick up a big white feather. Rob grabbed her arm just in
time to avoid her being hit by a car.

 Marty is crying harder now. She stops at the kitchen,
dumps everything on the swirled mossy green and bronze
colored marble counter top. She opens her purse and takes out
two plastic prescription bottles. There are about twenty pills
total. Marty takes them all.

 Marty picks up her things and leaves out the front door
into the cold rolling mist of night. She does not slam the door
behind her like most women would. She is too distrait for that,
she leaves it open.

 Marty steps around the side of the house were Rob
keeps a lawnmower and other equipment. She picks up a red

gallon container and walks over to his 1968 Porsche. It is in mint condition as it has been fully restored. Marty's eyes are numb, vacant as she approaches the car. 'Gluck, gluck, slosh, slosh,' Marty pours gas over it, and then drops the container of gas in a limp despondent manner at her feet. The gas trickles down the gutter. She stands there for a moment breathing in the fumes. She likes the fumes. She thinks about pouring gas over herself and lets out a small huffed laugh at the thought. Then her eyes are left numb again. She looks up at the sky. The mist whirls and rolls then parts momentarily exposing a cluster of stars. And the moon crescents sympathetically to her and a gleeful smile forms to Marty's pale lips, then all is occluded in the consuming viscous haze. Marty reaches into the breast pocket.

Marty pulls out an old book of matches from her and Rob's favorite restaurant. She takes one match and lights it then lights the whole package with it. She tosses the flaming book on the hood.

Fwah! Whah! The Porsche erupts in flames. And Marty turns with a jerk, walks calmly down the sidewalk.

The medication that Marty takes to correct and deal with her 'imbalance' begins to separate her from her senses, one by one. Every neurotransmitter assembly within her mind that could be enhanced was enhanced. Every negative impulse that could be blocked was blocked. Future repercussions ignored. Granted, she does begin to feel a measure of euphoria because the serotonin re-uptake inhibitors are responsible for doing just that. The psycho-pharmacologist just loves to make the brain do all sorts of tricks regardless of the damaging effects. The other medication Marty takes to draw her bipolar

condition under control makes her feel as though she is
confined in a mental straight jacket.

Marty is losing herself now. She drops everything on the
sidewalk. But there is no sidewalk. She is amazed that she can
see stars and the heavens beneath her feet, Marty laughs. She
stretches her arms out wide and laughs harder. The pills that
she takes and just took are designed to separate her from
sensations and failures that are just too troubling.
Unfortunately you can not tell a pill where to stop. Marty is
being separated from every vital mental function one by one:
good judgment, reason, reality, futures, self reliance, on down
the line. The mind is very smart though, it is very aware there
is something foreign to the extreme in its intricate workings.
When a mind is molested in this manner a reaction is triggered.
And that reaction is suicide. That which governs life and the
mind considers it a necessary separation.

The apartment Marty came from is only a block or so
from Pacific Coast Highway. Marty slowly makes her way with
an erratic shuffle to her steps and only Rob's dress shirt
covering her in this now heavily fogged frigid morning. With
her arms now gently falling to her sides she becomes transfixed
on her destination. The palm trees that line the road catch fire
in tandem. But the trees have turned to crystal and the large
furious flames appear in pastel casts. The road is not a road
any more. It has become streaks of light that encourage
following and will soon demand it. The telephone lines that
crackle and run speak to her. They tell her not to worry about
the automobiles that speed out on the highway.

She is told in whispering haunted tones that the cars are warm and generous friends, go greet them. A man in a powder blue Jaguar sees Marty with her vacant eyes as she steps into the street. He stops quick, jumps out, grabs the tail of her shirt drawing her back from the traffic. One more step and Marty from Tennessee would have been no more.

Karen's place

Karen is in her bathroom looking at her anti-depressants in the medicine cabinet. John is sitting in the kitchen. Karen's expression is blank and numb, she closes the cabinet. She looks to her left out the window. The clouds are cast in colors that give them a bruised, vulnerable feel; Karen frowns in sympathy. She walks into the kitchen.

"Poor Marty." Karen says, eyes to the floor.
"Yes, poor Marty." John replies.
"Wind chimes?"
"I don't like you anymore. Hey, I'm going to Tahoe for about ten days. I'll send you the final chapter in route or whatever."
"Tahoe, god that sounds good."
"I decided to write the ending of the book the way I think it should go—ok? I'm getting out of the fairy tale business midstream. No hard feelings?"
"Fine, but you know it's not that bad. Poor Marty."
"Yes, I know—she—I—know."

FINAL
CHAPTER

Sunday Morning

The Moffords step down from St. James church in
Costa Mesa after a glorious Sunday service of uplifting epistle
of spirit, from their good god that is. Amy thrills in three steps
at a time while grasping firm with both hands, the sturdy right
hand of Scott, her father. Robin takes hold of her free hand
and Amy merrily swings between the two of them. There is a
consummate blend of joy, sunshine, peace and spirituality that
is more than in the air, it is the air they breathe. Pastor
Donaldson stands stoic yet amiable by god's grace, waving his
hand gently to his flock offering kind sentiment.

About once a month or so the Moffords follow up
church with a very special excursion. After a stop for chocolate
chip ice cream and Scott's favorite pistachio at Thrifty's, they
head on over to an industrial park off a street named Redhill.
They weave their way through the one story complexes all the
way to the back in their 1994 Ford Fairmont. Scott parks the
car right up against the chain link fence with placards fastened
stating 'No Trespassing' as punished by law. At this vantage
point the massive John Wayne Airport runway is just on the
other side of the fence.

Amy climbs up and over the seat and onto Robin's lap,
of course she could have opened the door, got out and up to
the front seat that way. But a child is seldom hemmed into that
sort of practicality.

"Honey napkins quick!" Robin snaps.

Scott hands Robin five or six.

"There's more in the glove box if you need them."

"Carefull sweetheart." Robin says, with no upset in her voice or anywhere in her being for that matter.

There they sit a happy threesome waiting to see the big airliners land as this is the best place in the area to do that. And the planes do not disappoint as they land like clock work (literally) and every landing is an exciting accomplishment that Amy cheers on. It's the stuff joyous childhoods are cast in.

Excerpt by Dr. Charles Malworth- **Newport** *Gazette*

We are gonna fix what the good Lord screwed up.
It is all no more than a chemical imbalance, trust me.

Charles Malworth MD
Behavioral Medicine Research
Boag Hospital 1990

Across town at Boag Hospital—Emergency

Kaisty is huddled, knees up tight to her chest as Neil drapes her fuzzy blue wool sweater over her bony trembling shoulders. She doesn't say anything. Kaisty whimpers, with her face buried in her thighs and knees, arms wrapped around her shins. "The doctor will see you now Mr. Landitt." The nurse speaks kindly, soft smile.

"Thank you—just stay right here honey in this exact spot while I have a talk with this idiot."

Kaisty gives a muffled sob with a few incoherent words as Neil walks over to Kaisty's Psychiatrist. Neil's loafers making the usual and annoying 'squirsh squirsh' sound on the cold white industrial tiles as he crosses the room. There is only a scattered few waiting to be seen and one man is sitting directly in front of Kaisty about six feet from her.

The waiting room is quiet except for the 'hursh murr' sound of the air conditioner and an occasional paging over the intercom for a doctor.

Neil follows the doctor down the clean, wide sterile corridor to his office. Neil's eyes are blood shot, his face drawn tight and focused on the back of the doctor's white smock. Neil is holding his shoulders tense and drawn up, fists clenched. He will unload on this so called doctor but not until the door is closed and they are alone.

The man across from Kaisty is waiting for his wife to give birth and is quite calm as it happens to be their third. So whatever attention may be balled up in worried anxiety for most new fathers is free to be placed on the desperate looking woman directly across from him. Kaisty is a mess as she lifts her head to wipe her tears, he notices her swollen eyes from crying smeared with mascara, hair tangled unmercifully, face blotchy red, lips smudged with dark red lip stick. She places what little attention available to her somewhat in the direction of the man across from her, only because he is across from her but gives no indication -from her expression- that he even exists. Her eyes are vacant and blood shoot, deep brown, pained and sorrowful. She buries her head back into her knees and the man smiles to himself, out of empathy for her.

Neil shuts the door behind them hard, which gets the doctor's attention.

"What the hell is this crap!" Neil yells as he throws six bottles of assorted anti-depressants and anti-psychotics on the doctor's heavy maple desk.

The doctor slips his glasses on with a tense grin, his face pasty and gaunt, emotionless.

"Now hold on, just hold on Mr. Landitt just calm down."
"She is a God damn mess!"
"Alright, alright what have we got here, ok, sure." The doctor picks up a bottle with his superbly manicured, fat pale fingers.

Neil is still clinching his fists as his knuckles whiten, jaw jutting outward, lips crammed together tight, eyes intense and fixed on the doctor's hands. The doctor looks at Neil over the thin top brim of his glasses.

"Your wife is very ill Mr. Landitt."
"Granted, how is this crap you're giving her, help her. Risperidone, Olanzapine, Depokote, Lithium, Paxil, Effexor?" Neil fumbles with the bottles. "And there is more at home. This is ludicrous! You should read the poetry she's writing, it's

freaking me out. I love my wife dearly but it is like I can't find her anymore, even when she is standing right in front of me. "

"Your wife has a severe chemical imbalance."

"Bullshit, that's bullshit!" Neil barks.

"Now Mr. Landitt—you're going to have to calm down."

"You have no idea what that shit does in those bottles or what's really wrong with her do you?"

"Mr. Landitt your wife—she's manic depressive, which we call bipolar now, with agitated semi-delusional episodes and of course neurotic, bordering on psychotic tendencies. Mix in a generalized anxiety disorder and she is quite the mess. And the poetry, well, that is a written expression disorder. It's a medical issue, a biological condition and these pills here are her medication, period—Mr. Landitt."

"Now wait just a minute, besides being bullshit, all that crap you just said sounds more like symptoms of something else rather than sole conditions all to themselves."

"Well now, that's the debate, you've done your home work Mr. Landitt."

Back in the emergency room

The man sitting across from Kaisty knows from experience a case such as this is better off opened than left closed. He knows this because he is the minister for a church in Tustin, a City about fifteen miles east of Newport.

The lissom, hushed sounds of Mozart's concerto No. 21 in C Major pours from the speakers in delicate measured procession above their heads. Kaisty does not pay attention to it but something within her does as it begins to relax her if only slightly.

He asks her a direct question:

"What or whom is ruining your life young lady." His standard question for anyone of youth.

"My Uncle." Kaisty pops her eyebrows up as if to say 'Wow where did that come from, that was weird but there you go.'

"I'm going to ask you another question and I want you to give me the first answer that comes to mind."

"Do I have to?"

"Yes." He states firmly and compassionately. "How old are you?"

"Eleven." Kaisty replies then raises her head with the same perplexed look in her watery red eyes. "That's weird because I am thirty two."

"Any trauma you can think of when you were eleven?"

"I don't know I was just a kid, are we done?" She places her head back in the crevasse made by her thigh and knees.

The man takes a deep breath and rubs his hands together slowly and hard as if to say 'here we go.'

"Whatever is ruining your life right now is locked up in an incident or chains of incidents with similar events which can have a tremendous effect on someone even many, many years later without any apparent memory of them. I want you to look at that eleventh year of your life, can you recall any major upsets?

Kaisty is silent for a full three minutes.

"Like I said, maybe my Uncle or something."

As crude as this counseling session may be in this setting or may become, he knew he had to try to help this girl because he also knew she was probably here to fill a prescription which will only separate her further from her senses and maybe life altogether.

"Go to the beginning of the incident then go through it and tell me what you see and feel as you go through it."

Kaisty shakes her head slowly from side to side in an 'Oh this going to be just great' manner with her eyes closed, wipes under her eyes with the back of her knuckle and asks the man for his hanker-chief. He hands her one. She lets out a 'Ughff' as she readies herself.

"I don't know why we should bother, it was just that one summer, I don't remember anything terribly awful......."
"Go to the beginning of the incident and tell me what you see and feel as you go through it."
"Alright, alright. My parents are dropping me off at a train, a big old huffing and puffing train in Santa Ana. I'm standing on the platform with my suitcase at my side waving good-by. Gorgeous day, big clouds.

223

As she speaks there is sun light at the feet of the man across from her that has shown through the large window to his right.

Rebuttal by Dr. Larry Culp- *Newport* **Tribune**

The only chemical imbalance that exists anywhere is that there are too many drugs being marketed and subsequently prescribed and crammed down trusting throats by 'authorities.' It is a scam. No—no it is crimes against humanity. It is crimes against humanity because these so call medications like the SSRI variety, cause permanent brain damage. Depression and neurosis is an emotional response to one's life, think about it.

Further more, Dr. Malworth, there is no scientific instrument for measuring chemical imbalances in the brain, it is fraud. Bipolar, wonderfully crafted marketing on that one. A condition that doesn't even exist the way they claim it does. But if you market it well enough, well, you sell a lot of pills, a whole lot of pills. And they pin a diagnosis on you that stays put. Oh sure they may say one has changed from this condition to that but make no mistake they are concocting a customer for life.

Dr. Larry Culp
Psychiatrist
Private practice

Doctor's office

"Don't you think maybe just maybe something may of happened to her, maybe several things to make her unstable and have difficulty coping?" Neil calms slightly but intensely.

"Sure, oh sure, things happen to people all the time, triggers the chronic condition caused by the underlying chemical imbalance, brings it all to the surface. No need to try and change what happens to people, can't do it, been proven. In fact there is a new drug on the way that can even......."

Neil stops him cold. "How much do desperate people spend a year on this so called 'medication' you cram down their throats. I'm no idiot Mr.," Neil says through clinched teeth and brutal glare.

"Oh, lordy, it should be well into the tens of billions now I would suspect." The doctor unabashedly admits.

Emergency room

"I recall turning around on the steps of the train waving good-bye. The big steam locomotive began with that slow burdened thumping noise, you know." The man shakes his head in acknowledgment. "The man who sits people, I forget what you call him, helps me to my seat. I scooted over to the window, wipe it clean with my sweater and waved to my parents one more time. I could see my face in the transparent reflection of the window, my big smile and long curly mousy blonde hair. I was a cute kid. The thrust of the engine came out from underneath the strain with quick powerful steam punches as we labored for speed. I can still hear that heavy strained squeal of the metal wheels against the iron rails. Flimsy ash and tiny red hot embers swirl past in a dirty steamy gust outside the window and the funny little whistle blasting a steam shrill. Oh! And as we are rounding this big sweeping turn I can see the white smoke billowing out of the stack from the engine at the front of the train. It was so wonderful.

Three weeks with my aunt and uncle, I was so excited, so excited. They picked me up at the train station in Modesto about three hours later. Big old truck, big old, dirty, beautiful truck. We threw all my stuff in the back and down the dirt road we went to their farm or ranch or whatever it was."

Kaisty looks up to see if the man is still with her and he is, very much so.

"It was what childhoods are made of you know. Horses, ponds, hills, milking cows, running through the fields and collapsing for fun, things like that."

"Ok, return to the beginning and see if you can uncover more data."

"Oh brother, I don't know, nothing to add to the train ride or the truck ride or the horsing around. I had my own room, it was great, antiques and junk all over, thick patchwork quilt to lay on. My aunt and uncle would tuck me in every night. Then my uncle would come back and tuck me in again, much later.

The man across from Kaisty, the one prying this open, has a gut feeling where this digging around will end up and is worried he may throw her into a full blown restimulation of the incident. A nurse is approaching him with news on his own wife and he waves her off to not interrupt.

"Kaisty, tell me about that, when your uncle would come back in."

"Oh, I don't know, he just came back in, gave me a kiss on the forehead."

"Ok, start from the beginning and try to uncover more data."

"Do I have to?"

"Yes."

"Alright, alright. Train ride, truck ride, running up hills, swinging from trees and swimming in ponds......."

When Kaisty combs over the incident about four more times she gradually then suddenly becomes sullen and withdrawn. Her voice begins to crack. She has returned fully to the moment and cumulative moments when her uncle rapes her almost nightly after her aunt is long since asleep and as Kaisty has entered a state of never sleeping well again or having much else go right for her. She can see her uncles feet under the door in the unholy light that is an unwelcome illumination emanating from the hallway. Kaisty is gripped by fear and confusion and is unable to speak or protest. She feels as pain the thick coarse fingers of her uncle penetrate her. His other hand is over her mouth. He tells her in stern hushed tones not to tell anyone or else, you'll forget about it, stop fidgeting.

The stranger unlocking this hell waves off his wife's nurse once again.

"Keep moving, what happens next?"

Kaisty is held in the grip of the shock and pain of the act. But she manages to continue with much struggle.

"Ok, very good, you are doing fine, let's go over it again, tell me more about it."
"No, no I can't, it's horrible, I hate him."
"Kaisty, go to the beginning and tell me what is happening as you go."

Kaisty does just that several more times and slowly but surely and eventually chunks of the painful emotion start to breakaway and a long since suppressed peace finds its way back to Kaisty's face and she holds her body with less tension as she goes over the incident again. Unbeknownst to Kaisty that trauma has carried over through time and life affecting near all decision making and definitely most all reactions she would display. All moments to some degree are that moment, yet she has been unaware of that fact. All time, current, past and future is that time. During the recounting of the incidents a separation occurs. From present time adult to child. From child to present time. Which places the injury and trauma in its proper time and exclusive to its own event, which allows Kaisty to see for the first time that it is something that happened in the past and is not happening currently. This brings her peace.

She is able to face the incident and inspect it sanely for the first time ever.

Back in the psychiatrist's office.

"Mr. Landitt you are going to have to calm down, it is merely a chemical imbalance. The right combination of anti-psychotics and such, that's all we are looking for here. And quite frankly Mr. Landitt what is the alternative to psychiatric care anyway?"

Neil says nothing as his eyes are the source of communication that is of piercing anger and hatred. Neil is still hung up on the doctor's previous statement that the beauty of psychiatric care today is that you don't have to really know what happened or what is going on with someone to help them, just take your medication.

"What is the alternative? The alternative? That's like saying what is the alternative to rape?"

"Hah, Mr. Landitt, quite frankly, it is a matter of moods of uncertainty and extravagant whims that trouble most women of Newport Beach. But you have to give them something and now a-days its pills, pills, pills." The doctor states without a hint of restraint.

Emergency room

"I'm lying in tall grass of this—this field and I want to die, I'm only eleven years old and I want to die."

"Did you make any considerations at that point?" The man asks.

"Ah, yes, I—I wanted all men to die with me." Kaisty stammers.

The minister stands up, steps over to, and sits next to Kaisty. He intends to offer prayer but he does not get the chance.

'Squirsh, squirsh, squirsh, squirsh, squirsh,' Neil comes quick, grabs Kaisty's arm and yanks her off the seat. He grabs her purse and sweater and darts for the exit with Kaisty in weak sloppy protest. As they near the glass automatic door Kaisty's doctor speaks out from the corridor.

"Mr. Landitt, Mr. Landitt! You can't cut her off from the medication cold, it has to be very slow with a doctor's supervision! There are terrible side effects!" The doctor blurts in a rare show of concern.

Neil does not loose a step and Kaisty can barely stay on her feet in tow. Neil raises his hand and makes a sturdy, middle fingered, gesture to the doctor without looking back.

The man who was talking with Kaisty hopes he helped her some.

The doctor hopes he hasn't lost another patient, literally and figuratively. He hopes this because there are standards of existence that must be met in Newport, especially in the doctoring of Newport. The two men are left with the silence of their concerns and the 'hursh murr' of the air conditioning unit and the light that shown at the minister's feet forty minutes ago arrives at the seat Kaisty occupied a few moments earlier. But she has left.

"The chains of fear and deception are anchored in darkness and disintegrate by the piercing frequency of light that reveals every shadow's secret."

Alishia Fry
1929
Newport Poet

Back at the Industrial park

The Moffords pull out of the industrial park. Amy looks at her list of all the different airlines that landed this morning. She names them off softly to her self, wiggles her toes and gently pats her mother's left forearm. Scott places his rough hand over the back of Robin's smooth, delicate one. Robin smiles airily, for this is merely another blessed, happy morning the good Lord has graced them with.

Karen's place

Karen is balled up on her couch in a fetal posture, lights are out, she is crying. Karen tries calling John in Lake Tahoe. She sobs harder, tightens further into a ball and presses send again. John is in the middle of Lake Tahoe on a houseboat—no reception. As fortune goes Karen shares a similar past with Kaisty.

———————————

Neil pulls in the driveway and Kaisty is asleep. Her face is uncharacteristically peaceful with a weak smile accented with an occasional sigh.

"No more pills, no more psych pills honey." Neil says just above a whisper as he picks Kaisty up and carries her in. He carries her over the same threshold as he did on their wedding day seven years ago. The moment is not perceived by Kaisty and Neil does not give it a thought. He lays her down on the bed and pulls her favorite thick dark purple and beige comforter up and tucks it under her chin. Her face is a mess but there is beauty there and there is a peace. Neil wonders where the relaxed serene almost mystical expression has emerged from.

He has never seen this expression, asleep or awake.

"No more pills honey—that bastard." Neil says gently in Kaisty's ear. He walks out of the room.

The house is sensed by Neil as relief, cool and dark, only slivers of light intrude through the closed shutters or a gush from a high window where the light has found a way to pour itself in like water entering a sinking ship.

Neil never drank in the morning, never even thought about it. He opens the refrigerator and pulls out a beer. He walks heavily over to the stereo and looks over very slowly, deliberately, his music collection. Neil has not listened to The Beach Boys Sunflower record in years. The record came out in 1970 when the boys were dead in America. He loves it though. He plays it low as Kaisty's cat enters the room in a fluid silky gait. He jumps on the couch and takes immediate inventory of Neil as he places his chin on his folded paws.

Neil hears a little patter on the roof. "Rain?" He whispers incredulously as he stares up at the vaulted ceiling. Neil sits on the arm of the couch like all men do. And like all women hate them to do. The dripples of rain on the roof give way to a hard down pour. "What the hell!" He hopes it does not wake Kaisty. It does not.

Neil begins to hunch his shoulders in a numbed stupor, reflectionless. Futureless. He is struck with the stark coldness of present time. It is a bad place for a man to dwell too long in. Neil falls a notch from melancholy to a heavy dose of self-abasement. He has worked hard to bring Kaisty's dreams into being but at times he thinks his efforts are pathetic and impotent at best. Neil gets another beer. The downpour stops just as quickly as it started.

Neil walks back to the stereo and sits down on the carpet, leans back against the console. He draws his knees up to his chest, wraps his forearms around them, beer in his right

hand. He lets the album play out. The first time he heard this
album was on an 8-track. He exhales and adds an amiable
smile. Neil lets it play out, he wouldn't think of stopping it
until it was finished.

Neil's eyes drift around but a great portion of his
attention is inward. He does happen to notice Kaisty's DVD
with her four commercials and her 'America's Most Wanted'
crime re-enactment on it. His smile broadens. If there was
ever a right time to watch the collection now would be it, Neil
thinks. No insistence from Kaisty for them to ponder what
may have been if she continued acting. Just his own quiet
desire. He crawls over, pushes it in and presses play. Kaisty's
smiling face appears instantly, she is mopping a floor with
some damn soap they still have a case of under the sink. Neil
exhales again, a small huffed laugh. Neil slips into a wistful
state with regard to his wife and her smiling face and amiable
movements. His eyes well up some as he watches
the next three. Then came the crime re-enactment role. Kaisty
thought of this as her big shot. She plays some woman
criminal on the run. She is just awful. Neil laughs softly,
lovingly.

Neil crawls back over to the stereo to turn it off when
he spots a set of cassettes. He bought them for Kaisty a year
or so ago. They are of the 'self help' variety. She never listened
to or even appreciated being given them. Neil blows the dust
off opens the package and sets one in the cassette player.
Kaisty's cat gives Neil a look that says he has been sized up and
a final opinion formed, surely to his detriment.

Neil presses play >

"Mechanisms—the mind is full of mechanisms. For example all our emotions run along a track. Boredom, fear, interest, thrill, apathy, they are all stops along this track. One is strapped onto this track at birth and has no choice but to slide up and down it like a ride at the fair. One senses, feels and reacts with whatever emotional notch is slipped, caught and locked into as life is thrust upon them. And one reacts to the current environment and situations with a modified point of view drawn from snarled up past painful emotions. These bundles of prior experiences that make one *react* irrationally to life in present time. One sees a cute kitten and that is a cheerful experience, another sees a cute kitten and that is an awful reminder of the one that was lost and spent weeks looking for, one feels sad even years later (relatively mild example). And these losses, traumas if you will, accumulate over time, which can reduce ones ability to enjoy life. The kicker is that eventually one may get stuck chronically in one of these *lower* emotional notches. So, therapeutically speaking, you have to go to the past incidents where the attention is snarled up tight, as a permanent fixture and free it.

Maybe even love and rejection and maybe even something like insanity and depression are mechanisms. Maybe one has these mechanisms bolted all over him. And all one has to do is trip a mental wire to bring it all in upon himself. Maybe he is buried in these things. Where is the human being in all this? Is good judgment and rational thought something entirely different? Is the spirit the current that runs all the machinery of life? Is an evil mind simply at the effect of one nasty not very well thought out survival mechanism? Or is

235

there true evil? You will find out on side two of this cassette. And we will also discuss how psychiatric drugs gum up and jam up the delicate intricacies of the mind and make true recovery nearly impossible and not to mention cause irreparable harm to the brain itself.

What is troubling you can be traced to: 1. Those things *you* have done to yourself or others. 2. Those things *you* should have done but did not carry out. And lastly number 3. Those things that happened to you courtesy of others. And how a relatively simple but very effective therapy and training on how to handle life can keep one thriving in life. And, of course, how all this must be dealt with by *you* and not some pill designed to separate one from their senses even if prescribed by the holy divineness himself in a clean, white, knee length doctor's smock.

Basically we will delve into what accumulates over time as one goes through life and how it all becomes occluded and pushed way, way out of view but still have tremendous affect upon you. And if you are willing to change your mind about a few things that would also be helpful."

Neil shuts off the tape, puts his face in his hands and rubs hard. He says quietly but tensely to himself "What is wrong with my wife my beautiful wife?" Neil gets up off the couch with a heaviness and effort. He walks through the kitchen to the back patio. Neil opens the door and steps out into the back yard. The dampness and warmth strike his senses delicately, fully. Neil always wondered how it can pour rain one minute and be totally clear the next. There is a wonderful fragrance in the air, an amplified fragrance. Neil breathes in deep, eyes scrunched closed, makes an attempt at a smile but the smile finds its way off his face as soon as it arrives. It is as though the quick drenching and warmth of the late morning draw out the best of the earth to smell, Neil figures. He steps back in closes the door, thinks no more of it.

Neil walks down the hall. He stops in front of a picture of Kaisty and himself in Big Bear on a ski trip ten years earlier when they were only dating. The smiles are genuine and broad. Neil's tear ducts begin to well. He continues down the hall to the master bedroom.

Neil is standing in the doorway of the master bedroom looking at Kaisty with a weighted sympathetic gaze. She appears to be resting peacefully to him. He walks over to the bed and lies down next to her. Kaisty is on her side as he conforms his body to her positioning, his knees to the back of her knees, his stomach to the small of her back. Neil wants to take a nap with her, fully clothed, not even bothering to take his shoes off. He gently brushes her hair to the side and kisses the back of her neck, his warm breath framing the kiss sweetly. A tender sight.

In lying there, Neil appears relaxed as he gently runs his hand down Kaisty's shoulder and upper arm. But his mind churns and races even harder than ever. After a mere three minutes with Kaisty Neil is off the bed and headed for the bathroom.

Neil lifts the toilet lid up quick and picks up a bottle of anti-depressants. Neil opens the bottle. "Let's see who the doctor is again, oh sure it's Dr. Reedman. Hey doc my toilet is depressed." He pours the pills into the water; they congregate at the bottom of the bowl. Neil picks up another bottle. "Hey doc my sewage line is psychotic *and* depressed." He pours about twenty tablets, they rush to the bottom. He picks up another bottle. "My septic tank is neurotic, what would you prescribe? Paxil? My thoughts exactly." Neil pours bottle number three. "Oh—yes, the boys at the sewage plant would appreciate sane and chemically balanced shit." Neil pours bottle number four. The pills hit the side of the bowl, fly all over the cold ceramic tile floor. Neil breaks down, falls to his knees. He cries quick and hard, sobbing bursts. He tries to gather the pills then falls over to his side balled up on the same cold tiles, crying uncontrollably. He covers his mouth. "Oh my god my baby, my baby."

There was one thing the doctor said that was actually right, true and important. Once someone has been taking anti-depressants and anti-psychotics they should never quit abruptly. Neil in his concern and despair has just thrust himself and Kaisty both into dangerous waters.

People say men should cry more. That may be true but those same people in seeing a man lying on his side crying his heart out look away, it is just too much to bear. Some people are eternal optimists. Neil was. Whatever those underpinnings were, they are now gone. He lies there still and rigid as the crying is replaced by a dreadful numbness. He is not sparred though, anxiety comes in sickening waves that consume his body and mind and he is then left numb again, then he cries again. He lies there through the evening and night. Kaisty within her peace does not stir at all.

Neil is buried now beneath a mountain of failures. Personal failures and even ones he had no control over. Even those crush him. The doctor's failures, the hospitals failures and his wife's erratic frailties are taken in as his sole ownership. They annihilate him, his confidence.

But as in a dream where the scene can change in weird, unexpected ways and within his torrent of pain and self abasement Neil hears a flute. The faint shrill of a flute. It did not come from the stereo, he was certain of that. The stereo in the bathroom was not on either.

A fraught hopeless breath screams through the instrument as angst and desperation sustains the lofty pitch. Sorrowful and dishearten like a lover's departing kiss or nation's impending doom. An army of violins and cellos steal the melancholy with strife and distortion and ultimately a bitter mood of conflict surges. Neil covers his ears and winces at the torn and jarring harmonics that pierce his mind. But there was no escape because the music was in him and it was him. There was no relief with any orchestral movement unless there is joy taken in the dramatizing of death and dying.

Ten years of struggling to please a women who was utterly baffling to him. The fighting with the doctors, the insurance companies, even her parents. Ten years of failure funneled into one man, one moment. Unbeknownst of the source of the trouble or solution and what lies in the future left Neil defenseless against the brutal brunt of the anguished chorus. A now single distressed and shivering cello transported him to the black abyss of his own tormented solitude. But as men do he fought, as and with thought, for any possible salvation, intense and sweeping thought. But as life does, his efforts hovered only slightly above a bed of desperate and dissonant horns which blew harsh and tore at him as they began to recede back and fade leaving only the single despondent flute.

The painfully solitary flute. The shrieking breath of hopelessness giving life only to death.

_____

The ceramic tiles are cold and hard to Neil's right side. The pressure he felt on his hip as a lump begins to aggressively vibrate demanding an immediate response. Neil rolls over on his back lying flat staring at the ceiling, unsnaps his cell phone from its harness.

Some phone calls can change states of mind, even alter entire lives with a few spoken words, this was one of those calls.

"Neil, Mrs. Binsent wants to sell, Harton wants you to go. Be at Wells Fargo conference room C in twenty minutes."

Neil sprang to his feet.

"I'll be there!"

A shot of adrenaline as thrill and determination shot through Neil's mortal body. He runs hot water and washes his face as the steam ghosts up the mirror, decides to us his electric shaver in route to Fashion Island. He fills his mouth with a blue wash and agitates it vigorously then spits it out all the while his eyes are wide in reflection. Neil darts out into the master then slows quick not to disturb Kaisty. He rips off his wrinkled dress shirt and grabs a freshly laundered one. He gives Kaisty a quick loving look. He takes a tie without notice for style, he loops and ties it fast but efficient while looking intently at Kaisty over his shoulder, via the mirror. He rushes for the door then stops abrupt, walks back to Kaisty, he sits down gently next to her. He brushes the hair off her forehead delicately with his fingers then lightly caresses her cheekbones then runs a single finger along the bridge of her nose. Her skin is as soft as the delicate texture of a butterfly wing he once touched as a boy, he smiles faintly at the thought. Neil leans over and gives her three kisses on her forehead. He gets up and leaves. He stops at the doorway turns around and softly says "For you my princess." Neil bolts down the hallway and toward the front door.

Neil opens the front door quick, stops, listens intently to hear if Kaisty said something, he thought he heard her. There was no sound, no stirring at all. Neil steps out. He is focused and intense, a tight coil of intensity that will soon find its release. Neil closes the door quietly. He takes a quick inventory of his immediate environment while he finishes clasping his cuff links. A tightly stretched grin forms to his face.

When Neil is standing outside of his worries he takes on a wholly different appearance to the casual observer. When Neil is purposeful, focused and set on righting the wrongs of his world he cuts quite and imposing figure. He stands a good six foot one, broad shouldered, narrow at the hips and all anchored to a washboard stomach. Hair, dark blonde from his mother's Holland roots and cut in a JFK Jr. style. He possesses his father's mossy green eyes, which are now ardent and determined. His high chiseled cheekbones are from his father's side again, which is Italian. His skin a naturally light tan and radiant, of which, Kaisty displays her jealously regularly. His nostrils flare taking in the dense, coastal air. The morning's warm saltin sweetness engulfed him as he engulfed it.

His slacks felt good against the skin of his legs. Those things in his immediate environment that were intended to be sensed as solid, felt so. Those things meant to be sensed as delicate, felt so. Sounds that were meant sooth, soothed. Noises that were meant to jar, jarred. Like the heavy breaking of the trash truck up the street. Neil felt wonderful, purposeful. He felt confident and maybe even a little prematurely triumphant. He led with swift eager strides to his Mercedes. Neil waves a fast hello to a neighbor jogging by.

In one fluid motion Neil opens, enters, closes the door and secures the seat belt. He turns the ignition on and sits, both hands holding the steering wheel firm. If a look from a man could burn a hole through matter there would be a big one in the garage door ahead of him. "This is it, this is our time, our place, our event. She wants to sell and Harton is sending me, *me* damn it. Tonight the champagne will flow. No—no tonight Kaisty and I will bath in champagne." Neil smacks the leather covered wheel hard with both hands, smiles quick and hard. Neil backs out of the driveway past Kaisty's Land Rover. "First thing I'm going to do is cancel the lease and buy it my dear, buy it for you."

Neil's smile softens now as he thinks of his wife. "The deal will solve everything, some women just need what they need, I see that now." Neil is heading to 6790 Newport Center

Drive, Well Fargo Bank about two blocks from Union Bank.
Half the bank is for banking, the other half is for real estate
transactions. Neil has done business there for Real Corp. a
hundred times, he knows everyone there and he knows what he
is doing. As Neil drives up Macarthur Boulevard he day
dreams of buying and putting case after case of Champagne in
his trunk, he sees himself laughing, Kaisty knowing nothing yet
of their good fortune.

Neil laughs out loud as he approaches Fashion Island.
Neil's exact route if one were ever inclined to visit Newport
shows off a grand marina. Sail boats of all shapes and sizes fit
with voluminous brilliant white sails dot the silvery blue Pacific
coast. Seagulls hang and dive in unabashed joy for thrill.
Occasionally, if the gods indulge, the mountains of clouds are
awash in a faint cooper and purple hue. The gods are so
inclined this August morning.

Neil pulls into the parking lot, grabs his briefcase and
heads for the entrance with long confident strides.

"Hello Macy." Neil gives a slick cheerful greeting to the
receptionist.

"Oh, hello." Macy returns unaffected by his good cheer.

"Are Mrs. Binsent's people here?"

"Suite 320." Macy looks up but only with a stripped
down version of courtesy and a smirky smile.

"Thank you my dear, did you know today is the biggest
day in Newport real estate history? A changing of the guard if
you will, Macy, big day." Neil flashes a broad smile and briskly
heads for the elevator.

Macy mumbles to herself "If I had a dollar for every suit that has said that I'd be................" She does not bother to finish the sentence.

Neil enters the elevator, spins around, presses number three. He sets down his brief case, straightens his tie and checks his teeth in the reflection from a polished metal plaque. He reads the plaque which gives elevator weight and occupancy restrictions while running his fingers through his hair. Neil moves to the also highly polished full-length brass paneling checking and pulling on his blazer for a symmetric fit. He stands quiet for a moment in reflection that is literal and figurative. As the elevator begins to slow to a stop Neil says "Classy not brassy." He always says that when he sees a lot of brass. He overheard Donald Trump say that when Mr. Trump spent a day with Mr. Harton and Neil was able to spend three minutes with him. The thought flutters away as light and easy as it had come.

Neil is looking at himself intently now. He feels the full magnitude of the event just at that moment, it has hit him squarely and thoroughly. He is ready for this, he is hungry for it. But a large measure of the satisfaction and determination is not self-motivated. This is all for Kaisty. No more having nice things at the expense of depleting their bank account. This will be real wealth, fabulous wealth. Mr. Harton has picked Neil especially for this and he will not disappoint.

The elevator door opens and Neil jets out, makes a right turn down the walnut paneled hallway. He knows exactly where suite 302 is. The door is open, Neil enters swiftly. Two men are seated where he expects them to be seated. Neil lays his brief case on the table with a confident thud, flicks the snaps to open it, lifts up quick.

"Hello gentlemen." Neil speaks professionally without looking up. No need for hand shakes either at this level of the game.

"Mr. Landitt." The men return in tandem.

"Mr. Landitt, Mrs. Binsent would like to talk to you, she is on conference call.

Neil is amused by a thought that flashes to mind courtesy of late nights and the History channel. He thinks of General Douglas MacArthur delivering the terms of unconditional surrender while aboard the USS Missouri to Foreign Minister Shigemitsu of Japan. Neil knows that Harton has hounded Mrs. Binsent for years over that twenty acres and Neil is very interested in what she has to say.

"Hello Mr. Landitt, I have never met you but I am sure you are a capable man. I am an old women Mr. Landitt and your Mr. Harton an old lion. My late husband and I use to grow pomegranates on that land and fig trees too—did you know that Mr. Landitt?"

One man across from Neil rests his elbows on the table and rubs his temples, he has been Mrs. Binsent's lawyer for years and has never really gotten use to her antics.

"Ah—no ma'am I did not." Neil throws a plastic smile at the two gentlemen across the seven-foot wide conference table.

"We even camped out on the property just for fun in the early fifties before all the building." Mrs. Binsent covers the receiver to laugh. Robin who is sitting next to her whispers "You're bad."

One of Claire's lawyers squirms in his seat, scratches the back of his neck.

"Mr. Landitt I am a frail old woman, forgive me I had to cough." Mrs. Binsent throws a waded up napkin at Robin. Robin has to cover her mouth to suppress her laughter.

Neil sits straighter than he already was and clears his throat quietly.

"No problem ma'am I understand."

He reaches into his brief case and pulls out an offer sheet and a pen, then sets them neatly and square in front of him and folds his hands into each other.

Kaisty has not budged an inch since Neil left her. The only change in the room are the fluid lazy movements of Kaisty's cat from the window sill to atop her hip. Kaisty's face is serene and beautiful. A sizable portion of her madness is gone courtesy of the stranger in the emergency room. As she sleeps a thin translucent, golden veil descends upon her as a dream. Within the gently rippling image is a writing by a famous Newport poet, Angie Bivelo. The words pulsate over and over

in whispers, which stand as an underpinning to her
peacefulness:

> She dreams in glass shapes that shimmer with
> flaming pastels, swirling white satin ribbons and
> soft gold bursts. Thoughts come as streams of
> light, stop abruptly at her feet, change in tone
> and subject. She becomes an unwitting passenger,
> drug along as she tries to jump on other streams
> of light which hold more cheerful tones. She
> cannot reach that far nor jump that far.

> I see the nurse coming my way with those pills
> in the little paper cup as I peek through my
> covers in false slumber.

> She is held aloft by the hurricane that is her life
> then descends through ethereal realms, her life
> again as tragedy. Very few contain sensations of
> past pleasures or future hopes of same. Yet within
> her hopeless abyss something is lifting her now,
> invisible entity. It lifts her through all suffering.
> Ideas she conceded to of beauty unattainable now
> discovered as a lie. Love and calm engulf her
> being of flesh robed spirit.

> The nurse stands in front of me, stern expression.
> I take two pills and scheme to hide them under my
> tongue as I know this is no solution for my anguish.
> But the nurse, she knows my tricks. I swallow in

silent protest. I will beat her—someday.

As wonder would have it and fate would demand it she rethinks all that she has concluded since youth. She is free to decide truths anew. She is free to construct realities of her own sensibility. And she is released to dream again in glass shapes with shimmers of flaming pastels, whirling white satin ribbons and soft gold bursts.

"Basically Mr. Landitt let's get down to brass tacks. The last offer from Mr. Harton will be just fine. I may be a stubborn old broad but I am not all that greedy."

Neil's face flushes as he tries to suppress the burst of delectation from coming to the surface, he will allow himself to indulge and revel when he gets home but definitely not here, not now. He knows full well the land is worth considerably more than Harton's last offer of nearly two years ago, before a good portion of the surge in property values. Then Neil thinks he might not of heard her right until he notices the facial contortions of the men across from him.

"Agreeable—that would be agreeable Mrs. Binsent." Neil manages between internal convulsions of absolute thrill.

It has been four full days since Kaisty had any anti-depressants or anti-psychotics. Neil's idea to wean her off cold turkey is ill advised even from the doctors who prescribed them in the first place. The poem by Miss Bivelo is smashed and scatters away as Kaisty is left huddled tight in a ball on a beach. She is alone. She feels the presence of something enormous, intensely powerful. It now has reached the height to block the sun. She senses that even with her eyes closed. A strength and need from the massive entity draws and sucks the air quick over her helpless naked body and towards itself as a show of dominance. Kaisty shivers painfully.

Kaisty opens her eyes. Standing three hundred feet high is the immense dirty turquoise curved water wall of a tidal wave. Its gigantic proportions give the false perception of moving slowly. Kaisty is not afraid. She stands up and gazes dreamily at the white and pale green frothy crest that towers high above her. She closes her eyes. Kaisty's face begins to harden as her biochemistry within her brain begins to contort and grind in revolt. The very 'medicine' that is intended to correct a supposed chemical imbalance has in turn caused a severe one. All color has drained from Kaisty's face, her nostrils flare from her minds sudden agony and her lips quiver and grimace with every neurotransmitter misfire. The years of SSRI inhibitors have created a serotonin sluggishness to develop, causing permanent brain damage. Her right cheek and eye begin to twitch ominously. Kaisty is still asleep.

"Mr. Landitt of course we will need much documentation. But I will tell you with all certainty—that I am certain. Certainty is important in all negotiations and all I have to do is put my signature to this. It is time to close this chapter in my life and let—let the man have what I have denied him for so long." Claire gives Robin a wink as Robin can barely contain herself while laughing tearfully into one of Claire's pillows.

"You are a gracious woman, Claire Binsent."

"And you a gentleman sir. Go ahead and work all this out Max, Gene. Let's have this done by the end of the day for them—alrighty?"

"Yes ma'am." Max and Gene reply in grumbling unison.

Neil leans back in his chair and exhales hard and lets out a sort of high pitched laugh he has never heard from himself before this moment of triumph. He tries to suppress it all but finds it impossible and useless. The men across the table are stunned. The property is worth far more that this. They find it difficult to even make eye contact with Neil.

"Oh Claire didn't you lay it on a bit thick at the end there? 'And you a gentleman,' sir." Ha, ha, ha, ha! Robin says in tears, mascara smeared all over her cheeks. They both are laughing now, that rich feminine laugh.

"Honey this is fun—Newport style. Oh I'll let them celebrate, what is it 11:30 am; right at five o'clock I will pull the rug out. Maybe when I was younger I'd let them celebrate all night before I broke their little black hearts but just a few hours will due. "

"That is so viscously wonderfully evil." Robin smiles as big as humanly possible while squinting her eyes into little smiles of their own.

Kaisty awakes in an agonized panic. At the full effect of the central nervous system horror of Akathisia. She lurches from her bed, sending her cat flying. Kaisty tries to run to the bathroom but all she can manage are jerky stabs at the floor with her legs and feet. She grabs her hair and tries to pull it out as she truly believes her scalp is on fire. She screams in wild bursts. She searches frantically for the bottles that line up on her side of the counter under the mirror and have for years, they are gone. "No, no, no!" She screams from the gut in spitting rage. Kaisty grabs the wastebasket and slams it against the shower door and the glass reverberates violently, empty prescription bottles fly out darting in all directions as they hit the tile floor. She collapses to her knees in front of the toilet where she sees several tablets partially dissolved at the bottom of the bowl. She scoops out a cupped palm full of the liquid muck and tries to ingest it. Kaisty begins to cry hysterically.

Kaisty pulls open her vanity drawer and without stopping in her pull lets it crash to the floor. She searches frantically for her razor blades in a psychotic induced panic. She must separate herself from this poisoned and warped mind. More neurotransmitters than the psycho-pharmacologist had planned on 'managing' have been molested. Molested to a state where the reaction of withdrawal is severe. Severe enough to trip the mechanism of separation—suicide. That being the nasty little secret with psychiatric drugs. You may trip this mechanism in taking them and by abruptly cutting off from them.

Kaisty must separate her self from her molested, poisoned mind. She stands now with a glistening sharp razor in her right hand. She avoids desperately catching a glimpse of

251

her own reflection in the mirror, the failure of her life and
living being way beyond her willingness to confront. And in
her highly aggravated state she slips on the water that had spilt
out earlier and hits her head on the porcelain toilet. Kaisty is
out cold.

Neil stands out in the parking lot of Wells Fargo in a
state of invigorated blossoming. He tries Kaisty with his,
seldom used, speed dial—no answer. Next is Harton.

"Did we get it Neil?" Harton blasts through the line.
"Your damn right sir, they are working on the
particulars as we speak." Neil replies brightly.
"Son of a bitch Neil, son of a bitch!"

A shot of excitement jolts through Neil's mere mortal
body. Harton makes four large steps across the deck and over
to the helicopter pilot berthing. "Rick! Rick lets go!"

"Neil, you son of a bitch! I'll be there in fifteen minutes,
meet me on the roof."
"Yes sir!" Blares from Neil's giant smile. His eyes emit
thrill and amaze as he looks up to the top of Union Bank two
blocks away.

Neil tries Kaisty again—no answer.

The sun is warm and generous in its blessing upon
Neil's face. He smiles to the heavens in thanks and dumb luck.
Neil does not quite know what to do with himself at this point.
He has never been separated from his senses and pressures like

this before. He stands with his hands on his hips grinning ear to ear. "Where the hell is Alec? He has got to hear about this." He ponders with a quick scratch to his eyebrow. After two more minutes of shear jubilation and that new high pitched laugh of his he rushes over to Union Bank.

Neil is alone in the elevator on his way up to the heliport on the roof. He cusps his hands together over his belt buckle and stands patient with a blissful grin, eyes projecting a conquer. He tries to remember the last time Harton said a kind word to him. He cannot. And it does not matter, not now. "We will develop this land together, Jack and myself," Neil mutters. At least fifty very custom homes, Neil imagines. He imagines greeting the construction crews personally early the first morning. He imagines himself inspecting the work personally after the crews have left for the evening. For the first time in Neil's life he gets a sense of what true success feels like. And it feels fabulous. Every ascending floor affirms and confirms the triumph and status which will surely bestow upon him. Burdens detach one by one as the white glow of a new floor number is reached, that burden falling away forever.

Kaisty would have it all and want it all. This will be no problem, not any more. With two floors to go Neil swipes with quick strokes the tops of his dress shoes to the back of his slacks. He checks his teeth in the polished plaque and spits out a breath mint. Straightens his tie and coat which is a repeat of what had already been straightened between floors 26-32. The elevator goes right up to the roof and opens directly facing the helicopter pad. Sunshine and wind thrown from the blades assaults Neil's perceptions with great pleasure. Neil smiles and covers his eyes as he walks swiftly and hunched under the revolving blades. Neil is separated from all senses save thrill and accomplishment as he makes out Harton's billion dollar smile gleaming his way from behind the windshield.

The door opens with urgency.

"Get in, sit down and strap in Landitt."
"Yes sir!"

The pilot takes off fast jutting upward and to the left, the way Harton likes him to. They are clear of the building and in open air within a few seconds. Neil's eyes bug and he suppresses a gasp as the building he was on three seconds ago is gone. Harton laughs.

"Well Landitt not a bad days work. How did you get her to go with the old offer?"
"Well sir—I learned from the master." Neil yells louder than he has to over the engine noise.
"Ha, ha, ha, yes, yes, you sure did."

The helicopter is over water now and dives down to within thirty feet of the ocean, another Harton favorite. Neil turns white.

"Ah come on Landitt, live a little."

Neil looks out the window as the silvery blue ripples and white caps whisk by.

"Sir I told Leslie to fax all documents to your yacht, we should have them in a few hours or so."

"Good work Landitt."

Mr. Harton's yacht in now in view, the 123 foot Palmer Johnson displaying a striking profile against the bright distance of the horizon. An inaudible "Wow" cracks from Neil's lips. "Boy if Kaisty could see this," Neil utters gently.

"Set her down Rick." As if Rick had something else in mind. The landing platform is no larger than a black dining table with white crosshairs to Neil, as anxiety creeps up his spine.

"Where the hell is Alec, Neil?"

"No idea sir, I have been calling him since yesterday."

"Maybe he found himself a little girlfriend to alleviate the stress from his mediocre efforts—ha!"

"He's—married sir—I."

"Christ, then he definitely needs a girlfriend. I don't know how you married bastards deal with it."

They exit the craft and step onto the finest ship south of 'The Nordic Star.' Jack's girlfriend is lying on a towel shielding her eyes from the sun as she greets them. She is only wearing the bottoms of her bikini. And there is not much material employed within that to speak of.

"Honey we have a guest, put on a robe for Christ sake."

She scampers away giggling with her left hand and forearm covering her bare breasts. Neil looks off to the south end of Catalina Island until she is out of sight.

"What the hell are you drinking these days Landitt."
"Ah—well—oh, I don't know."
"Jesus Landitt don't you ever relax? Two scotches pronto!"
The steward nods in acknowledgment.
"Let's go Landitt."

'Holy crumb this thing goes on and on.' Neil marvels in thought. 'Oh I wish Kaisty were here. Well on second thought she might demand a duplicate on the spot, ha!' Neil laughs to himself under his breath.

"Alright Landitt have a seat."

Neil takes a seat on a light tan leather couch with ivory piping on the edges within a capacious, opulent entertainment bar area. Solid teak everywhere with the smoothest deep gloss finish that a master craftsman may achieve. Neil is in a mild state of 'shock and awe' as he runs his finger along the leather.

"Oh get over it Landitt, with the money we are going to make you'll have a fleet of these."

Neil could not believe he just said that. Neil knew he was just kidding but still, he said it.

Scotches arrive.

The wind is brisk and electric on Neil's face. He hasn't stop smiling since they landed or to be honest since he left Wells Fargo Bank. It has been so long since he spent time on or near the water, he is amazed at the expanse of the Pacific Ocean.

"Landitt, wipe that wistful bullshit off your face and let's talk business."

Nothing Harton could say would erase the smile from Neil's face. The source was too profound, too deep.

"Mrs. Binsent is going to fax some documents over in a while I just got the call. I still can't believe you got her to accept an offer from almost two years ago."

"Well—I—I—you know." Neil shakes his head in modesty.

"Ah, Christ Landitt take some god damn credit once in a while."

"Thank you, sir."

The double malted scotch works its intended magic on Neil's already relaxed but still invigorated state. His normally rattled nerves are as calm as the dense purple blue sky, not a cloud in sight. 'Damn I wish Kaisty were here.' His only weight keeping him from floating off into the sanguine horizon. The enormity of the yacht is not affected in the least by the gentle massive swells, only an ever so slight lift can be sensed. Neil can see the coast of Newport in the distance. The yacht and today's success imparts a rare feeling of power for him. He spots a fishing vessel south a few miles, seagulls hover and swirl in hopes of a good lunch above it. His eyes grin at the sight. North about a half-mile Neil's attention is garnered by the thick grumble of twelve cylinders by Rolls Royce. The sleek lines of a domesticated race boat thunders up Newport Sound. It slits the calm waters as the reverberation of the engines off the coast adds to Neil's pleasure.

"My god this is wonderful." He says softly to himself as he takes in a deep intoxicating breath of the ocean's bouquet.

Two hours pass.

"Ope, ope, ope here we go, here we go Landitt the fax is coming through, coming through."

Neil straightens himself, sets down his third scotch.

"Ok, ok, what have we got here let's see, let's see. That god damn whore! What the hell is this!"

Harton reads aloud:

>>>>Basically I'll get right to the point. Mr. Harton— screw you. You will only see this property in your nightmares. You can kiss my fat old granny ass. You have harassed me and my late husband Edward for decades with your seedy, underhanded attempts in trying to acquire our precious land. You son of a white trash Hollywood slut. Have a nice day, bitch! Oh—I almost forgot, your boy couldn't negotiate his way through a Girl Scout cookie transaction! Did I say screw

you yet? Actually I have another word in mind but I'm
a lady, you prick!

Insincerely Claire Delane Binsent

"God damn it Landitt, you son of a bitch, what the hell
happened?"

Neil's body, mind, tensed insolvent.

"I—ah—I." Neil stammers.
"You are so damned fired! Get the hell out of here!"

Neil looks over the side of the boat transfixed but there
is no solace there, anywhere, inside himself or any where in the
immediate or immense wretched universe.

"Fire her up Rick. I don't want this loser on my ship one
more second!"

On the way back to Fashion Island Jack Harton did not
utter a word to Neil and Neil could not think of anything
meaningful to say. Harton stares out the left window, Neil out
the right.
A half second before the helicopter set down Harton
yells "Get out!"

And Neil does just that. He heads for the elevator
caught in the storm of turbulence by the blade thrusts and by
the internal hell that is the desperate numbing of utter failure.

If one were to ask Neil Landitt what happened within the next three hours he would not be able to recall much of anything.

But here is what happened.

As one might imagine Harton's pilot took off and up fast in the grey and yellow helicopter. The surge from the propellers nearly sending Neil over the side. The top of the building was now instantly calm. But Neil had no attention to give it and he paid no attention to the clouds that appeared as stark white cottoned plumes that recently shown out across the sky. And there were streams of same stretched thin and much higher or the warm and radiant sunrays dancing silver on the ocean's waves a few miles from the tower.

None of this mattered or was even noticed.

Neil pushed the down button, which was the only button available, the harsh symbolism not unnoticed by Neil. He stood there waiting, not knowing what to think, what to do or where to go. That much not knowing is a wrecking ball to a man's confidence. The elevator opens. The next seven minutes are a surreal, numb blur with a dash of viciousness by Neil. Only he and his self-abasement occupied the elevator until the 43rd floor. Two secretaries and an office manager enter, all three are women. Neil insults them all. Two cry and the other demands an apology. Neil has none to give, calls her a "Bitch" then "Whore bitch" and "You're probably hung like a horse under that skirt." She cries too.

Floor 39, man enters. Neil, not quite versed in modern technology takes offense at the man's apparent laughing at him.

Neil restrains himself for two floors then decks him. Knocks him out cold. Apparently Neil did not notice or understand the hands free earpiece which is wireless to his cell phone, attached to his belt. The rest of the way down Neil insults six more women, two men and threatens two others for laughing at him, hands free cell phone in use no doubt.

Neil staggers out into the parking lot, tries his key in three different gold Mercedes before he finds his. Neil is not computing with the same mind he was computing with an hour earlier. This mind is bent on survival by destruction. Basically if you make as many people as wrong as you can as quick as you can one doesn't feel so bad. Neil hurls an insult at a walker by and throws a sturdy middle finger at the fifty-two floor building. He starts the engine but a destination is needed.

Another seldom called upon survival mechanism within his mind kicks in. The 'where to go in such an injured state to re-group' computation engages. Before any meaningful reconciliation with ones self can occur or new plans drawn a man needs *that* place. And one can be assured if one is married—it is not home. He knows that place, all men know it. Neil heads for the first town east of Newport Beach which is Costa Mesa.

Ten minutes later Neil pulls into 'The Helm.' He speaks to no one, looks at no one. The sawdust Neil barely senses quietly smashing under his feet signaled the process of redemption and restructuring. Neil takes a stool at the bar. This is the place, all men from Newport know it. It is out of the way and out of the minds of most, except the anguished few that the big business of Newport has ground up and spit out.

Neil looks up at the television mounted in the corner. It just makes good sense, you win or lose then you just get on with it. It is a good place to start for a man and his complexities with no simple solution: Angels 11 Yankees 3. It is understandable, definable.

Now, and the consecutive moments that follow, are not the time to confront anything anywhere with regard to specifics. Now is the time for sweeping anesthetizing of mind and agony. This is the place, the place to drink.

Double scotch on the rocks, it gets one there swift and confidently. To the safety and serenity of thick numb oblivion. The state is akin to a self induced coma. Some traumatic injuries require such measures. No thinking, no suffering, no squirming, no pain, no plans. Thick numb oblivion, the mantra of desperate failure.

Three hours later Neil finds himself on a sporadically lit road in the sprawling agricultural town of Irvine fifteen minutes east of Newport.

Neil drove the big silvery gold Mercedes off the main road onto a gravel and dirt road used by agricultural trucks. The outside air itself seems dark and there is a rare August chill to the night. He slowly and gently maneuvered down the road between large fields of what appeared to be strawberries on one side and maybe lettuce on the other. Neil was not concerned with an accurate observation. They were quick and nervous low interest glances. Occasionally a rock would slap up under the wheel well and Neil would cringe. "I'll wash you first thing in the morning," Neil says with grievance.

Neil lost the deal for the property; that is where his interests were bolt to. He knew he had pulled it off just a few hours earlier, he knew he had it. He once told Kaisty 'The iron veil that once separated us from fabulous wealth will soon be lifted.' Those were his exact words, actually they were the exact words of an actor in some black and white movie, from the forties, he had been watching late the night before. But he meant it and Kaisty believed it.

Then some first year rookie pulls the rug out from underneath him, she pulled the whole world out from under him.

Maybe he put too much stake in that one property, the one deal. "For Christ sake it is only one deal." Neil mumbles to himself as the headlights illuminate the gravel road to an eerie depth. But it was *the* property, *the* deal and Neil knew it. He was finished, he knew Harton, he would call him back to his office, with a sliver of hope, then, in front of all would fire him, again.

The handgun that Kaisty made Neil buy a few years ago sat under the driver's seat, it did not make a sound. His concern for his wife was overwhelming at this despoiled point, all this hinged on her needs, desires, expectations and frailties. Neil slams both hands against the steering wheel and cursed her doctors and their sloppy and now harmful handling of her. He again slammed the wheel with tremendous force. "Damn it, damn it, fuck." He yells.

Neil fights back a tear, his jaw muscles become taut.

The thought most people never think and some people can not help but entertain was there for Neil. And in the same breath was really not there for Neil. "The gun is right underneath my ass," He spoke in a numb tone barely moving his lips. "Ah fuck this, fuck Newport, we've got about thirty grand saved up, we can move to—I don't know—maybe Northern California. I'll get my Brokers license, start by own company. That would be good for Kaisty, that would be damn good for Kaisty. This environment that's, that's the problem. I'll wean her off all that psychiatric med shit—heck, join a church, have kids. Damn good idea, that's what we will do."

Neil crept down a little further where some lemon trees stood hearty with large, bright, yellow fruit. His interest clawed out gradually from deep within to the lemon trees that went on for acres. He stops.

Neil opens the door and the Irvine evening rushes in. The hearty soil and strawberries on the left and what are now lemon trees on the right give off an inviting aroma. He accepts the invitation as he drops his rather expensive dress shoes upon the dusty gravel road. There is an occasional muddy puddle scattered about; he avoids those. Neil has a plan, an escape if you will.

Neil is now lightened by the alleviation of burden and he feels a welcome surge of confidence as he looks out over the rows upon rows of manicured vegetation. Neil steps out and walks in between the rows of lemon trees, the wide openness enhancing his new found liberation. Neil takes a delight in the gravel crunching under his weight. And the rich soil and semi sweet bitter redolence that engulfs his senses as he approaches a lemon tree. The sky above is vast and assuring as he reaches for a lemon then two. He holds one in each palm then places a lemon under each nostril. He closes his eyes gradually and breaths in deeply. A genuine splendor emerges bringing with it a pink blush on Neil's weary face. He drops his arms to his sides, lemons still clutched in his palms and makes a 360 degree turn enjoying thoroughly, the magnificent space and symmetry of man's manipulation of nature and natures passionate response.

Neil is now freed up to the degree that he can allow a concern outside of his current pressures to come in. "Where the hell is Alec?" He says with a twinge of irritation. Neil drops the lemons and snaps his cell phone off its harness and scrolls down to Alec's number. He presses speed dial. In the time it takes to bring the phone to his ear he hears a barely audible muffled ring which is separate and distant from the ring he hears within his own phone. The muffled ring stops. Alec's recorded message plays. Neil disconnects. He finds that sound curious so he presses speed dial again and again hears the muffled ring. Neil finally realizes it is not coming from his phone but from his Mercedes, he approaches tentatively. The ringing stops.

Neil redials and the muffled ring responds on cue. Every sense in his body is heightened, his knees tingle, eyes wide and intense. The hair on the back of his neck is alert. He steps around with light cautious steps to the rear of the Mercedes. Neil knows what will happen if he redials but does it any way. The response he expected confirmed the certainty with the same certainty. Neil's mind is now engulfed in wild speculation as he reaches to open the trunk. He stops. He stops to think. Neil slowly draws his hand into a limp fist. "Maybe the last time we went golfing his cell phone fell out of his golf bag. Oh—of course, sure, my god Neil relax!" Neil chuckles nervously to himself. "I'm such an idiot what a scardy cat, just open it." A bead of sweat trickles down Neil's right side burn, his collar now uncomfortably tight.

Neil pauses and grins with a heavy breathed huff then flings open the trunk. In Neil's trunk lays Alec's bloody, badly beaten, gagged and bound body. Alec's eyes are open and looking at Neil with a look that is frozen and fixed in death. Neil slams the trunk closed and steps back fast, catches his heal in a rut and falls flat on his back. For the brief moment he lay there he notices in further horror large drops of blood that had leaked out along the road from a drainage hole in the bottom of the trunk.

Neil scrambles to his feet and darts with arms and legs flailing to the driver's side and jumps in. "Oh shit, oh shit, oh shit, oh shit!" Neil blurts frantically. He floors it and whips the Mercedes around and considering the road is only wide enough for one truck going one way, whipping around means over and through the strawberry field. He rips out of the orchard and slides out onto Sand Canyon road in a four-wheel drift, tires burning and screaming for traction. "Oh Christ, oh Christ, what do I do—what do I do!" A man in just about any stressful situation or tragedy in this case, knows at least where he wants to be to figure it all out—his office. An office is probably more for pondering life and dire situations than business—truth in disclosure.

Neil in route to Fashion Island doubles the speed limit at ninety miles per hour. "Sweet Jesus Alec what happened? My trunk! How?" Neil pulls into the parking lot unlocks his seat belt, turns the key off, thrusts it in park, opens the door and gets out all in one frazzled movement. He hustles across the damp pavement. The usually imposing building is sensed as a safe harbor in his desperate state.

"Late night Mr. Landitt." The security guard inside the guard station says in an easy, friendly manner. His feet are up on the desk, hands twiddling his thumbs on his bulging stomach.

"Yes." Neil replies void of any pleasant emotion or social grace.

"How about those Angels, Guerrero hits for the cycle today, they are up 11-3 and the Yanks come back and tie it in the top of the ninth. Now it's the eleventh inning tied 12-12. And I think we're just getting started."

Neil does not respond as he waits for the elevator, his expression turning solid. His eyes glaze over, all thoughts are inward, sullen, desperate. The anxiety courses through his mere mortal body, chest is tight. His breathing strained.

"Go baby go! All the way, all the way! Ah shit—he caught it at the fence." The guard carries on as he stares into his tiny color television, his voice echoing through out the massive first floor entrance.

The guard station phone rings.

"Yes Mrs. Grendale, no, no I haven't seen your husband all day. Wait but Mr. Landitt is here."

Neil is frantically waving his hands and mouthing "No, no, no." Neil jumps in the elevator, his collar becoming unbearably snug to his neck now. He loosens his tie and unbuttons the top two quick. He begins to hyperventilate. "Shit, shit, shit! But I didn't do anything!" He smashes the brass paneling with his fist leaving a deep dent. Neil looks at his pale ghostly face in the dull stainless steel panel. "Just call the police, just tell them you found him in your trunk—my god I can't do that!" His reflection barks back.

Neil exits the elevator and takes quick tight steps in the direction of his office. He dashes over to the window and looks down. The mere sight of his Mercedes sends a burning shiver through his mind, he winces. Neil's window faces the interior of Fashion Island. But that is merely where his eyes are fixed, void of external emotion and interest. The reflection of the fog rolling in can be seen in the pained glaze of his eyes. The fog that creeps in leaves only the tops of the buildings visible or nothing at all. Neil has seen this fog a hundred times but tonight he senses evil, and evil flow of movement and presence.

Neil peers into the fog, the evil fog, thick and churning. He feels its damp misery rolling over him. He feels its cold apathy passing through his rigid body. Neil does not want to be here after all, he paces, his mind grinds, teeth clinched hard. He wants to go home to his wife, he needs a woman's comfort, Kaisty's comfort.

After a ten minute drive Neil has sunk deeper into his sullen numbness as he pulls into the driveway.

Neil enters the master bedroom tentatively with weary haunted eyes. The room is dark. He does not want to face his wife after all. The bathroom door is closed. Light luminesces out eerily from the gap at the bottom. Usually it is a warm glow but tonight it is eerie. Neil sits at the end of the bed, exhales. "Hi babe," Neil says softly minus most of the usual sweetness. There is no reply, Neil is somewhat grateful. He takes in a heavy breath, exhales, leaving his torso more hunched over than it already was, knocks off his shoes. He pulls his slacks off and sits again. He needs a break even from this menial exercise.

Kaisty has come to now from her fall. But she awakes into a tormented withdrawaled state. She awakes with pressure all around her, painful pressure. She must escape. The dynamics that comprise life have crashed in on her, all around her. Her neurotransmitters are desperate for their fix. The chemical imbalance caused by her endless stream of psychotropics and anti-depressants have wrenched her mind into a suicidal murderous state. Kaisty is awake but still lying on the cold tiles. She must escape.

Nothing can happen to a businessman that can alter the rigid automanticity of routine that he employs to unravel himself for bed. Neil drapes his slacks neatly over a wooden hanger in the closet. He takes his shirt off and balls it up and tosses it in the corner designated for dry cleaning. He takes his watch off, sets the watch in its usual position on the dresser. Normally Neil would take his socks off but he is exhausted, he just can't bring himself to it—he has a dead man in his trunk.

Neil sits down on his side of the bed and opens a drawer in a nightstand next to it. When he was a boy his father told Neil that at a time when he was greatly distressed he opened a bible right about in the middle. And he happened upon a passage that smoothed his father's troubles right out and salvaged him for a time. Neil at this moment has no recollection of which passage his father was referring to.

Neil pulls out a bible. He sees Kaisty's shadow whisk about under the door where the dusty silver glow emanates. Neil cracks open the seldom leaned upon bible. As one might expect what he is reading is part of a story and Neil is easily confused by it. He tries to take it out of context then back in context but the passage doesn't quite lift him out of his chasm. He closes the bible. He has attempted this shot in the dark with the bible once every few years since he was a young boy but was never saved by one passage on a lucky draw.

Neil steps over to the window, bible in hand. Newport twinkles in dull faint illusion to him now, he is lost. A light haze swirls as some leaves rise up from the grass and street in a weak gust. The leaves are helpless as they delight in the seduction. Neil opens the window. He can hear an occasional call crackle and run on the telephone lines above. He always wonders who makes calls so late at night. He sees and old man walking and a cat brush his black furred cheek against the back of his pant leg in its sensual satin movements; the old man reaches down to scratch the cat under his chin.

The night is unreal to Neil, murky and gray misted lacking any real solidity. The stars that usually stand high and approving for Neil hold no luster for him now. Neil closes the window; he steps back and sits back down on the edge of the bed. He stares at the cover of the bible, wonders what the

word bible means. He'll give it one last shot. He opens the
book with a filet cutting motion in the middle and reads.
Neil smiles wearily, mutters "Son of a bitch, serves me right to
go for the one hit wonder with the mighty bible." Neil lays the
bible in the drawer knowing he will never do that again,
considers he might as well go ahead and read the whole damn
thing some time and draws the comforter up over his nose.
There is nothing on earth he can think of doing with Alec and
must get some rest. Neil is exhausted from anxiety and worry,
he begins to drift off.

    Kaisty stands in front of the mirror naked, in a grinding
delusional craze, held firm and brought on by a psychotic break
of which her mind in its effort to survive had no choice but to
induce. In this state of mind there must be destruction,
destruction of self or any immediate life.

    Kaisty has her target and it is immediate.

    Kaisty turns off the light and cracks open the door. She
makes out Neil's balled up silhouette under the covers. But she
does not see him at all. To Kaisty it is an evil slumbering entity
that must be destroyed. She tip toes her naked body to the
closet, opens the dresser, fourth drawer. Kaisty pulls out a .38
caliber Colt. She is able to figure only one way out of this
collapsed internal hell. The molested circuitry that makes up
the functioning of her brain scream unmercifully for its fix,
Kaisty drops the gun, holds both sides of her head and winces
in pain.

    Kaisty, within her delirium and desperate condition
crawls up and onto the bed, eyes glazed over with a murderous

focus, her face stone and ghastly pale. Her stringy, oily hair sweeps across her cheeks as she crawls and a stream of mucous trails out of her nostrils. Her lips part and stretch into a sadistic smile exposing her teeth gnashing with hatred. The tunnel of her psychosis is crushing her now, she must escape and this despicable beast is blocking her. She climbs on Neil. Neil is not startled, men are never startled by women climbing on them. As Neil is only partially conscious, the pressure on him from her knees takes on a wholly different significance within a thick veil that separates full awareness from total sleep where Neil is held, an anxious reverie. The physical pressure of Kaisty adds to the impact of the passage Neil read from the bible and is now mouthing incoherently. And it reads him as he reads it and he becomes the verse and the verse becomes him, a melding of soul, as judgment. Every word having a profound affect on him. Self recrimination—courtesy of the Bible.

If I have made gold my hope, or said to fine gold, "you are my confidence." If I have rejoiced because my wealth was great and because my hand had gained much. If I have observed the sun when it shines, or the moon moving in brightness, so that my heart was enticed and my mouth has kissed my hand; this also would be an iniquity deserving of judgment.

Job 31:24

Neil is neither asleep nor awake and is susceptible to hypnotic suggestion, Kaisty Landitt style. From a reach in his mind he hears a command to open his mouth. He does so. Kaisty slides the barrel all the way to the back of his throat. "Good bye bitch." Kaisty says to the man who never could quite make her delusions into dreams that never came true anywhere, heaven or earth.

Kaisty pulls the trigger. Harsh crack of the revolver and sharp flash of white and red animates the room with a sudden horror.

The kick of the pistol knocks Kaisty's small frame off the bed but she springs to her feet and right back on top of him to inspect. His eyes frozen open in terror, blood streaming from both corners of his mouth. And since Kaisty placed the gun barrel deep in his mouth, smoke streamed out lazily from his parted lips.

Kaisty climbs off her very dead husband and tosses the gun into her purse. She walks into the bathroom with little apparent emotion, her face gaunt and features solid, eyes cold and unapologetic. She walks stiff with jerky little steps. She grabs the empty pill bottles and diet pills and whatever else made Kaisty—Kaisty.

She shuffles quickly now over to the closet and pulls out Neil's hanging cloths and laundry to get to the safe. She fumbles with the key, drops it twice. Kaisty takes out all of the money, about six thousand dollars. She stuffs it all in her purse. Lastly she put on a long over coat. "See ya later bitch!"

This being her personal eulogy as she hustled with erratic motions out of the room. Neil said nothing in return.

Kaisty made her way to the front door then tracked back to the kitchen to grab a small bottle of water and stuffed that in her purse too. As she turned around towards the door she noticed the bullet she had just fired logged in the counter top. She looked up. There was a hole in the ceiling. Above that there was a hole in the floor. Above that there was a hole in the box springs, then mattress. Above that there was a hole in the pillow and lastly a bloody mess of a hole. Kaisty tries to pry it out with her fingernail. The bullet would not budge.

Kaisty picks up her now heavy bag and ran down the hall toward the door—she stops again. To her right about shoulder high is a photograph of one of her cigarette ads. She takes it off the wall and stuffs it in her purse, frame and all. Kaisty runs out the door.

She fishes down at the bottom of her purse and pulls out her keys. Kaisty's beloved Land Rover chirps with anticipation as she now frantically pushes the unlock button. She pushes it, unlock then lock three times before she gets it right. She starts the Land Rover and revs it hard, backs up fast and crashes into Neil's Mercedes, which was parked directly behind her. She pulls up quick then maneuvers around the Mercedes only to take out the stone and mortar mail box at the entrance of the drive way.

She speeds off, eyes wide and crazed.

Kaisty was free of this man and his meager ability to please her and deliver them to sacred expectations. Kaisty decided to go to the beach where she spent almost every summer of her childhood, her mind unable to reason through to any other location of refuge. But as the simply necessities of life and travel dictate, she was near out of gas. She pulled into the Shell station at the bottom of the hill that happens to be open all night.

Kaisty stopped in front of pump number six because she always did and walked in stiff and hastily. Once she began to approach the counter she slowed her pace and tried to gather her self with the look of someone desperately attempting to do so. Kaisty then stopped abruptly and set her purse on the counter. The attendants jaw dropped then tightened right back up as fear raced through an expression of shock. For Kaisty's face and chest was splattered heavily in blood. Being completely unaware of this she smiled, albeit a clinched and ragged one, while she rummaged through her purse for some money. If the attendant wasn't already mortified at the sight of her he surely would have been (and most certainly panicked) if he had seen the handle of the gun which was in plan sight. But his eyes were fixed to Kaisty's bloody face. Kaisty kindly gave him twenty dollars and pointed to number six then calmly yet with erratic motions, made her way back out to the Land Rover. The attendant nonchalantly, yet very nervously, took the receiver of the phone and sunk down behind the counter to call the Newport Police station which only happens to be three hundred yards from the Shell station. Which also happens to be connected at the hip to the Land Rover dealer where Kaisty leased her new SUV.

Kaisty pumped her gas and took in a deep breath and grinned slyly, the night is cool and surreal to her. She was happy, happy about whatever chemically wrenched people are happy about but in no way did she understand or feel the true gravity of what she had just done. Somehow the execution of her husband is reasoned as therapeutic. Yet in her mind, which had been torqued and molested and ruined by years of antipsychotic and anti-depressant drugs, there was a delusional, synthetic peace. A temporary state at best.

Kaisty races down Macarthur Boulevard. She slides in hard a disc of her favorite band from the eighties, Depeche Mode. Kaisty flies through two stop lights without as much as a glance in either direction. Then inexplicably she slams on her breaks for the third stoplight. A bottle rolls out from under the drivers seat—an old prescription of pain killers. Kaisty's squeals in delight.

Across the intersection traveling the opposite direction on the same street is the car the Ukrainian assassins are in. The ones that are to make a visit to Mrs. Binsent tonight. A heavy mist carries overhead then stops sluggishly, like a thick numb blanket and the streets are desolate, except for the killers. Like murderers passing in the night, one accomplished, one in scheming, they pass each other, slowly.

One Ukrainian checks his gun thoroughly as the other drives carefully in that an assassin's greatest concern in route to a murder is being pulled over for an improper lane change by the local police. Explaining two men well armed and dressed from head to toe in black is always a delicate issue.

Dragane knows when Yurrgi is very quiet on the way to a job he usually intends to hurt his victim along with that which he is paid to do. Why he would want to add undue pain and suffering to a seventy-five year old women is beyond Dragane.

"She's old woman Yurrgi, why hurt like that?"
"I hate old women."

Dragane smiles with a heavy huffed laugh. Thinks of the next angle to egg on Yurrgi, maybe something about the Swedish girl then decides against it.

"Did old woman rape Yurrgi when Yurrgi was baby?" Dragane says and follows with a robust laugh.

As misfortune would have it Dragane pretty much hit the nail on the head. And for Yurrgi every old woman is that old woman. Yurrgi does not respond, waits for Dragane to stop at the light. And when he does Yurrgi draws his knife quick and drives it through Dragane's thick Ukrainian neck. Yurrgi reaches to put the car in park in case Dragane smashes the accelerator in reflex. Dragane's fingers flutter around his neck in shock. Yurrgi slaps a clip into his gun hard then shots Dragane in the crotch and beneath his right ear.

Yurrgi did not appreciate the comment.

Yurrgi reaches over and opens the driver's door. He pushes Dragane out after retrieving the eight-inch military issue

blade from his neck and Dragane's wallet. Yurrgi curses
something harsh in Croatian, slides over and drives away.

Yurrgi pulls up in front of Mrs. Binsent's home with the
engine and headlights already off. The thick industrial dish
washing liquid squirted into the disc brakes before they left
keeps them from squealing when stopping. Yurrgi pulls out a
hand rolled cigarette. He takes a lighter out of his breast
pocket and dips his head between the steering wheel and the
door. Yurrgi does not want anyone to see the red and yellow
glow of the lighter. He cups the cigarette in his large rough
hand to hide the burning end of it. Yurrgi is a professional and
Yurrgi hates old women. After a few minutes of intense
relaxation and focus, Yurggi steps out and quickly finds
the darkest route to the back of Claire's home.

Claire knows her immediate environment. And she
knows when something is extremely out of the ordinary.
Sometimes Claire has trouble sleeping. She will sit on her back
veranda in the dark and watch the lights of the marina in their
dreamy twinkling nearly all night. She may sip some tea, maybe
chamomile.

Claire hears whispers of conversation. She
concentrates intently; she knows it is very close by. Call it over
confidence or a rare mistake but Yurrgi felt like calling his
girlfriend for some reason. At 2:00 am in California it is
11:00am in the Ukraine. "I'll be home next week I promise, a
little business to wrap up, to take good care of." Yurrgi grates
his teeth at the prospect then tells her goodbye. He is down
the walk way in Claire's back yard to her right about fifty feet.
Between the figs and the pomegranates. He is hunched over as

he creeps while putting his thin black leather gloves on. Claire
does not panic, she slips to her knees and crawls toward the
French style doors outside the master bedroom. She thanks
god there was no light on. She crawls quick to the phone, it is
dead. Yurrgi did not make that mistake.

Deep within Claire's closet Marisah lights a match and
tries to focus on a piece of paper with combination numbers
scribbled on it in three different color blues and a black ink
because of how many months it took her to get the numbers.
Pens came and went. She closes her eyes to remember the
clockwise and counter clockwise motions from watching Claire
those many times. Marisah sways her head back and forth, the
rhythm helping her to remember. Eyes scrunched closed in
recall. 18-9-4-25-8, the safe cracks open quietly and smoothly
as Marisah holds firm the cool metal of the handle. She opens
the heavy round door slowly and a light within ignites the
brilliance of the diamonds. Diamond bracelets, diamond
broaches, necklaces, diamond rings and several scattered gems
burst with fiery allure. And there is just enough gold to give
the diamonds room to dance upon. Marisah is transfixed. Her
eyes are held in mesmerized sparkle, her chin and lower lip
tremble, her body in uniform quiver. The diamonds come alive
in the fanciful gaze that her eyes now bathe in. One hand full
and her misery is over, just one. But within Marisah's deep and
entrenched Catholic upbringing she is broadsided by guilt,
unexpected guilt. She knows she cannot do this or even if she
did she could not live very long with herself, not like she
thought she could. She is overcome by beauty and the
oblivious whorl of diminishing self.

As Marisah's internal struggle rages she is startled by the closet door opening very slowly. Marisah closes the safe fast but not hard. The closet is large and she hides behind a row of silky gowns. She peeks through and sees Claire on her hands and knees. Marisah is baffled, surprised and confused all at the same sight. Claire takes hold of an old shotgun.

Marisah's eyes spike in terror and she nearly blurts out for Claire not to shot her. But somehow she knows Claire is not aware of her presence. Claire backs out with the shotgun and a box of shells. Yurrgi the assassin is making his way up to the veranda very carefully stepping close to the handrail to avoid the center of the wood planks, which may creak. He draws his knife, the eight inch army issue, sharper than a razor. He intends to torture the old woman first. All old women are *the* old woman to Yurrgi. The one who physically abused and molested him from the age of four to ten. Yurrgi is insane, viscously insane. In full disclosure after eight years in a mental institution they made damn sure he was insane.

Claire sits on the cold oak floor and slips in a 12-gauge cartridge, then another. She can hear her husband's voice from decades ago. "You know the boy's won't invite us back if you keep winning every year doll face."

Claire won the local skeet shooting championship from 1953-60. Every May just about every one of Claire's and Edward's friends would meet out at Gary Cooper's ranch which was about half the town of today's Costa Mesa. "My little Annie Oakley, give uhm a chance this time honey bun." Claire loved wearing her black boots that fit right up under her knees snuggly. And her light chestnut trousers that bowed out at the thighs. But the tasseled leather waist fitting jacket and long black billed cap brought the outfit together. "How do I look honey?" Claire would ask Edward as she stood next to their light coffee colored 1949 Packard. "Can you just miss once in a while, heck, let Cooper's wife win this year or Gables new girl. They're going to hold a grudge for months my sweet."

Claire crawls with shotgun in tow, her 1947 Benelli Montefletro. As quiet as Yurrgi is Claire is very aware of his current location. She can make out the top of his wiry blonde hair coming up the stairs of the veranda. She can now see a gleaming blade in his hand as he runs his thumb along the razor edge. His squinting eyes glint in the moon light with and evil stoneness, vacant of mercy and reason.

Claire scrambles as quick and quietly as her seventy-five year old body will respond to the front of her bed, which is about fifteen feet from the French doors. She can see him in his slumped gait moving toward those same doors. The knife flashes with a sharp glisten as he twists it. Claire has less than twenty seconds to prepare herself.

Marisah is now under a Catholic induced trance, a self-recrimination of intense shame. Her eyes glaze over withdrawn as the diamonds now twinkle in taunting of her desperation. The thought of disappointing her god this way becomes overwhelming. She hates herself, Marisah never thought that until this very moment, maybe she hates herself because in her own despondency she let them enslave her this way. She realizes there is really no escape even with the diamond necklaces. As oppressive as her environment may be the internal structure laid in Marisah as a child by her religion makes her, her own judge, jury and executioner.

Marisah reaches up to her neck and unclasps her $22.00 necklace she bought at a swap meet in Santa Ana. She kisses it and lays it in the safe next to Claire's then closes the thick metal door for all eternity. She sneaks out of the closet, through the bathroom and to the laundry room. Marisah steps out into the night clutching her sweater closed under her chin from the chill. And instead of turning to the street she makes a right towards the boat dock hunched over with hopeless tormented steps.

The Ukrainian assassin by the name of Yurrgi reaches with his huge callous hand and finds the door unlocked, he twists the knob slowly, he is pleased with his good fortune. A moment ago Claire set the butt of the shot gun against the base of the large mahogany bedpost. She times the cocking of the shotgun with the friction scrapping of the door opening. Claire had not yet scheduled for having the top of the door plained down and now she thanks god she did not.

A grin begins to stretch on Yurrgi's face as the intense sensation of sadistic destruction and distant revenge overcomes him. "I will hurt old woman." He whispers to himself as he licks his upper lip leaving a glistening trail of saliva. Claire is ready, patient and cool. Although her old heart is pumping wildly. Yurggi steps in. Claire sees his crazed eyes for the first time. But the assassin does not see her, his eyes dart around a few feet above her head. "Down here big boy."

Claire fires, the harsh bright flash temporally blinding them both.

The shot meant for his heart hits his right shoulder and sends him spinning down to his knees. With his knife still reached high, his face grimaces with pain and sudden unexpected determination. Now Claire feels fear, a lot of it, she does not think she can kill this intruder, this monster. He lunges for her as she lets out another blast. The shot removing

three quarters of his huge face, blood splats quick on the French doors and ceiling—a lot of blood.

Marisah is standing with much effort now and slowly sways from side to side at the end of the dock. The moon's gleam off the drowsy ripples of the bay calms Marisah as she figured Claire just took her own life. "The old bitch must have missed the first time." She mutters as she pulls out a single edged razor blade from her sweater pocket. She takes a numb solace in that Mrs. Binsent must of had demons of her own.
Marisah lets out an anguished scream "Oh Saint Christopher forgive me!" As she begins to slit her wrist the razor blade slips out of her fingers and falls into the water. She looks over the edge. "Shit!" Marisah jumps in after the blade, its stainless steel flickers in the moon light on its decent to the bottom of the bay.
Claire is brought out her shock by a woman's scream out near the dock. Claire now has the presence of mind to dial 911 as Yurrgi twitches in death lying grotesquely at her feet.

A glance of wandering, a misshapen haunting
of nights breached silence, the remaining laughter

As a creek flows and the moon lit bright, a neon
light flickers to welcome one from the long dusty trail

> Poem left by John Wayne
> on a napkin after losing
> his seat playing Texas hold'em
> at the Binsent's, 1958

Kaisty pulled up as close to the beach as she could,
grabs everything she had taken from home and stumbles out.
She did not feel any need to turn off the motor or the
headlights. As one might guess she did not bother to close the
door either. There was a lot going on in her mind and a lot
about to go into her mind as she emptied the bottle of
Oxycodone into her mouth. There were sixteen tablets. Kaisty
grabs the bottle of water out of her purse -the purse being
taken along by all women no matter their mental state- and
guzzled down the tablets. She drops the bottle in the sand,
wipes her mouth sloppily with the back of her hand.
    Kaisty got within fifty feet of the water's edge and
plopped down in the sand. She was feeling no pain. Her
future was bright as the moons beamed light that appeared as a
heavenly passage to the ends of the watery earth. The meeting
of light and water gave the passage an incandescent and inviting
shimmer. She fixed on the moon lit path that surfaced the
ocean.
    Then the most wonderful and strange thing occurred
for Kaisty to witness. The sky began to tear and twist and then
snarl into psychotropic yellow, pink and silver swirls as a gleeful

284

smile emerged on Kaisty's face. She was free, freed from the man who could not harness a shooting star for the ride she most certainly deserved, the ride she needed. Free from a life of mediocre wealth. All movement in the ocean ceased and a few night flying seagulls stopped in mid flight. Under the surface of the stilled ocean swells darting neon glowed pulsations of light raced in all directions. Kaisty's eyes glazed over in wonder with mouth agape as she stood up on her knees in the sand with amazement, her lips and chin quivering gently. The moon became a smooth golden disc and it gave warmth to the chilled shore. Then the moon began to make a thumping sound with deep jarring thuds. The thumps that reverberated along the entire beach began to speed up and then even faster and its pitch increased as it thumped even faster until eventually it became a thumped stream of sound that Kaisty could feel in her chest as she fell back onto the sand. Then it stopped abruptly and the moon began to melt and Kaisty began to cry, the gold molten moon penetrating into billions of gallons of suspended salt water that was still without motion except the darting pulsations of light.

Kaisty felt something moving up from under the sand. Yet Kaisty was not startled, she knew this was all part of her transition to her new rich and ethereal ascent out of a mediocre existence. A blue rabbit climbed out from the hole. And then two others climbed out too. They began to chase each other around and around Kaisty. Faster and faster they went until the chase became a blurred blue ring and Kaisty started to laugh, then cry. Then she began to cry while she was laughing then laugh while she was crying.

The rabbits froze suddenly like the seagulls above but the rabbits froze because they wanted to and the seagulls stayed froze because they had to and the ocean stayed froze because it had to as well. The rabbits were trying their best to stand perfectly still without moving a muscle, their eyes darting around. One rabbit, the one who first emerged from the hole, ran over to Kaisty's purse.

"Hello, is this your gun?" The rabbit spoke cheerfully.

"Why—yes it is." Kaisty returned happily.

"May I borrow it?"

"Why—yes, of course."

The blue rabbit grabs the gun from Kaisty's purse as the other two rabbits race down their holes.

"Damn, they're gone!" The rabbit yells.

Kaisty laughs through her tears.

The rabbit rushes over to Kaisty and places the barrel to her head.

"You're a bad egg, you know that don't you?'

"No, no please I'm sick!" Kaisty pleads.

"She's a bad egg, isn't she boys?" The blue rabbit yells down the holes.

The rabbits deep in the holes can be heard with, "Oh yes" and "absolutely."

The seagulls speak but still cannot move "Oh I could tell easily, bad egg no question" and "Yes I agree whole heartily."

"No—no, I—I just couldn't—he, he just wasn't." Kaisty cries.
"Come on Kaisty say it with me b-a-d e-g-g."

The blue rabbit has a cold squint to his eyes now and slips his little paw around the trigger.

"Please, please—I'll get help I promise."

"I'm afraid it's too late for that pumpkin."
"No, no my doctor says there is a new drug on the way and he wants me to change the combination of the ones I'm taking now and maybe electric shock therapy and................"
"Oh, that should fix you right up princess!"

The rabbit strains with his paw and foot to click back the hammer.

"You're not even from Newport, are you princess?"
"Yes, oh yes I am!"
"No, nope, no you're lying."
"No I promise."
"Oh very bad answer." Said the blue rabbit. "Indeed, very bad answer." A seagull agrees. "My, my, very bad answer." The rabbits down the hole chime in.

"You grew up in, ok let me here it, C-o-s-t-a M-e-s-a. Isn't that so princess?"

"No, I've never even been there, I'll never go there, please don't shot me little rabbit!"

"Oh—princess I'm not going to shot you, *you* are going to shot you."

"Ok, ok, ok, I will do it." Kaisty whimpers.

"That's the spirit!"

The blue rabbit places the gun into Kaisty's trembling hand, she slowly, very slowly, raises the gun to her temple.

"Right thing to do, right thing." The Seagulls praise.

The two rabbits in the holes pop their little blue heads out. "We agree, right thing to do, only fair ya know."

Kaisty closes her eyes, tears drop as the eyelids merge.

Something gently but firmly takes hold of her right wrist, the one holding the gun. Then something takes hold of her left wrist. The same entity gently pries the gun from her hand and the rabbits run down the holes and the seagulls fly away and the moon returns to white. And the sea turns back to ambient saltin fluid. And the sky turns from psychotropic swirled yellow and silver/pink to black and stars. The entity takes each of Kaisty's hands and pulls them behind her back and attaches connected sterling metal rings to her wrists and the entity is now speaking to her, which she still does not see. The entity speaks to her in sacred verse. And the sacred verse offers her 'The right to remain silent.' Which Kaisty accepts, gratefully.

Karen's place

John will be over later today but for now Karen is left to her solitude and standing in front of her bathroom mirror, naked. She is fractionally numb, her expression desperate under a blanket of apathy. Her eyes emit an exhaustion, her skin pale and sickly. Her hair is oily and tangled, some stuck pathetic to her cheeks. She never displays this look to her friends, at least she thinks she does not. Yet she feels a measure of optimism, it can be made it out faintly in her blood shot eyes and weak grin. She opens the medicine cabinet, takes out each bottle of anti-depressants and pours the contents in the toilet except for five tablets of each, which she lines up neatly on the glass shelf above the sink. "This is all I need to get off this shit." She says frailly but harsh.

......END OF STORY

As the sun yawns and climbs groggily out of the Atlantic Ocean, Robin dozes with a fairy tale read to Amy open and faced down on her lap. One of Robin's hands is lying on her thigh palm up. The other hangs limp at her side. Her head is tilted back and her mouth is open. A Norman Rockwell of sleeping mother in a chair pose. As usual she never made it in to spend the late evening with her husband Scott who is asleep on the living room sofa. His face grinning sweetly in slumber. Amy dreams wildly yet a measure more innocently than the fairy tale just read to her. She is balled up and hidden deep under her thick comforter.

There is quietness, a stillness, that few households can lay claim to these days. Either asleep or awake there is a peace in the Mofford home. The space knows it, the tiny dust particles held in the temperate rays of first light know it. The walls, ceilings and floors sense it, shelter it and ultimately have become it. The air they breathe is peaceful and calm yet stirs unseen.

Eyelids flutter, a hand reaches to scratch a nose then loses interest and relaxes across a forehead. Robin's dog Arial laps up water out of her dish then waddles back to her comfort and soon is asleep.

A newspaper hits the porch with force and the air tenses, then is enveloped in calm once again.

Light becomes more prominent now. Birds chirp, slowly at first, then faster. They simply must. Amy becomes restless but there is pleasure on her face, her dream must be good.

The light from Amy's window that has crept along the floor and up Robin's leg has reached her face. And it finds beauty. It is a beauty that finds its way to one out of a strong purpose for living and love for those who also live.

Robin awakes.

Most all mornings are sweet at the Moffords yet the DNA of this sweetness is far different from past Sunday mornings. For this morning is bolstered and broadened by the promise of fabulous wealth. Scott who has instantly transformed from gruffy contractor to well kempt contractor all the while retaining the devilish smirk, helps with the making of breakfast—he never does that. Robin burns the toast—she never does that. Her mind and spirit to a marked degree hover above the property in planning and strategies. There is a slight undertow of overwhelm, which manifests itself as sly stealthy smiles that appear indelible.

They hug each other and punctuate with a kiss and Amy seizes the opportunity and wedges her thin little body between the two of them in laughter.

Every one is bound and determined not to allow sudden successes affect them too much—it does.

"Let's have breakfast out back." Scott says, with rare animation to his gestures.

"Oh, I don't know honey, look at all the clouds up there." Robin replies.

"Oh my sweet, there are always going to be a few clouds up there."

Scott tickles Robin. Amy laughs as though it is her being tickled.

"Come on, come on, come on!" Scott attacks in good cheer.

"I'll set the table outside!" Amy blurts.

The power and authority of Democracy wins the morning.

Amy grabs the usual: napkins, forks, knives, spoons, glasses, plates, more napkins and dashes out. Robin displays wide-eyed worried wonder for how she was able to do it all in one trip. Once she arrives at the large round weathered table and gently dumps the load she goes into place setting mode. Amy rubs her chin in scheming—who will sit where? Her dog Arial and cat Symba are considered in the arrangement with equal respect.

As she lays out the utensils with her delicate little fingers in the exact formation her grand mother Margo taught her, something soft and cool lands on the back of her hand in gentle side to side floating. She knows what it is although she has never seen one, so there is an amazement and a blooming awe of surprise in her eyes. It is a freshly minted snow flake, the very first one since 1928 in Newport. Amy looks up at the sky in childish wonder. She spots another.

"Mommy look!"

Scott and Robin with eggs, bacon and pancakes in arm watch the snow flake's heavenly descent. Quick smiles for Amy's joy grace each of their faces. A snowflake lands on Amy's hand again right next to the first one. It is a perfect duplicate.

"Mommy, mommy no one will believe me—it's a perfect match!"

Scott squints to inspect Amy's claim, as it truly is a magical occurrence. Amy points to the sky in sheer delight. The sky is full of snowflakes now. All three run inside with laughter and surprise in their voices to grab their coats. It all melts by 2:00 pm.

Later that day the Moffords can be found at the Newport Auto Show. They peruse and hold themselves lighter and taller this year. There is a difference between admiring to admire and admiring with a mind towards purchase. One observes this bridged chasm in how they lean into something that has caught their eyes. The salesmen know the difference. The ones who can afford their desires don't laugh as much as those who cannot and the Moffords are no exception except for little Amy of course, the seriousness of the scene fails to register anywhere in her joy as the warm and generous sun dances and plays in her golden hair. Her parents may not laugh as much as last year but the smiles are a measure more serene, their joy carved in a bit deeper. For they are majors players now and all will know soon enough.

"Go ahead honey just point and it's yours." Scott gently nudges Robin.

Beethoven's 'Ode to joy' erupts through well hidden speakers and gathers whatever loose ideas of pleasure, however plentiful, from those enjoying the day and forms them into the ultimate musical expression. The air rings electric to the accomplished as all matter, energy, space and time take the immediate form as sonic pleasure. Spirits rise fast, some quietly and some not so quietly. Amy dances around her parents legs and laughs out loud. Scott catches her quick and throws her up to the sky three feet above his head. Robin's eyes stun with wonder at Amy's sudden flight. The clouds tower above yet seemingly without weight. The sky is blue yet the blue cannot be touched, only perceived airily as such. Amy is still up there, with the music. She laughs in fast shrills. And Scott is there, broadly smiling, reaching upward. He and Robin will be there to catch her as long as they can be—forever possibly. Amy will stay up there with the joy and the music as long as she can keep her happiness and thrill alive. As winds shift quick and fierce in Newport for the upcoming generation and it all begins with a mystifying human impulse to either enslave or set one free.

A great piece of music was written for just one word—
joy. That is a terrifically optimistic thing to do. For so many of
us have written our own private ode to pain. And that is not
hopeful or optimistic.

Robin's eyes excite as if awaking from a dream to the
reality that she is a princess after all and the kingdom she rarely
gave second thought to is hers to rule. It always seems to
happen that way in Newport Beach, California.

As all great fairy tales begin with an ending like this
one..............

The End

"Oh—good question, good question. The average
price for a home in Newport ? Millions and millions
of course."

Robin Mofford
Real estate mogul
Newport Beach

EPILOGUE

A family from Indiana is leaving today after three weeks in Newport. Mother and father are ready to leave; the departure is in their eyes, prepared for the first leg of their long trip home. They enjoyed their visit but they know Newport is only a dream, especially when one is wide awake and California is something one yearns for, not to truly have, they know better.

Their thirteen year old daughter thinks and day dreams otherwise. Newport has left a permanent impression on her, she is changed, mind, body and soul. The beach, the nights, the people and Fashion Island has captivated her. She is struck with wonder, a fanciful reverie for which there is no cure. She will dream and the vision will be rich and consuming. Whether driving home, in class, at church or with her friends, it will be all about Newport.

She will come back, alone. When she is twenty she will load up her car, drain her bank account and move to Newport. All this runs through her young mind as she peers out the back window intently as they drive up Newport Boulevard and to the freeway, the freeway that goes east. The boys, the palm trees, Fashion Island, it all speaks to her. They tell her to come back as soon as she can, alone. We will make you a princess. She smiles with a slight tremble in her cheeks. If her parents could see her eyes they would be concerned, for their baby belongs to a dream now and not to them anymore.

————————————

At Boag hospital the three criminals occupying the south end of the guarded ICU, the ones who stumbled into Newport several weeks ago, lay quiet in their respective beds. The ones who killed a state trooper on their way to Newport, after raising hell in Ohio. One of them remains in a coma, one stares out the window at the ocean—catatonic. The other, a young man by the name of Jim has a huge bandage on his head and is talking to a pastor, Pastor Donaldson.

"We're finished, why do you bother?" Jim says in an apathetic tone.

"Because this is only a brief breath in eternity. I am here to address your immortal soul, my son."

The young man strains to look out the window away from the pastor.

"It's all yours pastor."

Pastor Donaldson reaches for the young mans hand. He dips his head in prayer and Jim cries.

Pastor Donaldson loves his hobby. When his nose is not in scripture or in preparing for the next Sunday's sermon he and his assistant Miss Brown tinker with the tone and pitch of the ninety seven year old bell hoisted some eighty feet up in the tower above their church.

"Miss Brown I'm down here at the coffee shop, give the bell a good ring if you will, I'll see what kind of response we get."
"Ok, Pastor."

Bong.....Bong.....Bong.....Bong the bell rings sure, strong and clear.
The Pastor sits where he can see most everyone in the coffee shop, patrons and employees. No apparent reaction at all.

"Miss Brown thank you, good. Would you add five pounds please and give her another good ring."
"Ok, ok give me a minute pastor."

Pastor Donaldson loves people. He could and has spent all day observing them and thinking of ways to help or offer some support. He sips on his coffee. He grins above the rim of his cup as a group of students comes in. Three are laughing, one looks embarrassed the other two are talking about something else entirely. The Pastor takes keen notice and that is nothing new for this man of the cloth.
The Pastor is a tall thin man and Mrs. Donaldson defends her cooking regularly. His face is worn but kindly. He

has smiled so much since giving his life to Christ at a spiritual revival tent some sixty years ago that his eyes and the surrounding skin are wrinkled eternally into little smiles of their own. He has a full head of hair at seventy-three years young which has only a slight hint of its former fiery red. His lips are perched out some in a permanent crooked grin. His eyes are dark blue almost navy blue. His wife of forty years marvels at and loves those eyes. The Pastor's ears are quite large and he receives ribbing for those ears even to this day. "Sometimes the lord whispers and he wants to make darn sure I hear him so he gave the biggest ears he could find." Being the Pastor's favorite response.

Bong.....Bong.....Bong.....Bong the Pastor likes this tone a bit better but he does not make note of his own response, only the response of those souls around him. Pastor Donaldson has kept careful notes over the months and has stumbled across a separating pitch and tone. Separating in that seventy eight percent respond positively in some respect and twenty percent slightly irritable and haunted and the remaining two percent react the most intensely with a marked and definite degree of agitation, their eyes and demeanor becoming rigid and resentful. "Very interesting results, very interesting Miss Brown." The Pastor would often say.

It is Tuesday afternoon and Pastor Donaldson has two men from the 'Christian advisory board of Psychiatry' in his office. This is their third visit. They are trying to convince the Pastor that they can diagnose mental illness or chronic depression from the onset, or advance cases, and offer treatment to members of his congregation. They have brought in clinical reports of the 'proven' scientific variety for the third time now. The Pastor has honestly given it much consideration.

"Now run that by me again gentlemen. Chronic depression, ok, this is a medical condition brought on by a chemical imbalance which you can treat and correct with the little tablets here, the serotonin re-uptake inhibitors?"

"Right."

"And the poor souls afflicted unfortunately don't have enough serotonin running through their—their brains? A deficiency?"

"Correct."

"Now let me see, these little pills here." The Pastor rolls one in his fingers, eyes it with a good inspection. "Keeps the excess serotonin from going back to where it came from so there is more of it as a neurotransmitter to be used, corrects the imbalance?"

"Very good Pastor, very good."

"Ok, maybe I am stupid but if there is a deficiency in serotonin why are you blocking the *excess* from being taken back?"

"Oh—years of research, proven clinical trials."

Both men fidget in their chairs and eyes are alert, fake smiles.

"Yes, and please forgive me for my ignorance but what was the name of the scientific instrument used which can measure hundreds of millions of neurotransmitters and subsequent chemical imbalances in the brain again?"

"Ah—well—I don't."

"Let me help you old sport, there isn't one. I did some research of my own since our last visit. I happen to also have some medical journals with clinical tests here stating, in no uncertain terms, these pills of yours cause permanent brain damage and difficulties of all sorts."

He very calmly slides them over to the now gaunt and bitter looking men. One man in noticing the name on the journal mutters under his breath. "Doctor Breggin again, that son of a bitch."

"Now gentleman do you really believe that a god would create a mind that would go out of whack so easily like you claim it does and that we are fortunate that you bright caring souls were able to pick up on this, so tragic, design flaw? One has to wonder why you people are so determined to peg *all* matters of the human condition as lying within a heap of noodles, ½ inch behind ones forehead. And really, lets be honest with your bipolar and chronic depression, isn't that merely and *emotional* response to the failed purpose of ones life? It also states that the psychiatric profession is solely responsible for *causing* the symptoms of bipolar by giving stimulants like these pills here to depressed people. You make them go way up high, higher than they can manage then let them crash even lower than they were. So—it says right here—right here!" He points vigorously. "They put a new label on their own therapeutic disaster which they in turn treat with more drugs like Lithium and Depakote. And what's with your electro shock 'therapy' and—and this 'mandatory mental health screening' I keep hearing about? This is crazy! I don't want anything to do with you people! Take your 'clown act' to the hell that spawned it!

The Pastor gently raises his left hand ominously and Miss Brown who has been waiting patiently in the tower begins to ring the bell with a sly grin on her face. There is a seldom seen steel resolve that Pastor Donaldson's face forms into. The furrows that run deep within the lines of his face hold stories, stories of trials and tribulation and subsequent triumph by staying true to the path of the lord. And he knows when and where the resolve forged within him. It was forged when sacred scripture bore equal weight to sacred literature.

The year was nineteen hundred and thirty nine. He recalls standing on a grey weathered, dilapidated old porch hugging his mother's thigh and watching his father squatting and figuring something in the dirt with a stick and a man in a big black car with a dark brown brim hat rolling up his window as the car drove slowly off, leaving billowing, low slung dust behind it. What he was figuring in the dirt was how he would provide for his family, after just being informed to be off the property after three generations of his family owning and living on the land. Living off the land for eighty years. Bad crop years from years of soil depleting practices and drought had forced bank loans. Not paying it back led to eviction.

They lived and died on this land. Relished youth and grew old on this land. He sees for the first time and expression on his father's face his young mind does not recognize or understand as his mother gently caresses his wavy red hair. It would take until early adulthood to know that as the look of desperation. He recalls vividly the fifteen hundred mile ride to California and the unwelcome greeting once they arrived. At times and unbearably long journey at thirty five miles per hour and the countless stops from breakdowns in their old 1922 Ford.   .

The young man would read to his mother, father, and little sister from the bible and the newly minted 'Grapes of Wrath' at the tender age of nine. He read by fire light, by sunset, by sunrise. He read by storm, he read by hunger and he read by his mother's gentle sobs deep within her sleep. He read by flood and he read by despair. And he read to and for hope and promise, the promise of the rolling bountiful grassland of California. The message brazen clear and holding firm in his young mind. Then he would dream, as boys do. When he did he dreamed of cowboys and Indians. They fought high above him in the sky. And the clash tumbled angrily westward. And the clouds became buffalo and every one hunted them, everyone, and the Indians hated those who hunted them for sport. And when the Indians died the young boy felt great sorrow, unexpected sorrow.

Big locomotives charged overhead too, huge billows of smoke jutting out from the engine stack thrilled him, the sight and powerful sounds nearly overwhelming him within his animate sleep. The fighting, the buffalo and the Iron horse all storming above him westward. It all spilling over the tall sierras and into the promised land, California. And then it was over, life changing forever, a confused triumph, a bittersweet conquer. And when he awoke he would read again, on the road at thirty-five miles an hour. And within his young mind, as soul, sacred scripture bore equal weight to sacred literature.

Bong.....Bong.....Bong.....Bong as the bell rings out and exposes the true character of the heart with just the right pitch

and tone, the two men's skin becomes pale and grim giving off an unholy radiance. The two men try in vain to suppress their aggravation as their eyes emit a tight hateful glare directed at the Pastor.

The Pastor rises from behind his desk tall and strong. The strength available to him from a reservoir sprung to action by keen observation. That of evil. Evil that only knows the dark impulse to enslave and destroy. The two men look up at the towering pastor defiant. Pastor Donaldson slowly rounds the table and then quickly grabs the upper arm of the largest man.

He relives a moment in an instant with intense clarity. As his family approached the end of their land before the first leg of the long journey west his father stops the old Ford. He steps out and kneels down, with his large rugged dark and callus hand he scoops up a handful of the dusty red depleted soil. He brings it to his mouth and kisses with a gentleness that is curious to the young fiery red headed boy as the dirt sifts through his fingers. A tear drop falls broken hearted as it hits the soil and is consumed instantly. More follow and all are consumed. He and generations have drawn from it and now it draws from him but he cannot give it life. And the tough man can give only a few more before his face becomes rigid with strength and resolve, his son in seeing this does not understand fully as he lifts his young eyes to the setting sun which is on fire as thousand mile wide copper amber hues smolder and crimson flames ignite into a bold shimmer over the promised land of California. And the sun still burns but its strength is broken for the day as the decent begins. Birds with great wing-spans glide dreamily over head as the nights hunting begins and the multitude of corn stalks that now dominate the landscape crook and flutter dryly in the wind. The red dust swirls up again as it has for months and his mother holds a delicate handkerchief to her nose and mouth as his father steps in the automobile. He steps in with determined cold eyes and the journey begins as the young boy reads aloud softly but confidently, for sacred scripture bore equal weight to sacred literature.

Words come to the Pastor and touch him deeply, move him mightily as his grip tightens and the man winces in pain. And John Steinbeck's words come to his lips and he utters them quietly, confidently, just below a whisper. And the men who were glaring defiant are now confused and frightened. And the strength came as sacred literature:

> To the red country and part of the gray country of Oklahoma the rains came gently.........................

Miss Brown puts her entire body into ringing the bell now. Pastor Donaldson lifts the man out of the chair with only the one hand clinched tight. Their eyes lock, bitter, intense. The Pastor stares him down fiercely but true evil even in its cowardice is compelled to stand defiant. True evil while neither being alive or dead must attack.

"Christianity is bought and paid for Pastor, the game is already over. It moved east to west and your one of the last *big* men to take down. We have our people entrenched everywhere in your hierarchy, your own Diocese. Ha, the Mormons are the biggest cash cow for us *so* far and you're next. In fact….." The man shakes his free hand at the Pastor and spits his words harsh at him. "In fact if you do not let me go and let us do our work on your 'flock' our plan is in place to acquire this land right out from underneath your beloved archaic church. Just get it old man." The man tries to squirm out of the Pastor's grip. "Let go of me now!"

He lets go of the man immediately.

The Pastor calmly walks to a file cabinet. The bell up in the tower stops ringing. Miss Brown sits down panting, in a heap of exhaustion. The men still sitting exchange victorious sneers between them. The Pastor thumbs patiently through his files and lifts one out. A cool, tight grin finds its way to his face. As he turns to the men he says, "Looks like you're a step behind on this one. A beloved member of my 'flock' by the name of Robin Mofford has graciously paid the whole darn thing off. We've had our own plan in place, do you think we haven't noticed what you have been up to? "

Hate and resentment burn in the men's eyes, as their pupils dilate and blacken to an unearthly tone and depth and their faces contort into defeated grimaces.

Two young men enter the office. They are very big and equally strong.

"These are my sons Daniel and Robert, they will be escorting you out."

The two young men converge on the men quick, like the defensive lineman from USC that they are. They each grab a man by the back of the neck quick; they had talked about that move outside the door. They rip them out of their seats like rag dolls. One of the men spews evil, a spitting tirade. "You fucking piece of shit! I'll fuckin sue you cock suckin bastard whores! I will fuck this holy ground you walk on, I will grind a whore in this office, on your desk! This isn't over you fuck, you fuck!"

Pastor Donaldson has always wondered how he would respond in the presence of true evil, he is rather calm, in fact, he is very calm. He takes a solace in that.

One of the biggest and strongest hands god ever created slaps itself down hard over the man's mouth, firmly, securely. "Don't you speak to my dad like that mister!" His weak, pudgy body thrashes and flails then eventually writhes in the pain brought down on him as he is drug out of the office. The other man leaves in a similar fashion.

The Pastor is merely a spectator now. The men flail their arms and kick their feet as they're being dragged in weak protest. They disgorge profanities the likes of which the Pastor's sons have never heard; they seem not of this world, scarcely English. They resist and restrain the harsh impulse to strike the two men, the evil men. But are unable to restrain their powerful grasps which cause nearly as much damage as a blow might. Pastor Donaldson walks over to the thick maple double doors and closes them gently, with a confident glaze in his eyes. He strolls over to his bookshelf and to his salvation. Within all the books of uplifting epistle to his spirit are two books, which are the underpinnings to his strength and compassion as a minister. The 'Grapes of Wrath' and the Bible. He pulls out the old Bible with care. He caresses the slightly tattered binder lovingly and carries his huge rugged hand over the front leather cover. It feels alive to him, it speaks to him even unopened. Its message carves deep within him as soul. He kneels to one knee. The wintry Pastor eases off his glasses and with thumb and forefinger massages the inside bridge of his nose next to his deep navy blue eyes, the eyes his wife loves. He knows by heart the passage he wants to read. The Pastor hears the men and his sons, the evil men, fighting in the parking lot. He chuckles softly under his breath. He is not worried.

He speaks the passage aloud and his eyes smile with spiritual fervor, for the souls of Newport are his to salvage. The Bible remaining closed. He knows it by heart as sacred scripture...............

The Dream Escapes Me

The dream escapes me now as would life drain
from a flower by design and necessity.

A sorrowful smile portends a daydreams kiss, she
comes to me as spirit only, no fleshly restraints.

At times a bitterness may arise as sure as a baby's cry.
Yet all will pass and all will rise again and all will pass
again.

A thank you breaks from her lips. I accept in partial
deserving.

My girl takes thought and wrenched emotion from a
book scribed a long time ago, a thousand years. She
sheds tears easily, profoundly. For a castle maiden's
loss is no more tragic than a young woman's anguish
who has lost her soldier to fight on ships that travel
to the stars, far into the future.

Yet I sit unaffected for the dream once impaled me,
yet now escapes me as would life drain from a flower
by design and necessity.

Poem found in the
parking lot by a man
sweeping up at the
Ritz, the morning after
the party.
Author unknown

Karen's place

Karen is sitting on her porch with John's manuscript on her lap neatly squared. Her hands are folded into each other resting on top of it. She is wearing sunglasses, the large dark amber style. John pulls up in a 1961 Jaguar in need of much repair but a classic none-the-less. Karen watches John exit the Jaguar. She notices everything about him, studies him passively. John flashes a big smile once he spots her.

"Hey kiddo, looks like you've finished."
"I tried calling, texting, email, I even tried bribing the local sheriff with sexual favors to search for you on the lake."
"No reception on the lake, sorry."

Karen manages a faint smile. "Lets go for a walk John the dusk looks serene."

Karen steps down and along side John. She places her hand in the inner part of his elbow and John responds instinctively like men do with a quick stiffening of posture. He lifts his hand around to his belt buckle and jabs his thumb behind it, juts out his jaw with a cheery smirk, they walk.

"How did you know so much about what happened that summer, John?" Karen asks with mild accusation.

John laughs, throws up his eyebrows, rubs his chin with his free hand.

"Well, I've lived her a long time Karen, I know these people, it all happened right here." John points the thumb of his free hand around aimlessly.

"But some of it you couldn't possibly of known how— how it happened."
"A writer has to take liberties Karen." John responds with arrogance for effect.

They are silent for a block or so.

"I don't know about this story John. I mean it's good sometimes really good but I don't know. What's with the rabbits and—and cowboys and Indians in the sky and the train too, I mean *really* John."
"I agree."
"I wasn't a literature major but tell me you *didn't* introduce a new character in the epilogue—You agree?"
"I've been thinking about those three guys from Ohio, maybe there is a story with them; I had to write this one though."

Karen thinks about Kaisty and the hospital scene, the second one.

"Thank you John."
"For what?"

Karen shakes her head and looks at John as if to say 'How can a man do something right for a change and even then be a complete dope about it.'

"I'm going to make you dinner tonight, John."
"Oh goody, I like food. I think you're right, the story is a bit much and kind of a mess."

Karen looks at her feet walking then looks up at John with a sweet intensity.

"Yes, but it's a beautiful mess."